DOUBT ON A LIMB

THE LEAFY HOLLOW MYSTERIES, BOOK 8

RICKIE BLAIR

BARKLEY
BOOKS

DOUBT ON A LIMB
Copyright © 2020 by Rickie Blair.
Published in Canada in 2020 by Barkley Books.

ISBN-13: 978-1-988881-15-7

To receive information about new releases and special offers, please sign up for my mailing list at www.rickieblair.com.

Cover art by: www.coverkicks.com

DOUBT ON A LIMB

CHAPTER 1

HERBERT EUBANKS PLUNGED the black PVC pipe into the septic tank and held it steady as liquid pulsed up the three-inch plastic tube. From there, it traveled into the hose that snaked through the yard and out to his pumper truck in the driveway. It was a task he'd done countless times, in hundreds of rural backyards. There was no reason to think today's job would be any different.

But it was different.

For one thing, this split-level house had three-and-a-half baths. The tank he was emptying wasn't big enough for a house of that size. And certainly not up to code.

He'd been inside the house and knew it well—another reason why this job was different. It had one of those "great rooms," a home office, and four bedrooms—or five, depending on what you considered a bedroom. For his part, Herbert would never have slept in the basement room, because it had no windows. But then, it wasn't used for sleeping, as he knew. Hence the locked door.

While the pump on his tanker continued its work, he glanced around at his surroundings.

The sweeping, pristine lawn—punctuated with well-tended perennial beds and gracefully pruned trees—contrasted sharply with the weedy expanse of the garden next door. *If you could call it a garden*, he thought. More like a barnyard, really. From somewhere came the bleating of goats, an unlikely pastoral note in such a polished neighborhood. He smiled to himself. That was another advantage to his job. The odor of a well-maintained septic tank was nothing compared to the aroma of a freshly manured field.

The bright sun promised a hot day, but this early in the morning it was so cool that he'd thrown on a jacket before leaving his one-bedroom walkup in the village.

The landlady had handed him a cup of coffee when he came down the stairs.

"Just to get you going," she said cheerily, holding it out with wizened fingers.

There was a reason why she was that friendly, he knew. And it had been a stroke of genius on his part.

With a smirk, he pulled up the pipe and tapped it against the side of the opening. Then he carried it out to the driveway and left it on the ground. He would uncouple the hose and loop it onto the carriers on the tanker's side after he closed the septic tank lid.

But he had something else to do first.

Kneeling at the two-by-three-foot opening, he leaned over to reach in a gloved hand. There should be an attachment on the roof of the tank, beside the lid. His fingers scrabbled over the rough surface until they hit something solid.

Ah—there it was. Grunting, he reached another few inches, until his arm had plunged in up to the shoulder, to rip off the plastic bundle. *Almost there.*

A shrill voice sounded behind him. "You bastard."

Herbert twisted his head to look behind him. He frowned.

"What do you want?" he snarled.

"I warned you."

Herbert, groping for the bundle, gave an exasperated snort before turning his head to concentrate on his task. "Bugger off," he said.

He barely felt the blow that killed him.

Herbert Eubanks toppled, head first, into the septic tank.

CHAPTER 2

WHEN ZARA PRICE telephoned to beg my help in a "matter of life and death," I assumed she was exaggerating. How could a middle-aged hobby farmer whose elderly mother sold homemade jam to tourists possibly become embroiled in a matter of life and death? Especially one that required the intervention of budding detective Verity Hawkes?

In truth, I was still getting used to the idea that anyone might consider me a budding detective. I'm a relatively recent resident of Leafy Hollow, a picturesque village nestled at the foot of the Niagara Escarpment in southern Ontario. After arriving as a twenty-eight-year-old widow a year earlier, I had revived a failing landscaping business acquired from my secretive aunt. I'd also acquired a best friend, a nineteenth-century cottage, a handsome fiancé, and an inexplicable habit of stumbling over dead bodies.

All welcome surprises.

Except the bodies, of course. Although, come to think of

it, the fiancé component had also required some adjustment on my part. After spending two years crippled by grief and anxiety attacks, it was not something I ever expected to happen. Apparently, lightning can strike twice.

And now I'd been gifted with a potential new client for my fledgling investigation agency. Putting the past out of my mind, I strove to concentrate.

"Is it your mother?" I asked Zara in hushed tones. "Has something happened?" For one awful moment, I speculated that one of Mrs. Price's gingham-topped confections was suspected in a possible poisoning.

It could happen, I knew. Samantha Price—Sam to her friends—was a little...let's say scatter-brained. Recently, for instance, her famous sour-cherry jam had turned out a bit salty. Salty enough that it could have preserved cod in the pioneer days.

The resulting scene was etched in my memory.

It had been a week earlier, after Sam had transformed the first crop of the season into luscious berry-red jam. Lorne Lewins, my unfailingly polite landscaping assistant and dedicated foodie, had spit out a sample mouthful with such force that it sprayed Mrs. Price's hand-painted apron. I had stared, horrified, at the red splatters on the cheery farmyard scene.

"Oh dear," she said, wiping down her apron with age-spotted hands.

While Lorne spluttered an apology and turned as red as the jam with embarrassment, I dug into the jar with a plastic sample spoon and lifted it to my lips.

We had been standing at Mrs. Price's farm-side stand, under her sign—also hand-painted—You'll Relish Our

HOMEMADE JAM, after Zara had waved us down on the road. When I lowered the driver's side window of my Pepto-Bismol pink COMING UP ROSES truck, she came over to speak to us. "You and Lorne must try mother's sour-cherry jam, Verity," she said, pointing proudly to the stand's tiered rows of jars. "It's a new batch."

The jams stood at the end of a gravel driveway that led to the two-story brick farmhouse shared by Zara and her mother. It had been a working farm at one time. I remembered stopping on the roadside as a child to pat the silky foreheads of Guernsey cows as they looked up from grazing the fields to poke their heads over the wooden fence.

Over the decades since, those fields had been sheared away—sold to developers. The cows were gone, too. All that remained of livestock was a tiny herd of goats in a pen behind the house. Pets, I assumed, because Zara was a dedicated vegan.

Meanwhile, the subdivisions and monster homes were closing in on either side. I wondered how much longer the two women could hold them off.

Cautiously, I tested a bit of jam on the tip of my tongue. Grimacing, I handed back the jar. "I'm not much of a cook..." *That was an understatement.* "But I think you used salt instead of sugar."

Mrs. Price took the jar to stare at it, apparently baffled. "I wondered why it wouldn't set."

Behind her, Zara was hastily plucking jars from the stand and plunking them into a cardboard box. She tucked in the top flaps and shoved the box under the table with one foot, looking embarrassed.

"Was it a new recipe?" I asked her mother, trying to smooth over the awkwardness. "Something you were trying for the first time?"

"Oh no," she said with a shake of her head. "I've been making cherry jam for, let's see..." She counted on her fingers. "...near on seventy years. Never had a problem before." She leaned in with a conspiratorial air. "That strange man was here earlier. He must have tampered with it." She grumbled under her breath. "Always racing up and down the road in that blue car of his." She tilted her head, looking confused. "Or is it red? Then again..."

Zara ran a hand through her graying hair, looking exasperated. "Mom—"

"No harm done," I countered. "Let's forget about it."

But I was confused. Who was this strange man? Was he a figment of her imagination—or real?

"Spicy corn relish?" Mrs. Price had asked, breaking into my thoughts with a jar in one hand and a fresh sample spoon in the other. "Wonderful with toast and tomatoes."

But now, as I drove to their farmhouse to review Zara's "life and death" case, I recalled that incident a week ago with the salt. Her mother could have added something—if not poisonous, then merely inedible—to her jam without realizing it.

Still, how bad could it be? A little indigestion, most likely. People can be dreadfully picky.

Which meant I was unprepared for the scene that unfolded when my landscaping truck crested the hill before Zara's hobby farm. I halted the truck to take it in.

Police cars lined the road, a van with Leafy Hollow

Animal Services stenciled on its side had pulled up alongside the police cars, and two uniformed constables were unspooling yellow caution tape around the sprawling, split-level house next door to Zara's farm.

Flashing lights drew my attention to my rear view mirror. An ambulance was coming up the road behind me. No siren, though. I pulled over onto the shoulder and turned off my engine, watching as the ambulance drove past and into the driveway of Zara's neighbor. It wasn't moving fast, and no one hopped out when it stopped. It couldn't be a medical emergency. But why would an ambulance...

Uh-oh. My throat constricted.

Someone was dead.

I vaulted out of my truck to head for the nearest police cruiser. The officer behind the wheel was making notes on a clipboard.

He put it aside to lower the window when I tapped it with a knuckle.

"Verity. Nice to see you again."

Having a police detective as a fiancé meant I was on first-name terms with most of the force. This came in handy for a fledgling investigator. "You, too, Fred. What's going on?"

He looked grim. "You know I can't—"

I leaned an elbow on the window frame. "It's only between us."

He looked dubious.

"You know Jeff will tell me later anyway."

He sighed. "We don't know what happened. Not yet. Forensics is here."

"But there's a body?"

"Yes."

I sucked in a breath. "It's not Mrs. Price, is it? Samantha?"

Fred looked surprised. "No. It's not a woman." He studied his clipboard. "Herbert Eubanks is the name."

I tried to remember who lived next to Zara. I'd seen him once, during a visit to the Prices' farm. He'd been strolling around his garden with a coffee mug in his hand. He was middle-aged, physically fit, hair not entirely gray, with an air of reserve. I noticed a certain frostiness in the way he greeted Zara's friendly wave. Then she muttered something under her breath that was decidedly unfriendly, and I assumed it went both ways. Neighbors can be very trying.

But he wasn't called Herbert Eubanks. I would have remembered that.

"Is it the homeowner?"

Shaking his head, Fred pointed wordlessly up the road. I followed the direction of his finger. A red tanker truck was parked in the driveway of the split-level. From where I stood, only the back end was visible. I moved over a few steps in order to read the writing on the side of the tank.

EUBANKS' SEPTIC SERVICES
WE'LL TAKE CARE OF IT!

Pointing to the truck, I mouthed a query over my shoulder at Fred. *That guy?*

He nodded, then resumed checking off paperwork boxes.

I had promised to address Zara's problem ASAP. But there was no harm in making a quick stop at her neighbor's to see why it was the focus of so much attention. A natural death wouldn't draw a response like that.

With a brief wave to Fred, I crossed the road and started up the driveway. The split-level house was new, with elegant trimmings of slate stone and gray-stained wood. On the left, three large windows, ten feet high, marked the main room. I suspected its peaked roof sheltered a cathedral ceiling. The front door, its solid wood panels stained a trendy blue-gray, was set back under a portico in the middle. On the right, white wooden shutters were closed over two smaller windows —probably a den or home office.

Behind that, the slate-tiled roof rose and dipped to overlay a series of dormer windows on the second floor. As I came to the end of the driveway and rounded the corner of the house, the vista opened up into an expansive garden of at least an acre, with shade trees, manicured perennial beds, and stone pathways. The roof swooped down to cover a one-story sunroom that spanned the back of the building. Pink and white climbing roses wrapped the pergola that sheltered a flagstone patio and fire pit.

Despite the flowers, the backyard was definitely not smelling of roses. Sniffing, I noticed a sharp tang in the air. Earthy, perhaps.

Three people in blue disposable jumpsuits were bent over a spot in the backyard about ten feet from the house. I recognized one as the coroner, Dr. Rajit Bakshi, "a lovely man" who was fond of Renaissance poetry, according to our local librarian. I assumed the other two were members of the forensic team. All three blocked my view. When one of them moved aside, I gasped.

Two motionless shins, ending in a pair of scuffed running shoes, stuck straight up from the ground. The rest of the body was—

I clapped a hand over my mouth as I made the connection.

Herbert Eubanks had fallen to his death in the septic tank he'd been hired to empty.

I turned away, feeling faintly ill and wondering if I could simply slink off and pretend I'd never been there, when a woman screamed my name.

"Verity! Over here!"

The forensic crew turned in my direction. So much for a silent getaway. I tossed them a feeble smile.

"Stand back, Verity," called Dr. Bakshi before returning to his work. He looked peeved. Must be having a bad day.

"Verity!" came the woman's voice again. I turned around.

Zara Price was waving wildly from her side of the fence. I trotted over.

Before I could reach her, a chest-high gray blur thundered past, nearly knocking me off my feet.

I barely had time to regain my breath before two police officers swooped past, also at a run.

"Stop it," one yelled. "It's heading for those—"

"Look out!"

Too late.

The blue-suited forensic team scattered as the gray and white animal bounded toward them, head lowered. With impressive form, it leapt into the air, clearing the upturned, booted legs sticking up from the tank with room to spare.

The gazelle-like animal landed on the other side, did a

quick feint to elude a startled officer, then headed for the road.

One of the pursuing officers ran into one of the forensic crew, who toppled against the other two. The entire group hit the ground in a tangle of arms and legs.

"Bloody hell!" yelled Dr. Bakshi as he fought to extricate himself. "What the bloody hell is that bloody goat doing now? Why doesn't someone stop the bloody thing?"

Our normally unflappable coroner was decidedly flapped today.

"Oh dear," Zara called behind me. "I warned them not to get Waffles riled up."

I walked over, choking out a response. "Waffles?"

"My billy goat. He's a wether—a castrated ram. You've met him."

"Have I?" Mentally, I reviewed my former visits to Zara's hobby farm, recalling that she had introduced me to all of the goats milling about in their pen. Sadly, I had no memory for faces.

Meanwhile, people were shouting at the front of the house. "This way, this way," someone yelled. "Head him off…"

I inclined my head in the direction of the melee. "Shouldn't you—"

Zara stuck out her chin. "No. I will not help them. I hope Waffles eludes them. Poor baby." Absently, she rubbed the head of a small white goat nuzzling her leg. An even smaller goat trotted up behind me, ducked its head to give me a gentle butt, then clambered through a hole in the fence.

"Don't worry, girls," Zara said, welcoming the new arrival with a head pat. "Everything will be fine."

I furrowed my brow. "Zara? Why is there a hole in your fence?"

She studied the gap, looking perplexed. "I don't know. It wasn't there yesterday."

"I see. And the life and death matter you mentioned would be...?"

"Oh." She looked stricken. "I didn't tell you on the phone?"

"No. But now that I'm here, I assume it has something to do with that." Turning, I pointed to Herbert Eubanks' stiffened form.

We contemplated the dead man—well, his legs—while the investigators scrambled to their feet. The coroner slapped away a helping hand. "Leave me alone," he snapped.

"In a way," Zara said.

"It's too late to help Mr. Eubanks, I'm afraid."

"Oh. I'm not worried about him."

I raised my eyebrows.

"It's a tragedy, of course," she hastily added. "But I'm concerned about poor Waffles." She leaned in. "Did you see the Animal Services van in the driveway?"

"Yes, I did. Why are they here?"

Zara's lower lip quivered. "To take Waffles away. The police think that he...that he..." Sniffling, she wiped the back of a hand over her eyes. "They claim he killed Mr. Eubanks. Oh, Verity," she wailed, gripping my arm. "Waffles has been framed."

I stared at her. The silence that followed was broken only

by the plaintive bleating of the two goats at her side, plus some considerably less-rustic cursing from the road.

"Over there," a man hollered. "Look out," someone else yelled. "Blast!" shrieked a third. "Why didn't you warn me?"

"I don't understand," I said. "What do you mean—Waffles killed Mr. Eubanks?"

Zara rubbed a thumb across her cheek to wipe away another tear. "It's like this..."

A scrabbling noise behind and above me caught my attention. Whirling, I stared at the homeowner's slate-tiled roof, half-expecting to see a disgruntled squirrel throwing pine cones. Or a furious raccoon roused from his diurnal nap by the commotion—and throwing squirrels.

I did not expect to see a goat.

Correction. Several goats.

"Zara?" I asked, in the calmest tone I could muster, pointing to the roof. "Are those...your animals?"

She swung her troubled gaze toward them. "Who else's would they be? Verity, you're not listening to me."

"Right. But is that normal for them? To be on the roof, I mean?"

"They love to climb. They try to get onto my roof all the time. It's adorable. They scramble up onto the shed and then they—"

"Hang on," I said. "Could this be the reason you and your neighbor don't get along?"

She shrugged. "He is a little touchy about his stupid roof. But the thing is, Verity, the girls haven't been over there for ages. Not since I reinforced the fence last spring."

Dubiously, I eyed the gaping hole in the fencing.

"I know," she said with a sigh. "But I swear, it was fine yesterday. Someone did this..." She fingered one of the torn edges. "And it wasn't a four-legged vandal. It was someone with two legs."

I turned to consider the stiff, booted legs sticking up from the septic tank. The forensic team had brushed themselves off and resumed their scrutiny of the body. "Why would anybody put a hole in your fence?"

"Isn't it obvious?" Zara puffed. "To frame Waffles."

I nodded to imply I comprehended this, although it made no sense. But before I could question her further, a familiar voice caught me up short.

"Verity? What are you doing here?"

I whirled to face the superlative detective, and darkly handsome, Jeff Katsuro—also known as my fiancé. "Hi, hon," I said with forced casualness. "Just catching up with my pal Zara here." Jeff looked unconvinced, so I bent over the fence to pat the nearest kid. "And her sweet little goats."

"I see. Then your presence has nothing to with the..." He flicked a thumb in the general direction of the septic tank. "... dead body?"

"Goodness," I said. "What an idea."

CHAPTER 3

"JEFF, it's ridiculous to accuse me of planning my arrival to coincide with the discovery of a dead body. How could I possibly know that someone had taken a header into the septic tank?"

His eyebrows rose.

While I considered my next words, my gaze drifted a little. Which was when I noticed a red, swollen scrape on the side of his face. I reached a finger to point it out. "That looks bad. How did you...? Hang on. What's that on your uniform?" I squinted at his shirt. "It looks like grass stains." Startled, I raised my eyes to meet his. "You looked fine when you left the house this morning. What happened to you?"

"Waffles happened to me." He stepped nearer, with a definite limp.

"Is Waffles okay?" Zara asked, clutching the fence wire.

"He's fine. Animal Services is taking him away. They'll be leaving as soon as—"

Zara didn't hang around to hear the rest of that sentence.

Clapping a hand to her mouth, she darted for the road, rounded the end of the fence, and kept going across her neighbor's front yard.

The two little goats bleated plaintively before scampering after her.

"Should we stop those animals?"

"Why?" Jeff heaved a sigh of resignation. "We already have a murder suspect in custody."

"That was quick work."

He turned an exasperated stare on me.

"Oh. Sorry. You meant...Waffles." I slapped a hand on my cheek in mock regret, then held it there while I re-evaluated his stance. "Maybe you should go home and put ice on that knee."

"How did you know it was my knee?"

"It's always the knee. You're not getting any younger, you know."

"Thanks," he said dryly. "I'm not ready to be put out to pasture yet."

"Unlike Waffles."

"Not helping."

"Sorry," I repeated.

While brushing off his pants with both hands, he gave me a puzzled look. "Seriously. Why are you here?"

"Zara needs my help. She says Waffles is innocent and he's been...framed."

"Framed?" Jeff looked incredulous. "That goat is a menace. He head-butted several officers into the ground. Harry," he added with a shudder, "got it right in the crotch."

"Ooh," I said, wincing sympathetically. "Did it hurt?"

"I'll let you know once he's able to speak."

"Why didn't you wait for Animal Services? They must be trained to deal with barnyard delinquents."

He worked his lips thoughtfully, but said nothing.

"Oh, I get it. With your household pet-wrangling abilities, you thought Waffles would be a pushover for your charms." I chuckled, thinking how my one-eyed tomcat, General Chang, was putty in Jeff's hands. "A regular goat whisperer. Did you offer him the General's liver treats? That won't work. Goats are vegans." I chuckled again, then stifled it at the look of pain on his face. "You're not really hurt, are you?"

"Only my pride," he replied, ruefully rubbing the small of his back. "But it proves my hypothesis."

"Which is?"

"That Waffles shoved Eubanks into that septic tank."

"Where he died."

"Exactly."

"Speaking of which," I grimaced, noting the earthy aroma in the air. "Did Mr. Eubanks drown?"

"The M.E. can't be certain until he does the autopsy, but no, it looks like he didn't. The tank had been mostly emptied. He probably broke his neck."

"That's good."

Jeff raised an eyebrow.

"Comparatively, I meant."

"It's not true," Zara cried.

We whirled to see her standing behind us, hands on hips. Her eyes and nose were reddened even more than they'd been before.

"Waffles didn't do anything. He would never do something like that," she insisted. "He's a good goat. Friendly. And now they're taking him away."

She paused, once again wiping tears from her cheek. "Verity, I need you to clear Waffles' name. You have to help us. There's talk of having him *put down*." The last words came out as a garbled cry.

Jeff cleared his throat. "Miss Price..."

He'd known Zara and her mother for years, but Jeff was always formal on a case.

"Miss Price," he continued gently. "Herbert Eubanks had been in the septic tank pumping business for years. He would be well aware of the dangers of hydrogen sulphide and taken all the recommended safety measures. It's simply not credible that he fell in accidentally."

Zara thrust out her chin. "He might have had some sort of medical event. A heart attack, even."

Jeff nodded. "It's possible. We won't know for certain until the autopsy. But he was a healthy individual with no obvious medical issues. Even if he had suffered a heart attack or a stroke, he would have fallen onto the ground—not head-first through a two-by-three-foot opening. He would have known to stand well back from the tank."

Zara chewed on a fingernail. From her furrowed brow, I could tell she was thinking.

"I'm sorry, Miss Price," Jeff continued. "It's much more likely that Mr. Eubanks was pushed, or in this case, *butted* through that opening."

"Maybe so, but not by Waffles. I'm positive."

"Are you saying one of your other goats might have done it?"

"Never!"

Two goats wandered by, headed for a climbing rose bush on the pergola over the patio.

I winced. "Zara, shouldn't you corral the rest of your herd?"

"Oh," she said, waving a weary hand. "They'll come home on their own."

The goats on the ground paused mid-munch to assess the progress of the two animals on the roof, then scrambled onto a storage cabinet and from there to the pergola, ripping off more roses as they climbed. They scampered onto the roof, dislodging slate tiles with each tread of their hooves.

The tiles clattered onto the patio, tearing off more rose branches.

I turned my eyes away. For a gardener, it was a painful sight.

Zara tugged at my arm. "Verity, you have to help us. Please say you'll take the case."

Jeff's eyebrows rose again. They were getting a real workout today.

"What's going to happen to Waffles?" I asked.

"If he's deemed a danger to the public, I'm afraid..." He left that thought hanging.

Zara sucked in a breath, looking miserable. When one of the goats rubbed up against her, she crouched to circle its neck with a protective arm. "My girls are innocent. *Waffles* is innocent. It must have been an accident."

Jeff took a deep breath. "Miss Price..."

Leaving Jeff to argue with Zara, I walked nearer to the group around the septic tank, taking care to stay well back. For all Zara's concern about Waffles, there was only one victim here. I had never met Herbert Eubanks, but he had a business and a community presence. He probably had family. He didn't deserve to die like that.

Then I wandered over to the broken fence. Scores of cloven hoof prints trampled the perennial bed that lined the homeowner's side of the fence line and made a beeline for the patio and the garden beyond. But the rest of the fence was intact. Even given my rudimentary knowledge of construction, it looked like a substantial barrier.

I bent to study the huge, jagged hole in the wire fencing. It was obviously the work of a human miscreant wielding a fairly substantial wire cutter. Not only that, but...I peered more closely. The cut links were bent inward, toward the homeowner's side of the fence.

I rejoined Jeff and Zara. They were still arguing.

"I'm sorry, Miss Price, but that billy goat is a menace," Jeff was saying. "There's nothing I can do."

"There's another possibility," I said.

Zara turned excited eyes on me. "Do you have a theory, Verity?"

When Jeff opened his mouth, I held up a hand to stop him. "I'm not interfering, but since Zara is my client now—"

"Thank you," she said.

"It seems obvious her fence was damaged by humans, not goats. And done deliberately."

"That doesn't change the fact that Waffles—"

"What if someone pushed Eubanks into that tank on

purpose, and then cut open the fence so the goats would trample any evidence? Maybe the whole thing was planned in advance, and the killer took advantage of the goats next door to cover up his deed."

"No one could possibly know the goats would even notice a hole in the fence, or come through it if they did. Never mind how much damage they might do," Jeff pointed out. "They could have gone in an entirely different direction. It would be leaving a lot to chance."

"I bet anybody who lived in this neighborhood was well aware of the destructive power of a gaggle of goats."

"A tribe," Zara said.

We turned to look at her. "What?"

"A tribe. That's what you call a herd of goats."

"Anyway," Jeff said, ignoring this caprine lore, "that would imply one of the homeowner's neighbors did the deed."

"Or the homeowner himself," I pointed out. "Have you thought of that?"

"Yeah," Zara broke in. "He's got a hell of a temper."

Jeff swiveled to face her. "How do you know that?" he asked in the even tone I'd long since learned to recognize. His *Officer On Duty* mode, I called it.

I had no time to warn Zara, though. She walked right into it.

"You should have heard him screaming at Waffles the last time he..." Too late, she noticed my frantically slashing hands.

"That would be the last time Waffles broke through your fence and decimated your neighbor's yard? Is that what you're saying?" Jeff asked, still in that no-nonsense tone. He whipped out his notebook and pen.

This was not going well.

"Zara, why don't you take the goats back to their pen," I suggested. "If you go around by the road, they won't do any more damage to the perennials. I'll meet you out front in a minute."

"And we'll go this way," I said, taking Jeff by the arm and pointing to the far side of the house. We talked while we circled back to the driveway.

"Who lives here?" I asked.

"Clive Yeager. Retired. Former military," Jeff said in clipped tones.

"Where is he now?"

"We're looking for him," Jeff said.

"That's suspicious, don't you think?"

"No. He's probably out shopping."

I started at the sound of a vehicle being driven very fast up the road. "Not anymore."

A metallic blue BMW sedan shrieked to a halt at the end of the driveway, which was still blocked by Eubanks' tanker truck. The driver's door opened and a tall man, about six-four, in khakis, a polo shirt, and deck shoes, vaulted out.

"What the hell is going on?" he blustered, striding in the direction of the officers standing outside the front door. When he saw Jeff, he swerved to confront him. "Are you in charge? What the hell is going on?"

Because repeating the same question usually works.

I tried not to roll my eyes.

His cropped hair was salt-and-pepper, his eyes clear, his

bearing erect. There was a suggestion of middle-aged spread at his middle, but only a suggestion.

This, I assumed, was Clive Yeager.

I breathed a quick prayer to the Lord of the Goats, hoping there were a few rose blooms left on that pergola— and tiles on the roof. Otherwise, I didn't give much for those animals' chances.

"Mr. Yeager, I presume?" Jeff didn't allow him time for a response. "I'm afraid there's been an incident on your property. A man has died under suspicious circumstances."

Yeager's cheeks grew red as he formulated his reply. Finally, he said, "What are you saying?"

"A man has died—"

"I heard that part. Details, please." Holding up a hand, he snapped his fingers. "Who is dead?"

Jeff nodded at the tanker truck. "We believe the deceased is Herbert Eubanks, the owner of Eubanks' Septic Services."

Yeager blinked at the mention of Eubanks' name—twice —but his erect bearing did not slump even a second.

"Do you know Mr. Eubanks?"

"Certainly not."

"Was he scheduled to pump out your tank today?"

"How should I know?" Frowning, he took in the crowded scene, hands on hips. "I don't look after the mundane stuff. You'll have to ask my man."

Jeff flipped out his notebook. "Where can we find him?"

"Isn't he here?"

"I'm afraid not, no."

Glossing over Yeager's mention of a "man," Jeff zeroed in on the pertinent detail. "Have you been out all morning?"

Yeager rubbed the back of his neck while fixing Jeff with a calm gaze. "Yes."

"Can you tell me where?"

"I was visiting a friend."

"Who is this friend?"

"None of your business."

We were distracted by the gentle clip-clop of cloven hooves on pavement, accompanied by Zara's soothing tones. "Come along. Don't you worry about Waffles. He'll be back soon. This way. That's right."

Yeager stiffened, his hand still clamped to the back of his neck. Slowly, he turned to face the driveway.

His eyes widened at the sight of Zara Price bending over a gaggle—sorry, *tribe*—of tiny goats, urging them along. Perhaps sensing a disruption in the Force, she looked up. Her own eyes widened.

With a thunderous roar of, "What the devil is she doing here?" Yeager started toward Zara at a furious pace, waving his arms. "Get those lousy animals off my property!"

Unfortunately—as I could have predicted, but no one ever thinks to ask me—his outburst produced the opposite effect. The goats scattered, bleating in confusion. Three of the bigger ones sprinted for the road, their legs kicking up behind them as they ran.

"No," Zara yelled. "Head them off. They'll get hit by a car."

The goats were in no danger. They had no intention of doing anything as mundane as hitting the road. Higher ground was their aim. And they found it—by scrambling onto the hood of Yeager's very expensive-looking BMW.

Every human male in the vicinity flinched at the sound of hoofs denting, scraping, and scrabbling over the hood's expensive metallic paint.

The goats consolidated their position by scrambling onto the car's roof. Men turned away in horror, unable to watch.

The goats' rectangular pupils swiveled widely as they regarded the humans below them. One of the goats chewed placidly on a hank of white climbing rose dangling from its lips. I identified it as *Rosa* 'Iceberg'. *A good choice.* The other two merely bleated, no doubt regretting the fact they had not brought their own snacks.

Yeager wheeled on Zara. His face was purple. "You —*maniac.* I warned you—"

As he started toward her, Jeff held out a warning hand. "Mr. Yeager," he said, in a voice stern enough to make his former clipped tone sound like a friendly greeting, "I advise you to hold your ground. Better yet..." Jeff indicated the front door. "I suggest we take this inside, where you can explain to me where you've been all morning."

Yeager worked his jaw so furiously I half-expected to see blood. "I told you. I was visiting a friend. And now I'm going into my house. *Alone.* I will talk to no one other than my solicitor. And move this *circus* off my lawn." He drew himself up into a picture of dignity before walking up his front steps, unlocking the front door, and stepping inside.

I braced myself for the inevitable slam. But instead, the door closed with a barely audible *click.*

CHAPTER 4

WE STOOD, staring at Yeager's closed door, for a long moment.

Finally, Jeff spoke. "Miss Price." I recognized his frustration by the set of his jaw. "Kindly corral these goats and return them to their pen. Now, please."

"I was just going to do that," she replied defensively.

As Zara turned to go, I touched her arm. "I'll help you," I whispered.

She nodded before walking away, uttering strange cries of "*bup-bup-bup*," followed by shouts of "Olivia! Buttercup! Tatiana!" Then more "*bup-bup-bup*."

The nearest goat looked up from its inspection of a trembling hybrid tea rose, then trotted happily after her. I puffed out a breath. One flower saved, at least.

Jeff's mouth dropped as the goats filed after Zara. "How does she do that?"

"I'll find out and let you know. By the way, that 'man' Yeager mentioned—do you know who he is?"

"Not yet." His eyes narrowed. "Don't get involved, Verity."

Holding up my hands, I assumed a look of mock outrage.

Jeff turned on his heel and strode off to confer with the forensic team.

While the bulk of the tribe went placidly, it was more difficult to persuade the three goats atop Yeager's BMW to relinquish their vantage point. Even repeated *bup-bup-bup*s from Zara did not dislodge them.

The Animal Services team didn't hang around to help. Given the teary streams of abuse they'd endured from Zara, I couldn't blame them. They closed the rear doors of their van on Waffles' panicked bleating and drove away, leaving his owner sobbing in the driveway.

Meanwhile, we had attracted a crowd of onlookers, including several uniformed police officers who assured us they were on hand only for crowd control.

Self-control, apparently, was harder. They smirked broadly in our direction. Occasionally one turned away, shoulders heaving, before resuming an erect posture with his expression wiped clean.

Neighbors and passersby—several of whom had parked their cars along the side of the road to watch, leaning against their vehicles—felt no such reluctance. Their hollers of "atta girl," "thar she goes," and "try a lasso," were not helpful.

Occasionally, Yeager came to a front window to scowl at

the chaos, then disappear. He probably couldn't bear to watch, either.

Eventually, we coaxed the goats off the car and onto terra firma. By then, the car's hood was so dented and cratered I doubted it would be possible to start the engine.

After we returned the goats to their pen behind the farmhouse, Zara latched the gate and leaned over it, watching them mill about.

I patted her shoulder. "They're okay, aren't they?"

"No," she replied sadly. "They miss Waffles. They can tell he's gone."

I squinted at them. They looked the same to me. "Poor things," I said. Pitching my voice a shade higher, I called to the nearest animal, "He'll be back soon, don't worry."

The goat stared at me, its expression inscrutable. It made me a little uneasy, to be honest.

Zara was counting them, her finger outstretched. "...seven, eight. One's missing. It must be..." She scanned the pen again, leaning over the gate. "...Agnes. The littlest one. We have to go back and find her."

"I'll come with you. Maybe I can figure out what happened."

Zara looked uncomfortable. "Are you going to talk to Yeager?"

"I doubt it. He won't come outside while the police are here. Even if he does, I'll be with you if he tries anything. There's nothing to worry about."

Frankly, I was more worried about what Zara might do to Yeager than the other way around, but I kept that to myself.

We set off down the driveway. By the time we reached

Yeager's backyard, the forensic team had loaded Herbert Eubanks' body onto a gurney. Yellow caution tape surrounded the septic tank and an area behind the house, but there were no stiff, booted legs to stare accusingly at us. Still, I kept my view averted while the gurney trundled past.

"Zara," I asked as nonchalantly as I could. "Who found the body?"

"I did. Then I called the police."

I assessed the sight lines between Yeager's septic tank and Zara's farmhouse. There were spruce and cedar trees in the way. "But you couldn't see him from your place, could you?"

She shook her head. "No. It was after I headed out to feed the goats—I always do that before breakfast. I saw they'd escaped and I was frantic to find them. When I checked the perimeter, it was obvious where they'd gone. So I went after them."

"Through the hole in the fence?"

"No. I didn't want to do any more damage to Yeager's precious perennials. I went around. I was kind of hoping to get them back before he noticed anything, to be honest."

I scrunched up my face at this, wondering how Yeager would not notice the damage to his property, even if the goats were safely back behind the fence. Unless he was blind—and I saw no indication of anything other than 20/20 vision. He hadn't even been wearing sunglasses when he got out of his car.

"You said the goats escaped. Did you mean through the fence?"

"No, from their pen." Zara straightened up, her brow furrowed. "That's the strange part, Verity. I built that pen specially. They couldn't possibly have broken out by themselves. Come over and take a look, then you'll see what I mean."

"I will. But you mentioned the perennials. Is Yeager a dedicated gardener?"

She rolled her eyes. "Supposedly. Those roses of his won top awards at the Canadian National Exhibition." In a low tone she added, "He probably sprayed the other entries with weed killer."

"That's harsh."

"You don't know him."

"He doesn't look like a gardener, I'll give you that." As the proprietor of a landscaping business, I could usually spot fellow enthusiasts. They had dirt under their nails, scuffed and battered shoes, and red necks from kneeling in the sun. Yeager, on the other hand, was immaculately turned out. And that BMW had never seen anything even resembling a bag of manure.

I amended that to, *until recently*, thinking of the goats.

"He doesn't do the work himself," Zara added with a snort. "That *man* of his does it all. Yeager just gives him orders."

"You mean he tells him what to plant?"

At this, she looked thoughtful. "I don't think so. I've overheard a few of their discussions and it seemed to me that his hired helper was the real gardener. I'm not sure Yeager knows a rose from a rhododendron."

"Then why bother?"

She shrugged. "Bragging rights, I guess."

"Do you know his man's name?"

"No, but my mother might. She's talked to him a few times. When Yeager wasn't home, of course," she added, scowling at something behind me. "That man," she spat out the words, "refuses to speak to either of us."

I spun around to see Yeager looking out a window in his sun room. He had a glass in his hand and was glaring at us. I tried a friendly wave, but he merely turned away.

"I'm going to leave before he comes outside and starts yelling," Zara said. She pointed to the bottom of the garden, where a tiny goat was nibbling the lower branches of a flowering spirea. "Can you get Agnes? You only have to take hold of her collar and lead her gently along. She's very sweet and will follow you anywhere."

"Of course." I headed off on a zigzag trajectory that would allow me to double back behind the kid, in order not to spook it. But as I got farther from the house, it struck me that the septic tank in which Herbert Eubanks died was very close to the back of the building. Too close, in fact. Having discussed the possibility of revamping the ancient septic system at Rose Cottage—the eighteenth-century, rundown fieldstone home I'd inherited from my aunt—I knew that was no longer allowed.

Not only that, but an older septic tank like that would not comply with the current code. It might have been grandfathered, like Rose Cottage's septic system, but Yeager's home was fairly new. It must have been erected after demolishing a much older home. The shrubs around the current residence, which would have been planted once the house was built, looked to be about ten years old.

A permit for new construction like that would have

required an updated septic system. And the new tank would be a lot bigger.

Then where was it?

After scanning the yard, I spotted telltale black pipes sticking out of the ground about twenty feet from the house. The new tank.

Why, then, was Herbert Eubanks pumping out the old one?

Soft bleats and a gentle head-butt to my thigh drove that question from my mind. I bent to caress the velvet fur of the gray and brown kid. "Let's get you home," I said, pulling gently on the leather collar. "This way."

While herding Agnes back into the pen, Zara took pains to point out the "safety features" that kept the goats secure behind sturdy posts and wire fencing. "They couldn't have gotten out on their own," she said.

"Are you sure? They seem like real escape artists."

She sighed. "They are. But even if they found some new route out of the pen, it hardly seems likely they would have had time to break through the fence. They would have been sleeping. It was early when I went to feed them."

"It does look as if they had help," I agreed.

"Besides," she continued. "It rained last night. Goats hate to get wet. They wouldn't have left their shed."

We stood, watching the goats. One of the bigger ones was butting around a big blue exercise ball. "That's Ethel. She loves doing that," Zara said with obvious affection.

"She's very cute. I'm afraid I have to go, Zara. I left Ethan by himself at a job site and I need to check in with him. We'll talk later, okay?"

She nodded absently, chuckling at Ethel.

I studied her, wondering how best to word my next question. I decided to be blunt.

"Zara, who will pay for the damage to Yeager's car? And his roof?"

"I don't know. I hope my homeowner's insurance, although last time they threatened..." Wearily, she ran her hands across her face with a sigh. "They said they wouldn't pick up the bill again."

"Last time? Is that the incident you told Jeff about when you described Yeager's temper?"

She nodded. "I can't afford to pay for that car." Tears sprang to her eyes.

"I'm sure you won't have to. Yeager must have insurance. You'll probably only have to pay his deductible. It can't be more than a few thousand."

At this, she started to wail. "I don't have even that much. Oh, Verity—I might have to sell the girls."

I patted her arm consolingly. "It won't come to that. We'll find out who's behind this." Inwardly, I had my doubts. That car of Yeager's was worth over a hundred grand. His deductible might be equally hefty, not to mention any civil suit he might decide to bring. I walked to my own vehicle—a twenty-year-old bright pink pickup, worth about three hundred—leaving Zara slumped on a bench behind the farmhouse. It struck me that Zara had a good reason to blame the tribe's mysterious escape on someone else.

Anyone else.

Ethan Neuhaus was puffing his way around the half-acre lawn of our first job of the morning by the time I pulled up in the Coming Up Roses pickup. I'd dropped him and the mower off with a promise to return after checking out Zara's alleged life-and-death scenario. Ethan's own vehicle, an aging Camaro, was "in the shop."

He stopped the mower to wave at me as I walked across the lawn. Then he pulled a rag from his pocket to mop his brow. He looked beat. Since it was barely 9 a.m., I was surprised. Ethan Neuhaus, a wiry bag of bones with shorn hair, scars on his scalp, and a missing finger—lost in a child-hood accident, he claimed—was generally more energetic.

Today, that shorn scalp revealed a large purple bruise that extended onto his forehead. I peered at his bloodshot eyes. "Had a hard night?"

"I'm fine." He tucked the filthy rag back into his pocket.

"You don't look fine. How did you get that bruise?"

"Walked into a door."

"Ethan." I adopted a level tone. "With Lorne out of the country, you know I'm relying on you. You promised you wouldn't let me down."

"I won't." From his other pocket, he pulled a can of caffeine-heavy Red Bull, snapped off the tab, and took a long swallow. "I'm fine, told ya."

His words were slurred.

My jaw dropped. "Are you drunk?"

"No," he blurted. "Course not." He drained the can before dropping it in a pail hanging from the mower's handles. "Told ya. I'm fine."

"You're not fine. You're under the influence. And operating heavy machinery. Get off that mower. Now."

"I haven't had a drink," he said, carefully enunciating each word while yanking out the mower's key and dismounting.

"Maybe not this morning. But I'm willing to wager you had quite a few last night. Enough that you're still drunk." Another thought struck me. "Is that what happened to your car? Was it impounded? Did you get into an accident?"

"No," he shouted. "It's not—" He lowered his voice. "My car is in the shop, I told you. Transmission trouble."

Because the car in question had barely a single operative door, this wasn't surprising.

I studied his face, recalling that I'd dropped him off at the job site less than an hour earlier. He hadn't seemed drunk then, although he was more quiet than usual.

Which wasn't saying much, since Ethan Neuhaus was not sociable at the best of times.

I watched as he popped the metal tab on another Red Bull.

"How many of those have you had?"

"Does it matter?" He took a long swig, paused a moment to swallow, then another. But as he was raising the can a third time to drain it, a strange look came over his face. He burped. Burped again. His eyes grew wild. Then he bent over, vomiting violently on the lawn.

Fortunately, he missed the mower.

But not my shoes.

"Oh man," he said, straightening up and pulling that rag from his pocket again. "Sorry. Let me clean those for you."

"No." I shook my head. "Go home, Ethan. I'll talk to you tomorrow."

I brushed the top of my running shoes over a clean bit of grass, then climbed onto the mower. "Keys," I said, holding out my palm.

He handed them over. "I'm sorry, Verity. I'll make it up to you."

Having heard this before, I merely sighed.

"Wait," he said as I inserted the key. "What happened to Zara Price?"

"Nothing. But Herbert Eubanks is dead." I turned the key and the engine sprang to life.

"What?" Ethan screamed over the noise. "What did you say?"

I turned off the key. "Herbert Eubanks is dead. Zara found his body this morning. In Clive Yeager's back yard."

Ethan looked more shocked than I'd ever seen him. More shocked than even the time he'd narrowly escaped a street brawl during a busker festival.

"Herbert Eubanks?" he asked.

"That's right. The septic pumper guy. Did you know him?"

"Yeahhhh. How did he...?"

"Fell into a septic tank. Accident, the police think."

Ethan looked incredulous. "That's impossible." He shook his head, staring off into the distance.

"Ethan, if you know something that might assist the police with their enquiries..."

He gave me a sharp look.

I raised both hands in a gesture of surrender. "I know.

You're not a fan of the police force. But if Herbert was a friend of yours—"

He snorted. "Herbert Eubanks was no friend of mine." He frowned. "Why are you involved?"

"I'm not," I said, wondering at this sudden interest in my investigative sideline. "I'm a friend of Zara's. She's concerned her goats might be at risk. They made quite a mess of Yeager's back yard." Knowing how fond Ethan was of his Camaro, I decided not to mention the desecration of Yeager's BMW. Ethan was already under the weather. Details of such an automotive tragedy might push him right over the edge.

He was still frowning at me.

"Go home," I said, reaching to twist the key.

"Verity, I'm not kidding. You should steer clear of this."

"What are you talking about?"

"Eubanks. And Yeager. Steer clear."

I was aware that Ethan's background included a few unsavory details and a minor criminal record. Jeff had warned me against hiring him, although he admitted that Ethan was not violent—merely...How had he put it? *Unreliable.* And I'd discovered that for myself.

But Ethan had proved his worth. Not only by showing up for work and doing a good job but also by providing a vital clue in a previous investigation—at considerable personal risk.

Besides, easy-going Lorne Lewins, my regular employee and personal friend, had no problem working with Ethan. He liked him. And I trusted Lorne implicitly.

At least I did until he and his beloved, bakery owner Emy Dionne, took off on a three-week adventure to Bermuda, where they were currently sunning themselves on the pink sands of world-famous Horseshoe Bay beach.

I knew all about Horseshoe Bay because Emy sent me—her bestie—a photo. Every. Single. Day. Wouldn't you think blue skies dotted with fluffy clouds, soft pink sand, and luxuriant Gulf Stream surf would get boring after a while? Apparently, they don't.

I climbed down from the mower to face off with Ethan.

"You know something about Clive Yeager. If you tell me what it is, I might forget to tell Jeff that you were operating a riding mower while intoxicated."

To be honest, I suspected reckless lawnmower activity wasn't a felony. Or even a misdemeanor. Probably not covered under the Highway Traffic Act, either. Still, if it exposed his fiancée in any sort of risky behavior, Jeff would not look kindly on it.

A fact Ethan was aware of. He sucked in a breath.

"It's only rumors. Honestly. And even if I did know what they were up to, I couldn't tell you."

I parsed this sentence before replying. "If you don't know what it is, how do you know that you can't tell me?"

Ethan looked confused. That made two of us.

"Well..." he started, looking nervous. "Look, I'm not kidding. Just steer clear, that's all I can say." He turned on his heel. "I don't feel well. I'm walking home. I'll work the rest of the week for nothing to make it up to you."

"That's not necessary—"

But Ethan was already yards away. He raised one hand in a backward salute before disappearing down the road.

CHAPTER 5

AFTER AN ENDLESS, exhausting day cutting lawns and edging flower beds by myself, the only thing on my mind as I wearily mounted the front steps of Rose Cottage was a long, hot shower. Followed by a nice cold drink on the back patio overlooking magnificent Pine Hill Valley.

I hadn't counted on Boomer, the energetic terrier mix that shared the cottage with Jeff and me. Boomer had been indoors since the pit stop I made over the lunch hour, and he was raring to go. The moment I turned my key in the front door lock, the little dog started bouncing with excitement. By the time I actually had the door open and stepped inside, he was alerting the entire neighborhood to my unprecedented return.

Arf-arf-arf. Arf-arf-arf. Arf-arf-arf.

Whereas General Chang, the one-eyed tomcat that had adopted me mere days after my arrival in the village, was reclining languidly on the back of an armchair, tail swishing, watching the dog with his usual sangfroid. I wasn't fooled. I knew The General was happy to see me—he had, after all, picked the chair nearest the door.

"Come on, then." I unhooked Boomer's leash from its hook. Might as well get it over with. If I delayed long enough to take a shower, or fix a drink, he might explode with suppressed excitement. Plus, once I collapsed into a chair, I might never get up again.

I attached the leash to Boomer's new leather collar. Jeff had purchased a hand-tooled rawhide number, claiming the bejeweled one I bought was "too girly for that poor dog." I suspected it was actually too girly for Jeff, since I was pretty sure Boomer couldn't care less, but I held my tongue. I deferred to Jeff's opinions on all things sartorial, to be honest. Human and canine.

We stepped out the door, locking it behind us. Normally, I wouldn't bother, but Jeff—and my Aunt Adeline, who shared a home next door with her long-time companion Gideon Picard—were adamant about "security measures." It was easier to comply than object. Although I did smirk a little behind their backs.

Even though I'd put in one of my longest work days ever, it was still broad daylight. It was well past the dinner hour, but sunshine flooded Lilac Lane, filtering through the overhanging branches of chestnuts and maples. Blue jays flittered across the lane, and chattering red squirrels darted from tree to tree. The days of late June were the longest of the year. I couldn't decide if that made my day better, or worse.

Boomer trotted by my side, occasionally pausing to utter a warning *arf-arf-arf* at the cheekiest rodents.

"I don't know why you bother. They don't look worried to me."

Boomer tossed me an incredulous look before resuming his steely surveillance.

My cell phone rang, eliciting a fresh round of *arfs*.

I slipped it from my pocket to check the screen. Wilf Mullins, Leafy Hollow councilor, proud Hummer owner, mayoral candidate, and my lawyer, was returning my call.

"Verity! Great to talk to you again. It's been ages. I have to make this quick. Giving a speech on village history at the retirement home tonight. Campaign stuff, you know."

"How's the campaign going, by the way?"

"Well..."

My question hadn't been a serious one. It was intended as an icebreaker before I divulged the real reason for my call. I'd expected Wilf's usual effusive optimism. But instead, he sounded downcast. It must be more than a mishap at the campaign pamphlet printer's to depress Wilf. "What's wrong?"

He groaned. "I was expecting an uncontested election. That's what everybody said. *Don't worry, Wilf. You're a shoo-in. Who would run against you?* That's what they told me."

Uh-oh. "Wilf? Did someone else file a nomination form?"

"Yes. This morning. With the two-hundred-dollar fee. There are now two candidates in the race."

Technically, there were more than two, because the bumblebee mascot for the Strathcona football team had also filed, as well as a local medium, who promised to "awaken Leafy Hollow's team spirit." Personally, I found that one disturbing. And there had been one long summer weekend when someone spray-painted the bronze statue of the village founder, a dour-faced Loyalist in tight pants and riding boots, with the slogan, *"Vote Britches for Mayor."*

But I knew what Wilf meant.

"Who's the new candidate?"

"Martin Griffiths. He showed up at the village hall this morning. With a retinue, I heard."

Pausing to let Boomer dig frantically at a pile of rotted leaves beside a tree stump, I mulled this over. "I don't think I know a Martin Griffiths."

"You wouldn't. He moved back to the village recently after years living out of the country. Some Caribbean island, I think. Anyway, he came back last fall."

"Where does he work?"

"Doesn't. He's retired from some fancy corporate job. I'm not exactly sure what. He'll have plenty of time to campaign."

"Wilf, you shouldn't worry. You have a real presence in the village and years of service on council. Why would anybody vote for this Griffiths person?"

Even over the phone line, I heard his anguished sigh. "Because he's already been the mayor."

"Really? Then why haven't I—"

"You wouldn't know, Verity. It was years ago, and you weren't living in the province then. But Martin Griffiths was the village's most popular mayor. He'd still be mayor today if he hadn't given it all up because of poor health."

"Is he elderly?"

"Not really. He's not in his eighties or anything. After his stint as mayor, he started up some online financial business. Made a fortune, apparently."

"But he was ill, you said. Running a startup can be draining. Why did he attempt it?"

"Ha. I never believed all that stuff about his health." I could hear Wilf's fingernails tapping on his desk. He had me on speakerphone, obviously. "There were rumors that he—"

I didn't hear the rest because I was too busy trying to stay upright. An exceptionally bold squirrel had run across in front of us, pausing only to taunt Boomer with a loud *chirp-chirp*. If squirrels could raise a finger, I swear that one did.

Boomer launched into a missile-like attack, dragging me along with him.

"Stop it," I yelled, digging in my heels and trying to hold him back.

The squirrel darted up the nearest tree. Boomer clapped his front paws on the trunk, *arf*ing furiously, but at least he wasn't propelling me forward anymore.

Wilf was still talking. "I didn't put any stock in it at the time, but still, one wonders."

"Right," I said breathlessly. "Sorry, Wilf. I didn't get all that. Griffiths isn't entirely respectable? Is that what you said?"

Wilf muttered something inaudible before answering. "Unfortunately, he's straight as a die. Ethical, honorable, and completely trustworthy. It's a nightmare," he moaned. "And now he's back. Running on a crime-control ticket, if you can believe it. Crime! In Leafy Hollow. Ridiculous."

I didn't have a rejoinder for this, because in my experience crime—as in the lethal shovel-to-the-head variety—was, in fact, a bit of a problem for the sleepy village. "Yes, ridiculous," I agreed. "Where does this Martin Griffiths live, anyway? In one of those new condos by the river?"

"Oh, no. He bought the Harrison estate. Paid twenty million, I heard."

"Wow. Where is that?"

"You've seen it. The old stone place across from the entrance to the Pine Hill Conservation Area? The place with the wrought-iron fencing and the outbuildings and the locked gate and the waterfall?"

I sucked in a breath. I *had* seen it. Many times.

"Wilf, is that the estate that overlooks Clive Yeager's place?"

"That's the one. They're neighbors, although obviously they're not swapping tales over the fence because the Harrison estate is huge. Anyway, enough of my worries. You called because you had a question, Verity?"

"I did. But..." Watching Boomer stare into the branches of a giant oak with an intensity no human could hope to match, I paused to rephrase. "The fact is, Wilf, it's Clive Yeager I'm calling about. I wanted to get your opinion of him."

"Is Clive hiring you to do lawn work? I thought he had a man for that."

Again with the man. I was starting to take this personally.

"He hasn't hired me for anything. But his neighbor on the other side, Zara Price, asked me to look into a bit of an issue with her goats."

Boomer jerked me farther along the road as he darted around the tree trunk, obviously expecting the squirrel to sneak down the other side.

"Goats?" Wilf asked in a puzzled tone. "Is that a new sideline with you?"

"No. It's an investigative thing."

"Huh." More fingernail tapping. "Wait a minute—I've heard about those goats. Yeager hates them. He's always trying to get me to sue Zara Price, and her mother, and the truck they rode in on. I always tell him to let it go. Disputes between neighbors never end well. What has that woman done now?"

Two thoughts struck me.

Wilf had not yet heard about Herbert Eubanks' unfortunate demise.

And second—he was Clive Yeager's lawyer.

"Didn't Yeager tell you about the dead man in his backyard?"

Okay, a little brusque, but I was taken aback.

"Dead man in his...What on earth are you talking about? Oh, hang on, Verity. I've got a call on the other line. Look at that—it's Clive himself. Talk about coincidence. Can I get back to you?"

"Sure," I said, pretty certain Wilf and I would not be resuming this conversation. "But before you go—one quick question. Is Clive Yeager a respectable sort of person? Honest and so forth?"

Wilf uttered one of his customary guffaws. At least he was feeling better about his mayoral setback. I was happy to cheer him up, even at the cost of looking ridiculous. I'm good that way.

"Respectable? You're such a joker, Verity." He chuckled.

"I'd trust Clive Yeager with my life. Does that answer your question? Sorry, I have to go." He clicked off the call.

Back at Rose Cottage, I munched on a grilled cheese sandwich—I lacked the energy to attempt anything more ambitious—while contemplating my day and tossing baby carrots to Boomer, who snapped them up before they had a chance to hit the floor.

It had not been a good day.

I'd hired Ethan away from my main competitor, landscaper Ryker Fields, after Ryker ran into a spot of bother—actually, a lot of bother, and criminal bother at that. His business was on hiatus for a while and Ethan needed the work. I knew Ethan's faults. It was probably pique that led me to take a chance on him. I get my back up when everybody's telling me what to do, or what not to do. And I did that with Ethan. I couldn't admit it without looking like an idiot. Oh, wait—too late.

Then there was Hawkes Investigation Agency's new case. Waffles, the wayward wether. With a wince, I recalled telling Zara Price, *I'll find out who's behind this.*

What had I been drinking when I made that promise?

It wasn't merely another case of a missing pet. This pet had been implicated in a suspicious death. And that case had been assigned to Jeff.

I'd always promised to stay clear of Jeff's murder cases. Fortunately, he was working late at the station, going over evidence with his team. I wouldn't have to defend my choice tonight.

With a start, I dropped my half-eaten sandwich onto the plate. I'd completely forgotten to ask Wilf a crucial question. *What would happen to Waffles?* What would the authorities do to the billy goat if he was deemed a dangerous animal? And who decided what constituted *dangerous?*

I contemplated the sandwich, then tipped it into Boomer's dish. My appetite had disappeared. I was in over my head this time. I couldn't answer even the most basic questions about my new case.

To make it worse, any suspicion about Clive Yeager was unfounded, according to Wilf's assessment. But that brought me back to Ethan. What had he meant, *Steer clear?*

Steer clear of what, exactly? And why?

And looming over the whole sorry mess was the one very personal question I should be able to settle but somehow couldn't—our wedding date. Jeff and me.

Sliding the platinum chain over my neck, I unclasped its fastener to slide off my diamond-and-ruby engagement ring. I slipped it onto my ring finger, admiring the way the stones caught the light. Jeff had given me the chain with the ring, so I could wear it while landscaping without fear something would happen to it.

He was not pressuring me to decide. Jeff was happy we were getting married, but content to wait until I got around to the details. He'd even gone along with my professed desire for a big wedding, with "a bridesmaid and a cake and a band," although it was the second time for both of us. I think he found it endearing.

As for me, given my tendency to suffer anxiety attacks in crowds, I started to panic the moment the words were out of my mouth. But the more I admired my ring under the kitchen's unromantic overhead light, with Boomer munching carrots by my side, the more I realized I was being ridiculous. Jeff wasn't going anywhere. Also, he was supportive of pretty much anything I wanted to do.

But would that support extend to interference with his murder investigation?

Probably not.

Meanwhile, Ethan would return to work tomorrow and Lorne would be home soon. I'd been spoiled of late, with two strong employees to shoulder the workload. Today had been a good opportunity to get my hands dirty, to remember what it was like to be a working woman. My best friend, Emy Dionne, worked her butt off running the 5X Bakery. Five days a week, she rose at 4 a.m. to start prepping and baking, followed by a full day in the shop. Even on her days off, she was planning and sourcing. Emy never complained. And here I was, begrudging her a three-week holiday.

I should be happy I had so many clients. When I took over the business from Aunt Adeline, it hadn't been a priority of hers for years. That had changed, and my aunt was proud of me for bringing about that transformation. Ethan and I could hold the fort for the time being.

As for Waffles, I was being ridiculous there, too. Animal Services wouldn't sentence a poor goat to death over a misunderstanding. They probably had a nice little retirement farm for wayward wethers.

It couldn't hurt to make sure, though.

I made another quick call to Wilf.

He answered immediately. "Verity! How's my favorite client?"

I heard the *pop* of a cork, followed by the soft hiss of a beverage being poured. One with lots of bubbles.

"Thanks for taking my call again, Wilf. I hope I'm not interrupting anything." As I strained to listen, my eyebrows rose. *Was that feminine giggling I heard in the background?*

"No problem. How can I help you?"

"Just a quick question." I took a deep breath. "If a person's goat was found to be responsible for another person's death, would that goat have to be destroyed? Legally, I mean?"

That time I definitely heard giggling.

To his credit, Wilf took my question seriously. "The Dog Owner's Liability Act in Ontario allows for a dangerous dog —if it's injured humans or other animals—to be destroyed. After due process, of course."

"Does that law apply to goats?"

"I can't say the question's ever come up."

More giggling in the background.

"But, no. I'm pretty sure it doesn't."

"So the goat would be safe. What about the owner?"

"The owner would almost certainly be sued for damages. But the goat might not be safe either, Verity. Any animal that caused a human death could be considered aggressive. And aggressive behavior is one of the symptoms of rabies."

"How would they tell if it had rabies?"

"Ah...That requires a test of the animal's brain tissue." Pause. "Which requires the animal to be dead."

"Then it might be destroyed after all?"

"Possibly. Sorry."

"Thanks, Wilf." I clicked off the call, envisioning how upset Zara would be if that happened to Waffles. But there was no point worrying about that now. The best thing to do was to move forward and find a new suspect.

Too bad my qualms about Clive Yeager had been unfair. I knew it was petty to resent that. After all, why should it upset me that one Leafy Hollow resident was *not* a murderer? There had to be some innocent villagers. It was simply the law of averages.

The thing to do was to plot a new course. Go at the problem from a new angle. Reassess the situation.

And I had just the person to help with that—Aunt Adeline. She was never shy with her opinions.

CHAPTER 6

THE FOLLOWING MORNING, I found my aunt sitting under a vine-covered pergola behind the cottage she shared with Gideon. Her back was ramrod straight, her fingers tapped relentlessly on the wooden arms of her Adirondack chair, and her lips were clamped on a cheroot. She puffed out a stream of smoke. Then she removed the cheroot and waved me over, all without turning her head.

"Verity. About time you dropped in."

I took the adjoining Adirondack chair, careful to stay upwind of the cigar. Adeline smirked, then snuffed it out in the ashtray on the arm of her chair. "Your mother hated these things, too."

"Never stopped you from smoking them."

She chuckled. "I knew it wouldn't be cigars that got me in the end, although I never suspected Claire would be the first to go."

That thought hung in the air between us for a moment, creating a miasma far worse than the dissipating cigar smoke.

Adeline dropped the ashtray on the table with a clunk, drawing us back to the present. "What brings you here on such a beautiful morning? Checking in on the old folks?" She craned her neck to check the empty path behind me. "If this is meals on wheels, I'm not impressed with the menu."

"Stop it. You're hardly old. Speaking of Gideon, though..." We giggled in unison at the familiar joke. "Where is he at the moment?"

"You'll never believe it."

"Try me."

"He drove into Strathcona to attend a two-day miniature railroad convention."

I stared at her. "I don't believe it."

"Told you."

"No, seriously."

"That's where he is. After his last blood pressure reading, the doctor suggested he find a hobby. Something relaxing. So he went to the Legion to play billiards."

"What does billiards have to do with miniature trains?"

"Nothing. Except...First, everyone at the Legion bets heavily on those billiards games, so it turns out they're not all that relaxing. Especially given Gideon's somewhat competitive personality."

That, I knew, was an understatement.

"And second, one of those old geezers at the Legion is a model railroad buff. And he took Gideon to see his setup."

"You don't refer to Gideon as an old geezer, do you? I mean, when he's actually in the room?"

Adeline squinted. "Hmmm."

"Never mind. Continue."

"Well, he's hooked now. He's planning a big setup in the basement. Multiple tracks, tunnels, tiny little buildings, lights, crossing bells. The whole outfit. It's quite an art to set these things up, apparently. Hence the visit to the Strathcona convention. He intends to buy equipment and get ideas for his layout."

"That sounds nice. I actually dropped by to speak to you about—"

I didn't get to finish my sentence.

"But it's good Gideon isn't here, because it gives us a chance to discuss the mission."

"What mission?" I asked, feigning ignorance. I well remembered Adeline talking about her latest assignment for Control, the shadowy black-ops marketing group that she and Gideon had worked for.

But she hadn't mentioned it in weeks, and I'd hoped she had either forgotten, or the mission itself had been scrapped.

My aunt tilted her head, looking puzzled.

Before she could open her mouth to remind me, I plunged in. "The reason I'm here is because I need your help with a case. Zara Price hired me to defend her goat, Waffles, from legal ramifications."

"Her goat?"

"Yes. He's a wether."

She nodded. "I understand castration is a huge improvement. Something about the smell." Adeline slumped in her chair, looking longingly at the cigar butt.

I needed to up my game if I wanted to keep her attention.

"I wouldn't know. But I do know this goat was present when Herbert Eubanks was killed yesterday."

She straightened in her chair and shot me a piercing glance. "The septic tank guy?"

I nodded.

"He's dead?"

I nodded again. "He fell into an empty septic tank. Broke his neck, or worse. You haven't heard?"

"Nooo. I've been thinking about our..." Her brow wrinkled. "Wait. Why would Zara Price's goat be involved? Was Eubanks pumping out Zara's septic tank?"

"No. Next door. Clive Yeager's septic tank. And the police think Waffles was responsible. They believe the goats..." I trailed off at the look on her face.

"Clive Yeager?" she asked, her tone icy with suppressed anger.

"Do you know him?"

Her eyes flashed. "That bastard. Of course I know him."

"Good. Because I was hoping you might have some suggestions about how I should proceed. To clear Waffles, I mean. I think it's a matter of providing reasonable doubt, really, because it's not as if a goat can commit a criminal act. But Zara's afraid the authorities will designate him a dangerous animal and then—" I drew a finger across my throat. "She's upset."

But Adeline wasn't listening. She had leapt to her feet and was pacing the flagstone patio, hands clasped behind her back, mumbling. She whirled to face me. "Yeager's the main suspect, I take it?"

"No, not really. He wasn't even there when it happened."

She clicked her tongue. "A likely story."

It didn't take finely tuned investigative skills to sense that my aunt was keeping something back. "What do you mean?"

"I mean...if you want to clear—what is the goat called?"

"Waffles."

"Right. If you want to clear Waffles, you'll need to identify the real killer. And that must be Clive Yeager."

"The police think it was an accident. Waffles and his tribe didn't make many friends among the officers who tried to apprehend them." I shook my head sadly, recalling Jeff's groans as he sank into the sofa with an ice pack the previous evening. "It is possible Waffles head-butted Eubanks into the tank."

Adeline grew dismissive. "That's a smokescreen. Eubanks had been pumping out septic tanks for decades. He wouldn't have stood over an open tank with livestock in the vicinity." Her brow wrinkled again. "Why were the goats in the vicinity? Zara built an impressive pen for them. How did they get out?"

"That's the question. She believes someone let them out deliberately in order to cover up Eubanks' murder."

"Which the police say is an accident."

"Correct."

"Yeager's subterfuge worked, then."

"I guess." Given Wilf's assessment, I was uncomfortable pinning the whole thing on Zara's neighbor, even though he had been a tad obnoxious. Of course, it was easy for me to say that. There hadn't been any goats perched on the Coming Up Roses pickup truck when I left the scene. Good thing the animals didn't notice my colorful rose decals. They might have thought they were real. "What should I do?"

"That's easy. We have to confront the killer in his den."

"What do you mean, *we*?"

"Oh, I'm coming with you. We can go right now. Did you bring the truck?"

"If you're suggesting we visit Yeager, I don't think he'll talk to us. He wouldn't speak to the police."

Her mouth was set in a thin line. "He'll speak to me." She puffed out another breath, shaking her head. "Imagine trying to pin this on a *goat*. Idiot."

I scrunched up one eye. "I think you missed the part where I said Yeager wasn't around when this happened."

"I'm sure he'd like you to believe that."

"The police seem to believe it."

"That's the problem. The police have always believed Clive Yeager. Even when they shouldn't. That alone is suspicious."

"Aunt Adeline, I think you should know Jeff is in charge of the official investigation into Herbert Eubanks' death. He's a competent detective, honored several times for his work."

And my honey—so back off, I thought indignantly.

Her face softened. "Jeff is an intelligent man and an excellent detective." She patted my arm. "But I've been around long enough to know that what you see on the surface is not the entire force. There are...machinations. That's all I'm willing to say."

Oh no. I'd awakened my aunt's inner conspiracy theorist, when all I wanted to do was save a poor little goat from the gallows. Of course there are no gallows in Canada, but nice work on the alliteration, I thought.

"I can't see how visiting Clive Yeager will help Waffles," I countered.

"I'm sure this Waffles is a perfectly adequate goat. But he's not our prime concern at the moment. Let's go."

Sighing, I followed her to my truck, climbed behind the wheel, and cranked the engine.

Ten minutes later, we pulled up outside Yeager's split-level home. A single patrol car was parked in the driveway, its driver nodding over paperwork.

"Look. A cop. We should leave."

"Don't be ridiculous. That's only routine." Aunt Adeline hopped out of the truck, slammed the door, and paced toward Yeager's front door, tossing a friendly wave at the constable behind the wheel as she passed the cruiser.

He returned her wave. "Hi, Adeline."

"How's your mom, Charlie?"

"Much better, thanks. I'll tell her you were asking about her."

With a nod, my aunt started up the front steps. Rolling my eyes, I hurried after her.

She stood off to one side, inclining her head at the door. "You should do the knocking, Verity. It's your interrogation."

I wasn't planning to interrogate anybody, but I held my tongue and stepped forward.

My brief rap on the door was answered almost instantly. Clive Yeager must have seen us drive up.

He stood rigid in the doorway. "Yes?"

"Mr. Yeager." I held out my hand. "I'm Verity Hawkes. I'm representing the interests of Zara Price, your neighbor, after yesterday's unfortunate incident."

His brow wrinkled slightly. "Did you bring a checkbook?"

"Ahh, no."

"That's the only thing that interests me. Payment for damages rendered."

He could have shown more concern about the fact someone had died on his property, but I kept that thought to myself.

"We can discuss that. Could we come in?"

"Who's we?"

My aunt stepped out from behind me.

Yeager's lip curled. "You."

"Hello, Clive. Long time, no see."

"I have nothing to say to you."

"We need to talk. It might be mutually beneficial."

For a long moment he stared at my aunt, whose relaxed countenance gave nothing away. I could tell his curiosity was piqued.

He opened the door wider, motioning us to enter. "Ten minutes. No longer." Once we crossed the threshold, Yeager shut the door and indicated the den at the front of the house. Black filing cabinets lined one wall and an impressive glass-topped desk was centered in the room.

After filing in, my aunt and I sat in the low-slung leather armchairs. I was hoping for a beverage, if only so we could prolong our stay, but Yeager offered us nothing. He didn't even sit.

Leaning against the desk with his legs crossed at the ankles, he glared at my aunt and me in turn. "Well?"

"Miss Price is concerned that her goat Waffles will be euthanized as a result of the...incident," I said.

Yeager's jaw dropped. He seemed momentarily unable to speak.

"And so it should be," he finally blustered. "That damned animal is a menace. They all are. Good riddance." He emphasized this sentiment with a curt nod.

My aunt leaned in. Coolly, she said, "Despite the newer homes in this area, the entire district is zoned agricultural. Goats are well within the established parameters."

Yeager huffed. "Are they? Are they really? I take it those established parameters do not include my Series 7 BMW. Which those beasts all but destroyed."

While they shot daggers at each other, I tried to move on. "If we could return to Mr. Eubanks' tragic death for a moment..."

The combatants turned their attention to me.

"Miss Price believes that someone deliberately released her goats," I continued. "Do you know anything about that, Mr. Yeager?"

"You're not seriously suggesting I vandalized my own home and vehicle."

"No, but perhaps you know someone who might wish you harm. Someone who might also want Mr. Eubanks dead?"

Yeager blinked rapidly, but covered it with a sudden flap of his hand, as if he were brushing away a fly. "Of course not."

"Take your time. A man with as many business connections as yourself, not to mention an outstanding military career, must have made enemies over the years."

His voice was cold. "What are you implying?"

To be truthful, I had no idea. I wasn't even sure what type of military career he had. Or what business connections it might have sparked. I was basing my comment on Jeff's mention of, *Retired. Former military.* I'd hoped it would be enough to wrest something loose. But the man was too calculating to give the game away that easily.

"As I told the police," he said. "I was not home when Mr. Eubanks met his untimely end. I have no insight to give you. Or your client." He glowered. "Especially not your client." He straightened up, gesturing to the door. "If that's all you came to say..."

I rose to go.

"Where were you?" my aunt asked, still seated.

"What?"

"You said you weren't here. Where were you?"

"None of your business."

She leaned forward. "Come on, Clive. You know that won't work with me. I'll get to the bottom of it. And I don't have the scruples of the police, either."

They glared at each other. I had the impression neither realized I was even in the room. "You told the police you were visiting a friend," I offered helpfully.

Yeager never took his eyes from my aunt's. "That's right. I was."

"What friend?" she asked, unruffled.

If the air in that room got any more frigid, I'd have to send out for a parka.

"None of your business."

My aunt was unruffled. "Gillian's covered for you before, hasn't she?"

"Who?"

"Gillian Shadrach." Out of the side of her mouth, she added, "She owns the dress shop on Main Street."

"The one called Viola's?" I asked.

She nodded.

"If Gillian owns Viola's, then who's Viola?"

"Such a lovely woman. Passed away years ago," Adeline said, *sotto voce*. "It was a real loss to the village."

Turning back to Yeager, she said in a louder tone, "So. Did she?"

His eyes flashed, but his tone was icy. "I told you. It's none of—"

"She provided an alibi for you the last time." Adeline fixed him with a steely gaze. "Tell me—are you lovers? She's a little young for you, isn't she, Clive? I'm pretty sure that roll around your gut is middle-aged spread, not love handles."

"Get out."

Adeline rose, a half-smile on her face. "We'll speak again."

Yeager stalked behind us to the front door. I paused on the threshold, turning to ask one more question, but he shut the door in my face.

In the truck, Adeline was silent until I dropped her at Gideon's cottage.

"You have to tell me," I said. "What is it between you and Clive Yeager?"

She paused, her hand on the door handle, then turned to face me.

"Remember when I disappeared?"

"Of course I remember. The police told me you were dead. They said your car had gone off the road and crashed through the fence. They pulled it from the river and left it in my driveway." I shook my head. "How could I forget?"

"My car was forced off that road by Clive Yeager."

With a vicious twist of the handle, she pushed open the door and jumped out, closing it behind her without a backward glance.

CHAPTER 7

MY MIND REELED during the drive to my first landscaping job of the day.

Aunt Adeline had not mentioned Clive Yeager when she returned home the previous autumn. Not to me, at least. But surely if she knew the name of her attacker, she would have told the police. Why hadn't he been arrested?

I recalled her words.

The police always believed Clive Yeager. Even when they shouldn't.

Fortunately, I had an inside source at the police department. Jeff was careful to maintain strict confidentiality about his police work—a line he never crossed. But given that my aunt was involved, I hoped he would bend the rules just once.

In any event, Adeline's persecution complex had nothing to do with my quest to save Waffles. I was convinced someone freed Zara's goats on purpose. And now I had another lead to follow up—Gillian Shadrach, popular village dress shop owner.

I decided to check in on my main business first. Ethan had still looked a little green around the gills when I dropped him off that morning on the way to my aunt's. I gave him a call.

He insisted he was fully recovered. "Don't rush back. I'm fine. Besides..." He sounded sheepish. "I owe you."

"I have a couple of things to do. And our next job is right next door to the one you're on now. If you're certain you can cope with them both..."

Then I left him to it. Without even a twinge of guilt.

As I cruised down Main Street toward the dress shop, my cell phone rang.

"Is this Verity Hawkes?"

"Yes. Can I help you?"

"I hope so. You're the investigator, correct? The one who solved that Palmerston case?"

"It was a team effort," I said modestly. "But, yes, I am. And you are?"

"Liliana István. I'm a reporter for the *Bugling Beaver*."

"I don't think I've seen your name on the masthead. But then I rarely—"

"I'm not on staff. I'm a freelancer."

That made sense. As far as I knew, the village's online weekly newspaper had no employees, other than the editor, who worked part-time at the library to make ends meet.

"I'm following up on a story I think you can help me with," she continued. "On Herbert Eubanks. Have you heard about his death?"

"Yes, I have. I'm not sure I can help you, but...fire away."

"Is it true that you found the body?"

"No. Who told you that?"

"And you believe it's murder?"

"Um...I don't...what is your question, exactly?"

"You're investigating the case, correct?"

"Not really."

"What's your connection then?"

"I don't have a connection to the case, if that's what you're asking. I'm helping out a friend."

"Zara Price." It wasn't a question.

"How do you—" I pulled the truck into a parking spot and turned off the engine.

"Zara Price is the friend you're helping out, correct?"

"That's right. It's about her goat, Waffles. The police think—"

Liliana broke in enthusiastically. "That's what I want to ask you about. The police investigation. You see, I believe—"

"Hang on a minute. I can't talk about the police investigation. You'll have to ask them. I'm merely trying to determine if livestock belonging to Zara Price has been unfairly implicated in this poor man's untimely death." I sat back, pleased with my concise summation of the case. *I should write it down*, I thought.

"So it is murder."

"I didn't say that."

Liliana didn't notice my objection. Or if she did, she simply ignored it.

"I knew it," she said with an air of triumph. "It *is* murder. Can I quote you?"

"No! Don't quote me saying...what am I saying?"

"I'll read it back to you." She cleared her throat. "Herbert Eubanks was murdered, according to private investigator Verity Hawkes." She paused. "I should change that to *well-known* private investigator Verity Hawkes...or maybe even *outstanding* private investigator—"

"No. Listen. I appreciate the thought, but you can't quote me saying Eubanks' death was murder. I have no idea. It may have been an accident."

"Ha. Not likely."

"Why do you say that? Do you know something?"

I caught sight of a scowling meter maid pacing along the sidewalk in the direction of my truck. It looked like Fran, who was known for her unstinting devotion to duty. In the winter, drivers more or less ignored the parking meters along Main Street, confident the village's two meter maids were doing paperwork indoors. But once the nice weather attracted scores of tourists to the picturesque village, the gloves came off.

Residents told multiple stories of seeing Fran tapping her foot impatiently, leveling her steely gaze at a parking meter as it counted down to zero, an unwritten ticket poised in her hand. Sometimes she added a citation for "improper park," after carefully measuring the distance from the car to the curb.

Personally, I suspected meter maids Fran and Holly— known colloquially as Stan and Ollie, although never to their faces—worked on commission.

While eying the sheaf of blank tickets in Fran's hand, I

wedged the phone between my shoulder and ear so I could rummage through the coin drawer.

"You're jumping to conclusions, Liliana. There's been no official designation in that case. The police are still deliberating."

"Oh, thanks. I can use that. *The police are still...*"

"No," I said, rummaging. "Don't write that."

The coin drawer was empty.

Two cars ahead of me, Fran stopped to peer at the meter alongside a flashy, orange SUV. From my vantage point behind the wheel, I could see the SUV's meter was flashing red—just like the one beside my truck.

Fran pulled out a ticket, slapped it on top of her notebook, and started writing. She hadn't noticed my flashing meter yet. I upended my shoulder bag onto the bench seat beside me. The contents spilled out onto the cracked leather. Holding the phone with one hand, I reached for my wallet, which was teetering on the edge of the seat. I only succeeded in knocking it off the edge and into the footwell.

Liliana was still talking. "How about this? *Ace* private investigator Verity Hawkes confirmed she is probing the suspicious death of well-known Leafy Hollow resident, Herbert Eubanks. 'He was probably murdered,' Ms. Hawkes said."

"No. Wait, please." Setting the phone on speaker, I tossed it onto the seat, then ducked my head while stretching my arm into the footwell to retrieve my wallet.

"So we're good?" Liliana's voice came from the phone. "*Probably* murdered? What if I change that to, '*Most likely*, Ms. Hawkes said.'"

"No," I straightened up so quickly I hit my head on the glove box. "Ow." Wincing, I unsnapped the wallet, dumped two quarters onto my palm, and slid out of the driver's door. "Wait—I'll be back," I announced in the general direction of the cell phone.

I reached the meter seconds before Fran. She watched me suspiciously as I plugged in the coins. "Just topping up," I said merrily.

With a grim look, she moved on to her next victim.

When I regained the driver's seat, I realized Liliana hadn't noticed I'd left.

"That's great, Verity. Thanks for the scoop."

"What scoop?" My stomach sank. "I didn't give you a—"

"Too bad about Waffles," she said. "He was a fall fair prize-winner three years running. It's a shame. But with an owner like that, what can you expect? Animal Services should have stepped in years ago."

"What's that? What are you saying about Waffles?"

"Thanks, Verity. I owe you one."

In the rearview mirror, I noticed Fran peering at my truck's back end. She had a metal roll-up tape measure in her hand. *Damn.* In my haste to pull over and answer the phone, I may have failed to entirely nail my parallel parking.

"What about Waffles?" I asked. "And what do you mean *an owner like that*? Like what?"

"I thought you knew. Zara Price has a criminal record."

My jaw dropped. *Zara Price? The Gaia-loving, organic jam-making, brown-eyed animal lover? A criminal?*

"You can't be serious."

"Ask your boyfriend."

"How do you know about Jeff—"

"Verity, come on. The whole village knows you're engaged to Detective Katsuro. How are the wedding plans coming, by the way? Last time I saw your aunt, she said you're being indecisive. Check out Viola's. Gillian has *adorbs* bridal party stuff in the back. Gotta go!"

And she rang off before I could even open my mouth.

It seemed the whole world thought I should talk to Gillian Shadrach. Who was I to argue with the world? Because I was fresh out of quarters, I drove away from the curb to circle the block and pull into the tiny parking lot behind the 5X Bakery. With Emy and Lorne away, and the bakery's front door displaying a CLOSED sign for the first time in years, I knew there would be a vacant spot. And better yet, no meter.

I walked up the alley beside the building, sniffing sadly at the insipid air. Usually the aromas of chocolate, cinnamon, and freshly baked bread wafted through this walkway from the huge fan overhead. Not today.

Resolutely, I turned left to walk along the sidewalk and across the road to Viola's. Adeline had told me that Gillian had owned the shop for nearly a decade. In all that time, she'd never changed the sign. Some people—Emy explained in answer to my quick email—theorized Gillian was too cheap to pay the painter's bill for a new one.

As I stood outside, noting the peeling paint on the sign's edges, I wondered if maybe *Viola's* had not turned out to be a retail gold mine. Having wrested *Coming Up Roses* out of bankruptcy, I knew how difficult it was to keep a small business going. Gillian had my sympathy.

That wouldn't last.

I pushed open the front door. A bell jangled overhead.

The tiny store had faded chintz wallpaper, replica tin tiles on the ceiling, and worn carpeting. It looked as if Gillian hadn't updated the interior decor, either. Clothing racks lined both walls and another stretched down the center of the space, dividing it into two aisles. The front window showed signs of dust on the handbags displayed there, but the clothing racks were full to bursting with the latest fashions. At least, I think they were up to date. Without Emy—or Jeff, for that matter—I couldn't tell.

The young woman behind the counter—dyed blonde hair, blue eyes elaborately lined in kohl, tight dress—looked up from the keyboard of a laptop she'd been poring over. She closed the lid, smiling.

"You must be Viola," I said, although I knew perfectly well she wasn't.

"No. I get that a lot, but I'm Gillian. Gillian Shadrach."

I held out a hand. "Verity Hawkes. Nice to meet you."

"Ah." Her eyes widened in delight. "The investigator. I'm honored. Can I help you find something, or—" She gasped. "Are you on a case? How exciting."

"I'm only looking," I said hurriedly, pretending to assess the cut of a cotton jersey dress. The sleeves were only partially attached to the body, and there was a filmy length of fabric that could have been a...cape? An apron? A parachute?

"This is lovely," I said.

"Isn't it? New arrival. I *adore* that style." Enthusiastically, she swept out from behind the counter to pluck the dress from my hand and hold it up, draping it artistically over one arm. "It's flattering for many body types."

She pinned me with one of those *I-just-had-the-best-idea* looks employed by sales clerks everywhere. "You *must* try it on. It's perfect for you."

This was why I never went shopping for clothes by myself. The last time I bought a dress recommended by a sales clerk, it stayed curled in a heap at the bottom of my cupboard until I finally convinced a local charity shop to give it a decent burial.

"Why not?"

As I followed Gillian to the dressing room, I noticed a door leading to a back room. Overhead, an arched sign decorated with hearts and flowers read, Bridal Bower.

"Wedding dresses?" I asked, intrigued despite my better judgment.

"For yourself?" Gillian flashed a quick look at my naked ring finger. "Or...?"

I tugged the platinum chain out from under my shirt to show her my ring.

"That's gorgeous," she shrieked, five fastidiously lacquered fingernails clasping her cheek. "What a rock. You're a lucky girl." With a conspiratorial air, she gestured to the Bridal Bower. "Shall we take a look?"

Fortunately, I had an excuse ready.

"Sorry, no. My maid of honor would kill me if I looked at wedding dresses without her."

That was true. Emy had been hounding me about "the dress" for weeks. She routinely texted me web links with notations like, "How about this one?" Or "This one's pretty." Or "This is definitely the one."

I deleted those links. Something would turn up.

"Another time, perhaps. Let's try this dress on," Gillian said, flourishing the parachute-wear.

I followed, waiting while she swept aside a dressing room curtain.

"Gillian Shadrach, eh?" I chuckled. "You know, it's odd, but your name came up in a case I'm working on. About Herbert Eubanks' death. The septic tank pumper?"

Her shoulders stiffened, one hand still on the curtain. Then she walked into the tiny cubicle, hung the dress on a wall hook, and turned to face me.

I expected her to respond, but instead she fixed me with a quizzical glance. Clearly, the shoe was on my foot.

"I'm representing Zara Price." My voice faded as I added, "And her goat."

"Her what?"

I raised my voice. "Her goat, Waffles, who's been unfairly implicated in this man's untimely—"

My summation was squelched by Gillian's snorted, "Ha! That's funny." Her expression, however, did not depict mirth. Folding her arms in front of her, she regarded me with thinned lips. "That animal should be shot."

"Then you know the animal in question?"

"That depends. Are you talking about the goat, or Zara Price?"

I forced a smile. There didn't seem to be much point in adhering to conversational niceties at this point. Or in denying my real reason for darkening her door.

Gillian apparently agreed. "Let's get to the point. Why are you here?"

I took a deep breath. "Is it true you're Clive Yeager's alibi for Herbert Eubanks' murder?"

Her eyes narrowed. "Is that what Clive said?"

"More or less."

"Which is it?"

"He didn't exactly name you, but it was implied. Was he with you that morning?"

She shrugged, unwrapping her arms. "I don't see that it's any of your business, but why should I deny it? Yes, Clive was with me that morning." Her eyebrows rose. "And the previous night, as well. In my apartment, upstairs. Over the shop. Does that answer your question?"

"Thank you, yes. I'm sorry to have disturbed you." I turned to go.

"Wait." Gillian thrust out her chin. "I know what the villagers say about us. But they're wrong."

I had to start paying more attention to village gossip. Especially since Emy, my usual source for tittle-tattle, was out of the country. I had no idea what Gillian meant.

"Wrong about...what, exactly?"

"We're not lovers."

I felt my eyes scrunch up as I tried to interpret this. "But you said you spent the night together."

"I did not. I said he was here, in my apartment. Not the same thing."

"Is Clive Yeager often in your apartment?"

She frowned at me. "If, and when, that question becomes relevant to a police investigation, I might answer it. Until then—" She motioned to the front door. "I assume you're not actually shopping for a dress. Wedding or otherwise."

I crossed Main Street to walk back to my truck. When I looked over my shoulder, I saw Gillian through the plate glass of her shop window. She was on her phone, gesticulating wildly.

When she saw me staring, she whirled to turn her back to the window—after hoisting an emphatic finger in my direction.

Well. Gillian Shadrach was no *Viola*, that was certain.

CHAPTER 8

I STUDIED my best friend's heart-shaped face on the screen of my cell phone, smirking at the sight of her pink and peeling nose.

Served her right. Emy had won a three-week vacation in a contest she didn't remember entering. Whereas I was stuck in Leafy Hollow, corralling goats. It was hardly fair.

Putting my completely justifiable outrage aside, I zeroed in on what she was saying.

"Too bad you fell out with Gillian. She's cornered the market for wedding gowns in Leafy Hollow. We'll have to go into Strathcona now to find you something."

"Where's Lorne?" I asked, anxious to deflect wedding talk.

"He went marlin fishing. Or was it shark baiting? All I know is that it required a boat, a lot of sunscreen, and men in funny hats. Also beer. An entire crate of beer, in fact. I suspect the fishing part is optional." Lifting a glass to her mouth, she took a sip of something pink and fizzy. Ice cubes clinked as she replaced her glass on the table.

"Did he enjoy that museum tour you took him on?"

"Oh, he loved it. Best time ever, he said. He was lying, of course." She grinned. "He's adorable, isn't he?"

"So adorable. I don't know how you can stand all that adorable-ness, frankly. Doesn't it get dull after a while?"

She shot me a coquettish grin. "Not after dark, girlfriend. It's definitely not dull then."

"Oh, please. I'm nauseated and I'm not even drinking."

"Why aren't you drinking?" She shot a quick look at her watch. "It's after noon."

"I'm mulling over this case of Zara's. I can't get a handle on it."

"These are the goats with gall, right?"

"According to the police. They may have a point," I admitted, recalling the chaotic scene in Yeager's back yard, the indignant police officers, and the scratched and dented BMW.

"You don't sound convinced."

"I'm not. Someone cut a hole in that fence, and it wasn't the goats. It could have been Zara, but the links had been snipped from the other side. From Yeager's side."

"How do you know?"

"The cut ends were pointing inward."

"Wow. Nice work, Ms. Hawkes."

"Thanks. But that's not the only reason I think there's more involved than barnyard ruffians. Adeline claims—" I lowered my voice.

Emy leaned in, straining to hear. "What?"

"That Clive Yeager tried to kill her."

Emy looked puzzled. "Recently?"

"Last year. She said he was the person who forced her off the road. When her car went into the river."

"Did she tell the police?"

"They didn't believe her."

"What does Jeff say?"

"I haven't asked him yet." I glanced at my own watch. "He'll be home soon."

"Ah. That's why you're not drinking. You want to be sharp and clear-headed before mounting your attack." She giggled. "Or your opponent."

I *tsk-tsked*. "I don't think all that beach time is helping you appreciate the seriousness of this situation."

Emy smothered another giggle, then adopted a solemn expression. "Hit me with the details. Let's brainstorm. We can solve this case by the time Lorne gets back with the bacon. Fish. Whatever." She fluttered a hand. "Recap," she ordered.

I reprised my experiences with Zara's goats—glossing over the damage to Jeff's pride. Then I recounted the interview with Clive Yeager, as well as my conversations with shopkeeper Gillian Shadrach and the newspaper reporter Liliana István.

"Hmm. This reporter claimed Zara has a criminal record?"

"Yes. She didn't say for what, though."

"Hold that thought." Emy leaned out of the picture for a moment, returning with a refilled glass. "Liliana must be exaggerating. Or wrong." She took a sip before continuing. "I can't imagine Zara or her mother doing anything unethical, never mind illegal. Can you?"

"I don't know either of them well. Anything's possible."

"I guess. But why did the reporter tell you that?"

"To suggest Zara might be lying, I think. Maybe she meant to put me on my guard."

"About the fence?"

"Yes. What if Zara let the goats out herself?"

"Did she?"

"She says not. And why would she?"

"Maybe she wanted to annoy Yeager and it went too far." Emy took another sip, looking thoughtful. "But if her actions resulted in someone's death, even unintentionally, wouldn't that be manslaughter?"

"Possibly."

"Wait. I've had a thought—" Emy brightened, sitting up so suddenly that her drink slopped over the edge of the glass and onto her hand. "Oops," she said, licking it off with a grin.

"How many of those have you had?"

"Are you counting?"

"Somebody has to. Someone who can still count, that is."

She smirked at me. "Envy is not an attractive look for you."

"Ha. You never did tell me how you and Lorne won this trip."

"Yes, I did. Random chance. My name came up somehow and...here we are!" She downed the rest of the glass, put it down, and burped. "Sorry," she said with a giggle.

"Never mind that. What was your thought?"

"My...?

"You just said you had a thought," I said dryly.

Too dryly. I was craving a pink, fizzy drink myself.

Emy wrinkled her brow, thinking. "Oh. Right. I remember. You said Zara's afraid her insurance won't pay if the property damage turns out to be her fault."

"Yes, but I don't see how that's relevant."

"It's relevant because maybe Waffles really is the guilty party and she's trying to hush it up. Create a smokescreen."

I shook my head. "I don't think so."

"Why are you dubious?"

"There's more to it, I think. Yeager reacted to the mention of Eubanks' name. He denied knowing him, but I think he was lying. There was a definite flicker of something—if not fear, then certainly, annoyance."

"Who is this man he mentioned? The one who works for him?"

"Several people, Wilf Mullins included, confirmed Yeager has 'a man' to look after things. But no one seems to know his name." I paused as a thought occurred.

A rare occurrence, yes, but it does happen.

"I should ask Wilf to find out who he is."

Emy grinned. "How is Wilf, by the way? Has he ordered his inaugural suit yet?"

I snapped my fingers. "I meant to tell you. He has competition now. Martin Griffiths filed his nomination form for the election yesterday."

Emy looked thoughtful. "Martin Griffiths...wait, I know that name. He was the mayor, years ago. He had heart trouble or something and resigned. He's back?"

"Yes. Wilf is downcast, to say the least."

"Poor Wilf. He wants that chain of office so badly. But Griffiths will be a tough opponent. I remember Mom talking about him. He was a popular mayor."

Emy drained her glass, then stretched her arms languidly above her head. "I'm exhausted."

I rolled my eyes, which pleased her.

"After all that sightseeing, I need a nap. What's your next move?"

"I don't know, to be honest. Maybe I'll shift gears for a while and see how Ethan's doing. Given that I don't seem to be making much headway with the investigation agency, I should at least make sure the landscaping business doesn't go under. That's my bread and butter."

"Jeff doesn't care. You could sell *Coming Up Roses* and concentrate on the agency."

I raised a warning hand. "Don't you start. Besides, I owe it to Adeline to keep the biz on its feet." I heaved a sigh. "She brought up our mission again."

Emy was instantly alert. "The one for Control? Is it going ahead?"

"Apparently. I've been trying to distract her."

"Keep trying. That organization is...creepy."

"You don't have to tell me. I'm the one with the talking hologram in the basement."

She shook her head. "You should blow that thing sky high."

I grinned. "And Rose Cottage along with it?"

"You can figure something out. Lorne can help. He's good with explosives." She waggled a finger at me. "Don't go on any missions before we get back."

I snapped a salute. "Sir-yes-sir."

"Finally," she said coolly. "Some respect." And she clicked off the call.

———

When I caught up with Ethan at the afternoon's job site, he was standing by the side of the road, the mower turned off and forgotten on the homeowner's lawn.

"Now what?" I muttered, pulling up in the truck. My decision to let Ethan work on his own might have been a mistake.

When I got out of the truck, I saw the reason for his dereliction of duty.

Ethan's rusty Camaro was parked on the other side of the road. A man wearing baggy gray mechanic's overalls and a baseball cap pulled low over his face emerged from the driver's side. His attempt to close the door was not successful. After a couple of slams, he left it open.

He waved to Ethan, who hurriedly crossed the street.

My landscape assistant was so fond of that vehicle, I was willing to bet he'd named it. I never asked, because he was easily embarrassed. And he was likely to hide that embarrassment with a barrage of indignation. Even a swear word or two.

Then it would be downhill from there.

But today, he was clearly delighted.

Within minutes, the two men had the Camaro's hood up and were conferring in low tones over the engine.

I ambled over. "Hi."

The mechanic elbowed Ethan, who looked up.

"Verity. She's looking good, eh?" Stepping back, Ethan beamed at the car.

The mechanic lowered the hood with a solid thump and a pat.

It wasn't until later I realized I hadn't asked his name. Or seen his face, because it was shadowed by the brim of his cap. But I had been distracted by the condition of Ethan's car.

Far from "looking good," the Camaro showed unmistakable signs of a mishap. The right front bumper was crumpled, the headlight gone, and the entire right side scraped. It looked as if the vehicle had struck something and then bounced off it. Several times.

Noticing my gaze, Ethan waved it off. "That's nothing. Just needs a little touchup." He turned to the mechanic. "Next week good?"

He nodded. "Far as I know. Check with the office." Then he ambled over to an SUV waiting on the road behind us and shot Ethan a cursory wave while getting in.

When I stepped back to let the SUV pass, I recognized the logo of a local car repair shop on its door—the same garage that employed my father, Frank Thorne.

The driver pulled away.

I turned to Ethan, who was smiling as he ran a hand along the Camaro's gleaming—and so far, undented—roof.

I pointed to the damaged front end. "Did you hit something?"

"Scraped the side pulling into the garage the other day." He chuckled ruefully. "I was a bit under the weather."

I wondered if "under the weather" was code for *drunk.*

He must have hit the garage at high speed to cause that much damage.

"That's not funny, Ethan." Frowning, I added, "If you're drinking and driving, you can leave my employ right now."

He straightened up with a scowl. "I don't drive drunk. I only moved the car to get it out of the rain. Why do you always assume the worst?" Turning away, he mumbled something.

"What was that? What did you say?"

"Nothing."

"Ethan..."

He puffed out a long breath before turning to face me. "You'd never accuse Lorne of lying the way you do me. If I say it was a minor accident, that's what it was. This car is all I've got. I would never take the chance of damaging it." He bent to straighten the side mirror, his face wiped of his delight at having the Camaro back.

I felt guilty for a moment. With no proof of wrongdoing, I was being unfair.

But I reined it in. Ethan was on thin ice, and he knew it. I stood, watching him. There was something about him that rubbed me the wrong way.

Why couldn't I make up my mind? Either Ethan Neuhaus was a good employee or he was a liability. I couldn't have it both ways. Normally I wasn't this confused. I blamed it on the case of the wayward Waffles. It seemed like everyone I talked to in that case was hiding something. It was only natural to assume my new employee was doing the same.

Sighing, I contemplated the half-mown lawn. "Are you good to finish up by yourself?"

"Sure. No problem."

"I have something to do. Leave the mower and the trimmer in the driveway and I'll pick them up later. Since you have your car back, you won't need a ride, I assume?"

He gave a brief nod, pursing his lips.

Pulling away from the curb, I put the Ethan problem out of my mind in favor of reviewing my strategy for the next interrogation on my list. I needed help to sort out the witnesses' conflicting stories. If Martin Griffiths, newly returned village resident and beloved former mayor, was as respectable as everyone claimed, he would be happy to help a part-time investigator probe a serious threat to his community.

Wouldn't he?

CHAPTER 9

THE OLD HARRISON estate bordered a road that edged the conservation area's Young River Creek, surging with late spring runoff. As I drove along the road, overhanging maple branches filtered bright sunshine into dappled splashes of light, and birds flitted among the trees. Brilliant orange flashes among the branches revealed orioles staking out the highest perches for their intricate nests. Brown wrens hopped along the sides of the road, checking for insects.

After pulling up outside the wrought-iron gates that barred the estate's winding driveway, I halted my truck to study the scene. The sandstone house was a sprawling two-story, century-old building. A white-balustraded balcony on one side of the roof overlooked the road, as well as Young River Creek, visible through the trees. On the other side, a lush lawn bordered with azaleas and viburnums led the eye to a stream, dug out and lined with river rocks, that spanned the property at the back.

But the real jewel of the landscape was a three-story-high waterfall that emptied into that stream. I knew enough about landscaping to realize the waterfall was man-made. Someone —either the original Harrison family or a former occupant— had paid a lot of money to bring in the backhoes and expertise required to completely remake the original site. They'd commandeered a natural stream, which flowed through the property to a culvert under the road and from there into Young River Creek, and enhanced it with recirculating water pumps. Then they'd built a three-story waterfall chute at the back of the property. The entire scene was nestled into an arrangement of rocks, moss, mature trees, and water plants that made it seem entirely natural.

It was breathtaking.

And well beyond my abilities as a landscaper to even contemplate matching.

Lowering my side window, I reached out a finger to push the intercom button.

"Yes?"

"Verity Hawkes. I'd like to speak to Mr. Griffiths."

"What about?"

"I'd rather not say out here. But it's a matter of some importance to the village. And since Mr. Griffiths is running for mayor, I'm sure he'll be interested."

I held my breath.

A chipmunk darted across the driveway on the other side of the gate, jerked upright to stare at my truck, then scampered away.

I let out my breath. "Hello?"

I considered punching the button again, but as I reached out my arm, a metallic whine pierced the air and the gates slowly opened.

Shifting out of park, I eased the truck up the driveway, admiring the magnificent perennial beds that dotted the lawn. Briefly, I wondered who did Griffiths' landscaping, then banished the thought. I suspected my little outfit would not be up to the job.

When the solid front door swung open to my knock, I expected to see yet another mysterious "man," or perhaps a woman in a cap and apron. But unlike those British murder mysteries I loved to watch, there was no uniformed butler to answer this door.

Instead, before me stood an elderly man with a wild thatch of straw-like hair and startling green eyes behind black-rimmed glasses. He wore a rumpled plaid shirt untucked over baggy khakis. I looked down, fascinated. His big toe stuck out of a hole in one sock.

"Hello there," he said, throwing open the door and ducking his head out the entrance to gaze at my pink truck. "Is that Adeline's vehicle? She's spruced it up a bit since the last time I saw it."

"It used to be, yes." I thrust out a hand. "I'm Verity. Adeline's niece."

He pumped my hand vigorously, then clasped his other hand over it. "I see the resemblance. But I can't believe Adeline is old enough to have a grown niece."

I wasn't sure how to break it to this man, but my aunt was well into her sixties. "Ah..."

"I know what you're thinking. It's true. I've gotten a little older since I last saw your aunt. You must say hello for me. Anyway, come in."

Stepping over the threshold I asked, "Are you...?"

"Sorry. Where are my manners? We've never met, have we? I'm Martin Griffiths. Welcome to my home. This way, please. I'll see what I can do about getting us a beverage."

I followed him down a wood-paneled hall and into a dimly lit library, where I marveled, open-mouthed, at the ceiling-high shelves of leather-bound books that circled the room.

I recognized a few names on the worn but colorful bindings.

Poe. Dostoevsky. Munro.

"This is an impressive collection," I said, reaching for the nearest volume.

"Don't do that." Griffiths lightly tapped my hand.

I felt my face flush red as I yanked my arm back. "I'm sorry. I suppose they're all first editions. You have to handle them with gloves, right?" Inwardly I cursed my ineptitude. I'd had enough conversations with Emy's mother, chief librarian Thérèse Dionne, to know the correct way to handle old and valuable books. I just hadn't expected to see any.

Griffiths' face split into a grin. "Gets 'em every time," he chuckled. "It's impressive, all right—an impressive *trompe l'oeil.*" He ambled over to the huge captain's desk to angle the desk lamp until it shone on the nearest shelf. "Take another look."

I leaned in, feeling foolish. The spines of the books were real, but they'd been glued to the wall. The pages, even the shelves—except for the edges, which were wood trim, also glued to the wall—were painted in perfect 3D. "That's really something. Did you do it?"

"It is, isn't it? But no, it wasn't me. This entire house, as well as the grounds, has been used repeatedly for movies and television shows—costume dramas, mostly. It provided a healthy income for the Harrisons over the years. This room was done up for a Henry James novel." He wrinkled his brow. "Or was it E.M. Forster? I get those two mixed up."

The cost of that wickedly expensive waterfall was beginning to make sense.

"Now," he said. "If we were true to the era, there'd be a cut-glass decanter filled with brandy. Sadly, however, the movie folks took that with them. But I think I can rustle up something in the kitchen. Follow me."

Halfway down the hall, he stopped so suddenly I nearly ran into him. "I must show you this," he said, clapping his hands. "You'll get a real kick out of it."

We had stopped at a point in the wall that looked exactly like the rest of it—panels of rich brown walnut. Although, after the library *trompe l'oeil*, I suspected it was more paint than actual wood.

Griffiths grinned at me. "Are you ready?" he asked, leaning nonchalantly against the nearest panel.

I grinned back. "Give it your best shot."

Whistling, he ran his fingers over the top of the panel and halted, giving me a hesitant look. "Are you sure you're ready?"

The guy was a real showman.

"Yes," I said again with an air of impatience.

Griffiths pressed down on the top edge. The panel popped loose, opening a crack all the way to the floor. He reached in his fingers to slide it completely open.

"A secret door," I said. "Cool."

"There's more—take a look." He jerked his chin at the opening.

I placed a foot on the threshold, then hesitated.

"Go all the way in," he urged.

I took a step forward. Cold air drifted against my cheek, like a clammy, unseen hand, and I shuddered. "It's too dark. I can't see anything." A vein in my neck started to throb.

Then something brushed my arm.

With a gasp, I jerked back, my heart racing.

"Sorry," Griffiths said. "I didn't mean to scare you. I only wanted to give you this flashlight." He held it out.

"Right," I managed with a shaky voice. "I'm not usually this jumpy."

That was a lie, of course, but I saw no reason to discuss my anxiety attacks with a man I hardly knew—former mayor or not. I held out my palm, and he slapped the flashlight onto it. I turned it on with a soft *click* and directed the beam of light to the opening. A narrow circular staircase led down into...*what?* I wondered. Only the first half-dozen steps were visible. The rest were in darkness.

"This is creepy. I could easily see it in a movie."

"Go downstairs if you want the full effect."

"Is it safe?"

"Of course. I wouldn't take a chance on losing our leading

lady." He chuckled. "But I warn you—it's damp and dirty. And ultimately, pretty boring. There's nothing down there but a few old wine racks."

"I think I'll take a pass." Stepping back into the hall, I handed him the flashlight. "What's it meant to be?"

He pressed the top of the panel and the door closed. "It's supposed to be a priest's hole. They used it in some Elizabethan thing they were doing." He furrowed his brow. "Or was it a murder mystery in a haunted mansion?" Shaking his head, he added, "I don't know, sorry. I wasn't here then."

"I'm sure it was believable," I said. "Just standing in the opening gave me the creeps. I would hate to be locked in down there."

He chuckled. "That's not going to happen. I should nail it shut one of these days. Now, how about that beverage?"

After the priest's hole, I half-expected the kitchen to have begrimed windows, knife-scarred oak tables, and huge fireplaces with cast-iron cauldrons hanging from spits.

Instead, we walked into a bright, modern room with floor-to-ceiling windows along one wall, two marble-topped islands, a massive restaurant-quality gas stove with a steel hood, and white wood cabinets with carved silver handles. Peering at the nearest one, I saw it was in the shape of a fox's head.

"This is a beautiful room. Who does the cooking?"

"That would be me. The heating up, that is." He swung open one of two doors on a steel-fronted Zero freezer and, with a theatrical flourish, pointed to shelves stacked with white boxes bearing small, black-lettered labels. I recognized the logo of local upscale caterer *Bertram's*. "Meals for one," he said. "Already cooked. I just pop them into the microwave." He closed the door.

I glanced around the room. "And where is the microwave?"

He grinned again. "Guess."

I was determined to ace this challenge. Not only because Griffiths was clearly enjoying himself, but because I was, too. No wonder he was such a popular mayor. He was one of those people whose cheerful personality lifted the mood of anyone in his presence.

I strolled thoughtfully around the room, taking in the hand-crafted cabinetry, tiled backsplash, and original art. Pausing, I pivoted, then pointed to a watercolor of a bowl of fruit.

Griffiths walked over to tap the painting's bottom edge. It slid smoothly upward, revealing a microwave. He grinned. "Got it in one. How did you know?"

Grinning back, I said, "It's an odd place to put a painting, but the exact right height for a microwave. And if I'm not mistaken, that's a pullout shelf underneath. Perfect for heated dishes."

"What an eye for detail. No wonder you're such a good investigator."

"How did you know that I—"

"Oh." He shrugged. "I keep up with village doings."

"I thought you were out of the country."

"I was. Now, what can I offer you to drink?"

After Griffiths decanted two glasses of craft beer, we

settled into wicker chairs on the flagstone patio. Snow-white lilacs scented the air. Sipping my beer, I eyed the double-flowered blooms. "Krasavitsa Moskvy," I said, pointing with my glass. "Good choice."

"If you say so," he replied. "I'm afraid I'm not up on all the horticulture."

"No? Somebody was gardening here recently." I nodded at a muddy pair of Wellington boots at the end of the patio. They were lined up next to a basket of gardening tools and a pair of garden gloves.

"I can tell the difference between a dandelion and a tulip," he said. "But that's about it. It's relaxing, though."

"So you don't use professionals?"

"Of course I do. For the lawn. The rest of it takes care of itself."

I glanced at the sweeping perennial beds, with their picture-perfect blooms and carefully raked bedcovers of mulch. Those definitely did not "take care of themselves." I sipped my beer. Perhaps Martin Griffiths didn't want to risk a quotation from Coming Up Roses Landscaping, and the attendant necessity of shooting me down.

He could have said he already had help, though. I wouldn't have taken it personally. I wasn't here seeking work. Which reminded me why I was here, on the patio of a man I'd never met, drinking beer.

I decided to open my interrogation with a fairly innocuous question. "Mr. Griffiths—"

"Oh. Martin, please."

I smiled. "Martin. Have you noticed any speed racers in the neighborhood?"

He looked puzzled. "Speed racers?"

"Cars being driven too fast up and down the road. Street racing, I think they call it."

He rubbed a hand across his chin. "Not lately, but I've heard people talking about it. My last term in office, we tried to shut them down."

"Were you successful?"

"More or less. I've heard they moved their races to that old quarry out on Concession 8. At least they're off the roads."

"So you don't know any of their names?"

He looked startled. "I'm afraid not, no. Should I?"

"I guess it is an odd question, when you think about it. It was just a line of inquiry I was following."

"Inquiry into what?"

From the look in his eyes—and the way he edged forward on his chair, casting glances at the door—I feared Martin Griffiths might be regretting letting me in.

I began again.

"You already know I'm a part-time investigator, so you won't be surprised to learn the real reason for my visit."

Settling back in his chair, he feigned disappointment. "I thought you were looking for a date." His mouth turned down. "Don't deprive an old man of his dreams."

"You are quite the flirt, Martin. I'm going to ignore that."

"Too bad." He winked at me over the rim of his glass before taking a sip.

"I'm actually here about Herbert Eubanks—the man who was found dead in your neighbor's backyard."

"Clive Yeager's place," he said with a sad nod.

"So you know about it."

"Of course. But why are you involved?"

"It's a funny thing, but—I mean, not funny-funny, but a coincidence. Zara Price owns the small farm on the other side of Yeager's property."

"The elderly woman who sells organic jam by the side of the road?"

"That's her mother, Samantha."

"Ah," he nodded. "She makes excellent sour-cherry jam, by the way. It's hard to find."

"I guess. Anyway, Zara has a small herd—sorry, *tribe*—of goats. All females, except for one castrated billy goat—a wether, actually—called Waffles."

Griffiths' eyes were beginning to glaze over. I decided to skip ahead to the critical problem.

"The police believe Waffles butted Eubanks into the open septic tank, where he died."

He wrinkled his nose. "That sounds unpleasant."

"Got it in one," I said.

He smiled. "Go on."

"Animal Services took Waffles away. Zara is afraid he will be euthanized. She asked me to find out if someone deliberately set her goats free in order to trample Yeager's property."

His brows rose. "Surely the goat won't be sentenced to death over a few spoiled plants."

"The police maintain that Waffles is a dangerous animal. Whereas Zara believes he was..." I cleared my throat. "Framed."

Griffiths tilted his head with a puzzled look. "Despite my better judgment, I find this intriguing. Go on."

"Zara hired me to clear Waffles' name."

Martin Griffiths did not laugh, although he did twist his mouth in a way that made me suspect he was muffling a chortle or two. After a few seconds, he regained control. "What do you want me to do?"

"I want you to help me. I know it's a lot to ask, but with your knowledge of the village, and your proximity to the site of the alleged crime... Well... Would you?"

Griffiths assumed his most serious expression so far. "I'm running for mayor. Did you know that?"

I nodded. "I did."

"Which means I am duty-bound to offer my assistance when any of my would-be constituents is threatened. So my answer is—yes."

I smiled in relief. "Thank you. I'm very grateful. And relieved. But I think I should point out that no one has actually been threatened. Not yet, anyway."

"What do you mean? Is our young Mr. Waffles not threatened with death?"

"Ah, well, yes."

"And he's a Leafy Hollow resident."

I nodded.

"That makes him a constituent. And to be honest," he leaned in, "until the campaign revs up a bit, I find myself at loose ends. Not only that, but poor Mr. Eubanks died practically on my doorstep. Which makes me an interested party. Good lord—I could have been a victim myself." He held out his hand for a solemn shake. "Martin Griffiths, at your service. Where do we start?"

After putting down my beer to shake his hand, I extracted a notebook and pencil from my purse. "Let me set the scene," I said, sketching a rough map. "This is Zara's farm, and this is the enclosure for her goats. The pen is surrounded by a fence with a locked gate. The animals could not have escaped unaided."

Griffiths studied the map. "Unless someone left the gate unlocked."

"True. But the goats would have had to break through a secondary perimeter as well—the fence between Zara's property and Clive Yeager's." I sketched in the fence, as well as Yeager's house, pergola, and patio. Then I marked the location of the open septic tank with a large X.

"Is it a sturdy fence?"

"Very. Zara had it specially reinforced after a previous escape by the goats. I checked it over and it looked secure to me. Except for a gaping hole, but that's obviously new. I don't think even Waffles could have busted out without help."

On the other side of the map, I drew in the property line between Yeager's house and Griffiths' estate. "If you climb those stone stairs to the top of your waterfall," I pointed to the flagstone path that led from the patio, "you can see Yeager's house, right?"

He bent to run a finger along my penciled path. "I suppose. It's not something I usually do, though."

"Why not?"

"I don't need a lookout. I have enough to look at right here." He swept a hand at the flowers and greenery skirting the patio. "Plus, it's tedious climbing the equivalent of three flights of stairs. Hard on the old knees. If I want to take a walk, I'm more inclined to cross the road and follow a hiking trail through the conservation area."

"You've never looked at Yeager's house from up there? Waved to your neighbor, maybe?"

"I've spoken to Yeager once or twice, but we're not friends. He doesn't strike me as the friendly type, to be honest. More like the type that prefers to be left alone."

I couldn't argue with that. But it meant Griffiths couldn't shed any light on the strange manner of Herbert Eubanks' death. I must have looked dejected, because Griffiths straightened up with a rueful look.

"I'm sorry, Verity. I'm not much help."

"No, that's fine. I was hoping maybe you knew Yeager and could tell me whether he had any enemies. And more importantly, whether he knew Herbert Eubanks."

"I could ask around. I know people who might be able to answer that question."

"You wouldn't mind?"

"Not at all." He smiled. "We have to save Waffles. But tell me, Verity, what makes you think Yeager and Eubanks had any kind of relationship? Other than the obvious homeowner-hires-septic-pumper kind?"

I debated telling him about Yeager's reaction to the mention of Eubanks' name, but decided against it. It could have been my imagination.

"Nothing, really. It's a hunch."

"How would it help the goats?"

"What if Zara is right? What if someone pushed Eubanks

into that tank, and then released the goats to throw the police off the scent?"

He gave me a sharp look. "You mean murder."

I nodded.

"And you think the killer could be Clive Yeager?"

"It's possible, isn't it?"

His brow furrowed, and he lifted his glass for a sip. He stared at the lilacs with the glass frozen in his hand.

I was about to speak again when he put the glass down with a decisive gesture.

"It's true I don't know much about Yeager. But there is scuttlebutt going around—rumors, mind—that he's a retired military type who likes to keep his hand in."

"Keep his hand in? As in—" I drew a finger across my throat with a shudder. "That kind of hand?"

"It's only a rumor. You know how people like to talk."

"Who told you this?"

"I can't tell you that. You understand."

"Will you ask around?"

He nodded thoughtfully. "Count on it. Now—" Slapping both hands on his thighs, he rose to his feet. "I have some campaign strategizing to do."

I followed him to the front door. "Martin, I think you should know that Wilf Mullins is my lawyer and I consider him a personal friend. I thought I should mention it. In case it makes a difference."

Griffiths look puzzled. "Why would it? Wilf is an excellent councilor. I look forward to working with him." With a smile, he opened the door for me.

"But you won't be working with him, no matter how the

election turns out. Wilf had to resign his council seat in order to run for mayor. If he loses..."

Griffiths nodded politely. "I'm sure we can find him a committee to run," he said before closing the door.

Poor Wilf. I got into my truck for the trip down the driveway, feeling a little guilty.

CHAPTER 10

AS I DROVE AWAY FROM GRIFFITHS' estate, I realized there was a huge hole in my case. I'd made no attempt to probe the victim's background. Griffiths was right. There could be obvious suspects I'd overlooked—people who knew Eubanks, and hated him.

It seemed unlikely one would attract deadly enemies while flushing out septic tanks, but everybody has something to hide. Maybe Eubanks' death had nothing to do with his occupation. Perhaps it was coincidence that his killer caught up with him on the job. I tapped my fingers on the steering wheel, thinking it over.

Who was Herbert Eubanks? Really?

Maybe that reporter, Liliana István, knew something relevant. It couldn't hurt to ask.

Meanwhile, I had a clue to follow in my quest to find the mysterious street racer.

I had discounted Samantha Price's story of a street racer terrorizing the neighborhood, until Martin Griffiths all but confirmed it. If anyone in the village was likely to know who this racer was, it would be an auto mechanic known for having his ear to the ground as well as some dubious acquaintances.

My father, in other words.

Turning my truck in the direction of Leafy Hollow Auto Services, I marveled how easily former and present lives collided. Frank Thorne left my mother and me and decamped to Australia when I was eight years old. As a teenager, I changed my last name to my mother's maiden name in protest.

I never expected to see Frank again, let alone forgive him.

Until he reappeared without warning, along with a twenty-year-old mystery that ultimately revealed the truth about his sudden departure. And it wasn't what any of us had thought.

Our reconciliation had been unexpected, but not unwelcome. Still, I wasn't quite used to being a family again. It felt strange to be able to drop in on him at his job.

Visiting the garage where Frank worked as a mechanic was less uncomfortable than visiting the motel where he lived, however. The Sleepy Time Motel, set back mere yards from the highway that skirted the village, was also the home of my handyman and cottage restorer, Carson Breuer. The Sleepy Time, with its paper-thin walls, stained carpeting, and short-term rentals—very short term—would have been my absolute last choice for living quarters. The two men liked it fine. I'd often found them perched on camp chairs in the parking lot, beers in hand, contemplating the sun slowly setting over the highway as tractor-trailers rumbled past.

Carson's pet rooster usually perched on the back of his chair. Reuben wasn't interested in the sunset, though. He preferred scanning the scruffy strip of lawn for juicy grubs.

The three bays at Leafy Hollow Auto Services were always busy. I found my father in Bay No. 3, standing below the undercarriage of a black Pontiac GTO, a wrench in one hand and an oily rag in the other.

"Hi, Frank," I called.

He looked over at me. "Ettie. What brings you here?" After tucking the rag into the back pocket of his overalls, he set his wrench on a metal tool cabinet.

I ignored his use of my childhood nickname, having long since given up on that score.

"Nice car," I said. To be honest, I had no idea, but my father was sought out by vintage car enthusiasts to repair their cherished vehicles, so I figured it was a safe comment.

And accurate, apparently.

"A real beaut," he replied, tapping the sleek black body. "A '68. Pleasure to work on."

I studied the vehicle's sinuous lines, two doors, and exaggerated rectangular headlights. "V8?" I asked in what I hoped was a knowledgeable tone.

He gave a snort of laughter. "Yeah. V8. But you didn't come here to talk about cars. What's up?"

"Well..." I wondered where to begin.

He raised a hand while walking to the far wall. "Hold that thought." With his fingers poised over a series of buttons, he called over his shoulder, "Stand back," before pushing two in sequence.

"Why?"

Impatiently, he motioned me away. "Stand back. It's coming down." With the ominous creak and whirr of a hydraulic lift, the car descended.

Hastily, I backed up—straight into the wall. "Ow."

"Not that far," my father said with a roll of his eyes.

When the Pontiac reached the floor, he walked over to open the driver's door and climb in. "Meet me outside."

I watched as he backed the vehicle out of the bay and neatly tucked it into a parking spot with a one-handed twist of the wheel. He emerged from the car holding a clipboard, stopped to scribble notes on it, then brushed past me on his way into the office. "Have to drop this off. Be right back."

I sat at a battered picnic table outside to wait. The sounds of mechanics at work drifted out of the open bays—the whirr of electric tools, clang of metal against metal, and blasts of air from compressor pumps.

The office door opened and my father came out.

Standing with one hand on the doorknob behind him, he smiled at me. "Good to see you."

"Likewise. How are you?"

"Fine. Is this a social visit or did you want something?" After shutting the door, he glanced at his watch. "Not trying to rush you away, but we're busy today."

"I do have a question, but first—" Rummaging through the tote bag at my side, I pulled out a six-pack of Molson Canadian. "I brought you this."

He nodded. "Uh-huh. You do want something."

"Oh, come on. Can't a girl bring her long-lost dad a little gift without being accused of..." I narrowed my eyes. "What are you accusing me of, exactly?"

"Nothing." He shook his head ruefully. "But isn't it time to lose the *long-lost* bit? Are you ever going to let me forget it?"

I gave him a look that meant, *No*, and also, *Would you like me to recap?*

"Crikey," he said, tossing his cloth hat onto the picnic table and sitting opposite me. After running a hand through his rumpled, sun-bleached hair, he fixed me with vivid blue eyes and a sheepish grin. "What's your question?"

My father's breezy charm was lost on me, so I ignored it.

"I'm trying to find someone who owns a fast car, a street racer maybe. He was seen several times roaring at high speed past Clive Yeager's house."

"Where that guy was found dead?"

"That's correct."

"Why are you involved?"

"I'm looking into a few things."

Frank's tone turned serious. "You should be careful."

I sighed. When he looked at me, my father tended to see only the defenseless eight-year-old he'd abandoned decades earlier.

"Stand down, Dad. I'm not in any danger."

"Iffy. What about this street racer?"

"Do you know who it might be?"

"What kind of car was it?"

"Red. Or...blue."

"That's helpful."

"I don't know, do I? I've never actually seen it. And the neighbor's description was not exactly..."

"Precise?"

I nodded.

He drummed his fingers on the table. "There is a group of local street racers, but they don't race on public roads. They meet at some old quarry. I don't know where it is."

"Concession 8," I said helpfully. "Do you know any of them?"

"Maybe..." He looked uncomfortable.

"I'm not asking you to rat anybody out. In fact, I'm not interested in the racing at all. I think this person might have another reason to be in the neighborhood so often."

"Such as?"

"Such as being Clive Yeager's hired help," I said.

"Oh," he said, slapping his hand on the table. "I know who that is—Tyson Farrell."

"Who?"

"Tyson Farrell. He works here sometimes, when we're swamped. But that hobby of his is expensive, so he's always trying to turn a buck at something. When Clive Yeager brought his BMW in a while back, he mentioned that he needed help. Tyson volunteered."

"Help with what?"

"Yeager wasn't specific." He winced. "I got the feeling it wasn't cutting lawns, though." His eyes widened. "Otherwise I would have recommended you, of course, Verity."

"Thanks," I said dryly. "Is Tyson here today?"

"No. But he was here yesterday working on Ethan's car.

You must have seen him—he delivered it to one of your job sites." He drummed his fingers on the table again.

"Is there something else?"

"No. Except...when you mentioned a red car, I was worried it might be Ethan's. That kid's had enough trouble. I didn't want to land him in more."

"Even if it was his own fault?"

My father looked thoughtful. "He's a good kid, Verity. He thinks the world of you."

I gaped at him. "Are we talking about the same person?"

Without a reply, he rose to his feet. "Gotta get back to work. Anything else?"

"That's it. And thanks."

Bending to pick up the beer, he winked at me before disappearing into the garage.

Climbing into my truck, I returned to the question of the day.

Who was Herbert Eubanks?

He was a potential murder victim—so the police must have probed his background. But they hadn't arrested anybody. Did that mean they interviewed Eubanks' friends and family and couldn't find a motive?

Or that they'd been lied to?

Because if the police were convinced his death was merely a tragic accident, how hard would they look for motives? Or suspects, for that matter?

I dialed the reporter, Liliana István.

She picked up on the first ring. "Verity. I was just about to call you. You'll never guess what's happened."

"What?"

"The police closed the Eubanks case this morning. 'Accidental death,' they're calling it."

"That was quick. Any word on Waffles?"

"Oh." I heard her sharp intake of breath. "The goat's for it, I'm afraid. The timeline's uncertain, though. There has to be an inquest since, technically, Eubanks died on the job. A final decision on the animal has to wait until after that."

"An inquest might clear Waffles."

"Possibly. But you should tell your friend to prepare for the worst."

I had no intention of doing that.

"Liliana, do you know if the police talked to the victim's friends and relatives?"

"My understanding is that they couldn't find any. Eubanks was divorced, lived alone, and mostly kept to himself, from what they told me."

"That doesn't sound like they were very thorough."

"There's no obvious motive—no murderous spouse, no sizable inheritance, no recent arguments or known enemies. How hard would they look?"

"But that's just it. How hard *did* they look? Everybody has secrets. Herbert Eubanks may have seemed like the reclusive, withdrawn type. But that doesn't mean he was."

Another sharp intake of breath. "Ooh, you're right—let me get that down." I heard a noise that could have been a pencil scratching across paper. "How does this sound?" She cleared her throat. "Intrepid investigator Verity Hawkes is not willing to concede defeat. 'The police did not look hard enough for a motive,' said the dedicated sleuth. 'Herbert Eubanks may have had enemies.' No, wait, let's change that to, 'Herbert Eubanks *must* have had enemies.' I like that. What do you think?"

"No, no, no. Please stop. I'm in enough trouble over your last story."

With a pang, I recalled Jeff's astonished expression that morning when he'd read online, *Crackerjack P.I. Verity Hawkes believes Leafy Hollow resident Herbert Eubanks was almost certainly murdered.* "Don't quote me saying *anything.*"

"Okay. If you think that's better...I'll change it to, 'When asked if the police abandoned their investigation into the mysterious death of Herbert Eubanks too soon, spunky investigator Verity Hawkes delivered a terse *no comment—*"

"No! Please, Liliana, don't mention me at all." I paused for a mental rewind. "Did you just refer to me as *spunky?*"

"Too much?"

I sighed. "I called to find out what you knew about the investigation. But if there is no investigation, it's no longer relevant."

"Are you giving up?"

"Certainly not. Wait—that's off the record."

"No prob. I'll mark it as deep background."

"Thanks. Do you have Eubanks' home address?"

"Sure. It was on the incident report at the station."

As she rattled it off, I pulled out a pen to write it down. "Did you happen to check it out?"

"Yes. No one home. What are you planning to do?"

"I don't know yet." I did, of course, but there was no way

I would divulge it to intrepid reporter Liliana István. "Tell me, did you happen to interview anyone who might shed some light on Eubanks' character?"

"There is one person who might know something."

My ears pricked up. "Who?"

"Nicole Quilter."

"Who's that? Ex-wife? Girlfriend?" My third guess was unlikely, but still..."Business competitor?"

"None of the above. Nicole is a village garbage collector. And a good friend of mine. She works Eubanks' street. And, come to think of it..." She lowered her voice. "She picks up on Yeager's street, too."

I sat back, disappointed. "So she doesn't know either one of them."

"I wouldn't say that. You can tell a lot about people from their garbage. I'll send you her contact info. No—wait. Why don't the three of us get together at the Tipsy Jay later? Are you free?"

"Sure."

"Great. I'll set it up. And don't forget to let me know if you find out anything at the Eubanks homestead."

"I will," I said cheerily, crossing my fingers behind my back.

———

Eubanks' home was a modest affair, a small apartment on the second floor of a one-and-a-half-story house off Main Street in the village. I knocked on the front door, then stood back to study the wreath of faded plastic flowers and the banner that read, HOME SWEET HOME. A sheer curtain at the front window flicked back and a woman's face looked out. The curtain dropped. A few seconds later, the door opened.

An elderly woman with pinched and wrinkled lips, wearing stretch pants, slippers with worn-down heels, and a velour pullover, gripped the handle.

She looked me over. "Yes?"

I thrust out a hand. "Hello. I'm Verity Hawkes. I'm investigating the death of your tenant, Mr. Eubanks."

She continued to look at me.

I added, "On behalf of one of his associates."

"I didn't know Herbert had any associates," she said, ignoring my outstretched hand. "You might as well come in." She ushered me into a cramped and crowded living room. "I told the police everything I knew."

"I'm sure you were very helpful. It's just...There are one or two questions that have come up since, and I was hoping you might be able to shed some light. May I?" I gestured to a recliner nearest the door, figuring if I was seated, it would be harder to throw me out.

She shrugged. "Go ahead." Then she settled herself onto the sofa under the window. "What do you want to know?"

"How long was Mr. Eubanks your tenant?"

"Ten years, more or less. He lived here at first with his wife, but she walked out on him pretty quick. Can't blame her, either. He was quite the philanderer."

"Did you tell the police about his ex-wife?"

"They wrote it down, but I could tell they weren't interested. They said it was a long time ago." She gave a snort. "Like that would matter."

"What do you mean?"

"If you hate somebody that much, it doesn't stop, does it? In my experience, that kind of thing only gets worse the more you dwell on it."

"Are you saying Mr. Eubanks' ex-wife hated him? Mrs.... Sorry, I didn't get your name."

"I didn't give it." Her lips twitched, and for a moment I thought she was about to chuckle at her joke, but she resumed her sour expression. "Mrs. Peter Vaughn. You can call me Eileen." She inclined her head at a framed wedding picture on the wall. "My husband's been dead for years. Heart trouble."

"I'm sorry." I got up to take a look at the photo. A plaque attached to the frame read, PETER AND EILEEN, followed by a date.

I regained my chair, scheming how to return to the topic of Eubanks' ex-wife. "That's a lovely photo. Did Mr. Eubanks have a similar one?"

"Ha," she blurted. "Not likely. 'Good riddance,' he always said." She leaned in with a conspiratorial air. "He wouldn't even give her a divorce."

"Why not?"

"Didn't want to pay the lawyer."

"You must have known Mr. Eubanks well."

She waved a hand. "Oh, Herbert and me were good friends. We played Rummikub together."

"The game with the numbered tiles?"

"That's the one."

"You were on a first-name basis, then?"

"Definitely. I even cooked meals for him."

"Did he pay you?"

"Oh, no. We had...an arrangement."

I must have looked astonished, because she hastily added, "Not that. But I'm all alone in the world and so was he. We looked out for one another."

"Did you tell the police this?"

"None of their business." She look thoughtful for a moment. "The cops asked if he had any enemies. Paid his rent regular, that's all I know. And that's what I told them."

"Did Herbert ever mention any business difficulties, or associates who might been giving him trouble?"

She frowned. "Not that I recall."

A framed picture on the table by my elbow caught my eye, and I picked it up for a closer look. It was a faded color photo of Peter and Eileen, taken about ten years later than the wedding picture. A small boy stood in front of them, and Mrs. Vaughn's hand rested on his shoulder. "Is this your son?" I asked.

"No kids. That's my nephew. Auntie Eileen, he used to call me."

I replaced the photo on the table. "Used to? Is he...dead?"

She snorted. "Nah. But he's a good-for-nothing git. Always looking for a handout. I told him to clear out the last time he tried."

Meowww.

I jerked back as a fluffy white cat with the startling blue eyes and squashed nose of a Himalayan jumped onto the coffee table. Mrs. Vaughn stroked its head. "This is Mr. Snuffles." At my raised eyebrow, she added, "He has a sinus problem. Poor baby."

I smiled. "How do you do, Mr. Snuffles?"

The cat butted her hand.

"Can Mr. Snuffles have a treat?" I asked, reaching into my pocket for one of the General's liver bites and holding it out.

"Oh look—this nice lady brought you a snack, Mr. Snuffles."

The cat swiped at it, claws outstretched.

I immediately relinquished the treat, and he snapped it up.

Mrs. Vaughn smiled as the cat jumped off the table to regurgitate the treat on the beige carpet.

"Fur balls," she said, still smiling. "Poor baby."

I studied the carpet, wondering if it was beige by design. "Do you know where Mr. Eubanks' ex-wife lives now?"

"No idea." She looked up. "Mebbe I shoulda asked earlier, but why do you want to know all this stuff?"

"I'm making enquiries on behalf of a client whose goats have been...implicated."

"Goats?"

"Yes. From the property next door to the one where the body was found."

"Goats." She pondered this a moment. "Herbert would have been interested in the goats. He was a real animal lover."

We contemplated Mr. Snuffles, who had turned his back on the former treat and was licking a paw.

Nodding, I rose to my feet. "Thank you for your time, Eileen. I should get going." I leaned down to gingerly pat the cat. "Goodbye, Mr. Snuffles."

When I turned at the door to say goodbye, Mrs. Vaughn

had the cat in her arms. "There is one person who might be able to help you," she said. "I didn't tell the police."

"Who?"

"Herbert bought his business from an old guy who lives up on the hill. I think he's still there. They were friends for a bit."

By "the hill," I assumed she meant the Niagara Escarpment, as high as three hundred feet in spots, that enclosed the village. "Do you have his address?"

She nodded. "I think I wrote it in my book, the one I kept his rent checks in. Let me look." After placing the cat on the floor, she shuffled off down the hall.

She returned with an ancient Accounts Book, its leather cover worn and creased. Flipping it open, she ran a finger down the page. "Here it is. Terence Fidler."

Taking a pen and notepad from my purse, I copied the name and address. "Thanks."

On the way out, I made a mental note to drop off a whole bag of liver treats for Mr. Snuffles.

CHAPTER 11

SOMEONE WAS WORKING in the garden shed when I approached across Terence Fidler's weedy lawn.

"Hallo," I shouted. "Anybody home?"

A face, the head above it bald except for a sparse fringe circling the back of the neck, stuck out the open door to grin at me. "Hallo," he said. "What can I do ya for?" The rest of his body emerged in stages, until a wiry, five-foot-five elderly gentleman in a madras shirt, heavy work gloves, and rubber hip waders stood before me.

"I'm Verity Hawkes, a private investigator. I was hoping to ask you a few questions about a former acquaintance of yours for a case I'm working on."

He stripped off one glove and held out a hand. "Terence Fidler. Ask away."

I shook his hand. "Am I disturbing you? It looks as if you have some heavy work underway."

He chortled, holding up one foot. "You mean the hip waders. To be honest, the wife suggested I clean out the koi pond today, but I got sidetracked with this here squirrels' nest. Them damn fish will have to wait."

"Won't your wife mind?"

"Nah. She just wants to get me out of the house so she can put her feet up. Says I talk too much." He chortled again. "She's probably right. So. What can I do for you?"

"That depends. Are you the Terence Fidler who used to own a sewage pumping business?"

"That'd be me. Just the one tanker, though. Owner-operator."

"And you sold it to Herbert Eubanks?"

"That I did. Years ago."

"Was it a lucrative sale, if you don't mind my asking?"

"I did okay."

"How big a tanker was it?"

"Thirty-three hundred gallons. That used to be standard. But these days, those monster homes—the ones with five bedrooms and seven bathrooms? You need a four-thousand-gallon tanker for one house."

"Is it profitable?"

"You can make quite a bit hauling sewage if you're willing to put in the hours."

"Did Herbert Eubanks strike you as someone who was willing to put in the hours? I wondered—judging by where he was living—he didn't seem to have a lot of money."

I neglected to add that he might have been paying alimony.

Fidler thought this over, his wrinkled brow creasing even further. "Couldn't really say. He seemed serious enough. Hang on—is this the chap who just died?"

"Yes, it is."

"And you're looking into it? For the insurance company?"

"Sort of. I'm representing a neighbor. An individual who's been unfairly implicated."

He nodded. "Huh. I heard about the accident. Weird thing, that. He shoulda known better."

"What do you mean?"

"Anybody who hauls sewage for a living knows how dangerous it is. It only takes one good mouthful of hydrogen sulphide to knock you out. And while you're lying there..." He drew a finger across his throat.

"A lethal dose?"

"Fast, too." He shook his head. "You never take the chance of falling into a tank. Hell, I knew a guy whose son died that way."

"In a septic tank?"

"No. He climbed into the tanker. He was trying to fix something with the pipes. His dad told him to leave it until the next day when they could do it together, but there's no telling these young guys anything. It was hours before they found him."

"That's terrible."

"Yeah. His dad sold the business after that. Devastated, of course."

"I'm sure."

We stared sadly at the squirrels' nest.

I cleared my throat. "How does a septic tank work, exactly? I'm sorry if that's a stupid question, but I—"

"Not stupid a-tall. You'd be surprised how many folks don't get it. It's simple, really. Everything you flush down the pipes in your house goes into the tank, where it separates naturally into three layers. Solids at the bottom, where they eventually break down, scum on the top, and a middle layer of liquid that continuously drains away."

"And goes where?" I asked uneasily.

"Through a drainage pipe that leads to a series of perforated PVC pipes. They're laid on stone or sand and covered with soil. Most people grow grass over it."

"If the liquid drains off, why do you have to empty it?"

"Because the solid layer at the bottom builds up. You have to take it out before it clogs the drainage pipe. Simple." He straightened up, pulling on his glove. "Anything else I can help you with?"

"No, but...I don't get it. I mean, about Mr. Eubanks. What could have gone wrong? It's weird, like you said. Do you have any thoughts?"

"Huh." He flattened his lips into a straight line, thinking. "It only takes a second, I guess. If he wasn't paying attention..."

"Do you think someone pushed him in?"

He halted, his glove half off, to stare at me. "Is that what the cops think?"

"I have no idea what they think."

"It seems unlikely." He yanked the glove all the way up. "But it's a funny world."

"It is possible, then?"

"I guess." He chuckled. "In the old days, we used to throw road kill into septic tanks."

I gaped. "Does it dissolve?"

"Oh yeah. Toss a liver into a septic tank and it'll be gone in two days."

"So a whole body..."

"Hmm...it's not impossible."

In response to my queasy expression, he hastily added, "You can't do that anymore. It's against the law."

My eyes widened.

"The road kill part," he added hastily.

"Right. I knew that's what you meant."

When I walked under the huge purple bird of The Tipsy Jay sign and into the bar, Liliana hadn't arrived yet. I shot a brief wave at Katia Oldani, the proprietor of the Jay, the village's favorite hole-in-the-wall eatery. Katia had single-handedly elevated mac 'n' cheese to superstar status. Not to mention her trademark hot fudge sundae—a mound of raspberry sorbet nestled under a dome of white chocolate that melted as the server poured hot fudge over it. *Yum*.

Normally, I'd sit at the bar and shoot the breeze with Katia. But I didn't want my conversation to be overheard. Not that Katia was indiscreet. Not exactly. She was simply incapable of keeping a secret. Gossip was her lifeblood. After food, that is. She didn't mean it to be personal. But investigators on the prowl were wise to keep a distance.

I strolled past the bar to take a seat at one of the half-dozen tiny tables. With my back to the wall, I studied the day's menu. One of my favorites, *Creole Mac 'n' Cheese with Shrimp*, stood out. Tapping my feet, I burned a hole in the front door with my eyes. Where was Liliana? Would it be rude to order before she got here?

Normally, I found it difficult to eat a meal with total strangers. But since arriving in Leafy Hollow, my repertoire of social behavior had expanded more than I'd ever thought possible. The woman who'd spent two years holed up in her Vancouver apartment was long gone. Never to return, I hoped.

I was contemplating the freedom of eating with strangers —for one thing, you could order the exact same thing you always did without fear of being gently mocked by your friends—when a chubby, raven-haired young woman walked in with another woman, much taller, behind her. Liliana and her friend Nicole Quilter, I assumed.

After scanning the room, the first woman spotted me and waved.

They walked to my table and pulled out the other two chairs.

When they sat, they drew their chairs closer—touching, in fact. I smiled. Liliana's remark that they were good friends was obviously an understatement.

I'd never met Liliana in person, but I'd formed a mental picture from her voice on the phone. I expected a tiny woman, in her mid-twenties, bristling with enthusiasm. I was not disappointed.

"Verity Hawkes." She thrust out a hand. "I'd know you anywhere. You look just like your picture in the newspaper." She pumped my hand enthusiastically.

I tried to remember when my picture had been in the newspaper, online or print, then colored as I recalled the recent case involving my estranged father. It had definitely made the news—not only in Leafy Hollow, but in the neighboring city of Strathcona as well. "Thanks," I said, somewhat weakly.

Nicole was taller, darker, and older. Her short blond hair was damp, as if she'd recently showered.

"Nice to meet you," she said gruffly, opening a menu and carefully studying it. "Oh," she said with interest. "Katia's made her Creole Mac 'n' Cheese today. I must have that." Vaguely, she looked toward the bar, where Katia was chatting up a customer.

"Good choice," I said. "It's my favorite, too."

Nicole looked down at the table, fingering her napkin-wrapped cutlery.

As I studied her nervous movements, I realized Nicole Quilter was shy. Which hardly mattered because Liliana was effusive enough for two.

"How about a beer?" I asked. "To get things started? It's on me." Rising to my feet, I asked, "Local craft beer okay?"

Liliana could barely contain herself. "Oh, I love that," she enthused. "Thank you. I'll have the Moosehead lager."

"Nicole?"

"Same, thanks," she said without looking up.

"I'll be right back."

Once we'd had a couple of beers each and ordered the Creole Mac 'n' Cheese—Liliana opted for the house salad—our conversation picked up.

"Your job is an interesting one for a woman, Nicole."

"I get that a lot."

"Sorry. I hope that didn't seem condescending. Waste disposal is an essential service."

"It certainly is," Liliana enthused. "Where would we be without it?"

"What do people call you? Garbage woman? Trash collector? Sanitation engineer?"

"Mostly they call me Nicole." Her face broke into a sly grin and I realized with a twinge of relief she was joking. "But I understand the fascination. Not many women in my line of work."

"*Bon appétit*, girls!" Katia burbled, sliding three plates onto our table from a tray. After enjoying our enthusiastic reception, she withdrew.

Nicole put down her beer to pick up her fork.

"I'm a garbage woman and proud of it. I'd hate to work in an office every day. I get to work outside, and garbage cans don't talk back." She shook her head while spearing a forkful of pasta. "You have to keep an eye on traffic, though, when you're working the back, jumping on and off the truck. The lifters get hit by cars sometimes."

"I never thought about that. It sounds dangerous."

"It is," Liliana broke in. "I've written stories about it."

"It must be hard work, too. Aren't the garbage cans heavy?"

"Not usually. The trucks are motorized and we don't have to lift much anymore. But some people," Nicole rolled her eyes, "can't resist stuffing their cans to the gills. You know —" she gestured. "Those ones that are so full everything's sticking out the top? We call that 'snow-coning.'"

She grinned, picking up her beer for another swig. "And

before you ask—yes, it does take time to get used to the smell. Although, to be honest, it's usually the men who go crazy when things get gross."

"Like dirty diapers," I said, and we all laughed.

Liliana placed a hand over Nicole's. "Tell Verity what you found at Clive Yeager's place."

Nicole smiled at her friend, not taking her hand away.

I leaned in. "What was it? Does it have a bearing on the case?"

"I wouldn't know. But Liliana thought I should tell you."

I waited impatiently while Nicole finished another forkful of mac 'n' cheese.

"Thing is, we see a lot of strange stuff. Porn, for instance. You'd be amazed how many video collections I've tossed into our truck. Boxes of the things."

"Aren't people embarrassed?"

She snorted. "Not these days. Besides, it's all online now, isn't it?"

"I guess so."

"Anyway, what I'm saying is—it's easy to tell if a house belongs to a family or a single person or a dog owner or...you get the idea."

"Sure."

"And Clive Yeager is definitely single. But every once in a while he throws out a bag of—"

I leaned in. "Yes?"

"Women's clothing. It's usually a fancy dress, with high heels, lacy underwear, that sort of thing."

"How do you know this?"

"He's not good at tying up those bags. Stuff falls out, a spike heel splits the plastic—it happens."

"Sooo," I said, trying to take this in. "You're saying every so often Clive Yeager throws out an entire outfit, like the kind of thing a woman would wear for a night on the town."

"That's correct."

Liliana cocked her head. "Weird, eh?"

"How often?"

"I can't say, exactly. Every few months, I guess."

"But why would he do that?"

She shrugged. "I figure he shacks up with some woman, they argue, she moves out, he gets angry, throws out her stuff. Maybe. I don't know."

"He does have a temper," I said, recalling his reaction to Adeline. And his words. *I have nothing to say to you.*

"I don't know the guy. I only pick up his garbage."

"That is very interesting, Nicole," I said. "How about another beer? Then you can tell me about the other weird things you find in people's trash."

And we clinked our three bottles.

CHAPTER 12

WHEN I FINALLY ARRIVED HOME—I took a cab, for obvious reasons—Jeff was stretched out on the sofa. The latest spy thriller was splayed open on his chest, and the sound of gentle snoring filled the room. From his usual spot on the back of the sofa, General Chang was languidly batting a paw on Jeff's oblivious head.

Boomer was curled up on a cushion, fast asleep. That terrier had two speeds—on and off. I assumed Jeff had taken him out for a run earlier.

The tomcat looked up as I opened the door.

I raised a somewhat inebriated finger to my lips. "Ooh, be careful, kitty. Somebody's sl—sleeping." Then I slammed the door. I made a face. "Oops. Didn't mean to do that. Sorr-ee."

I had to hand it to my fiancé. He had nerves of steel. Jeff didn't flinch, although he did crack one eyelid. "You're home," he said sleepily. "Been drinking?"

Pausing to deliver a suitably shocked look at this outrageous comment, I dropped my purse on the floor and flipped off my sandals. One hit the wall with a thud. "Sorr-ee." I contemplated the fallen footwear. "I'll get that tomorrow," I said, before sinking into the nearest armchair.

And burping. Several times.

Before I could utter another "*Sorr-ee*," Jeff raised a hand to stop me. "How was the girls' night out?"

"What makes you think I was out with the girls?" I asked indignantly. "I could have been drinking with that handsome Adonis who's crazy about me. He's a firefighter, too." Weakly, I pointed a finger at Jeff. "You should be jealous." I let my head fall against the cushions.

"I dropped by Katia's for takeout on my way home. I saw the three of you in the corner, giggling like wild women."

"Oh." Thinking quickly, I added, "That was later."

"Right." His expression turned thoughtful. "Wait—what handsome Adonis?"

"I made that up."

He shook his head. "How did I fall for that?"

"Because you know how lucky you are."

"Come here."

I snuggled in beside him. Boomer jumped up and snuggled in beside me. The General stretched out on the back of the sofa and closed his good eye.

"This is nice," I mumbled. "Except for the room moving. Tell it to stop."

"I'd suggest coffee if it wasn't so late. What were the three of you talking about?"

"The case."

"What case?"

"You know—the case. Waffles. Eubanks. Yeager." I jerked upright, twisting my head to look at him. "Is it true the police have decided it's an accident and they're no longer looking into it?" Regretting the hasty movement, I slumped back, waiting for the world to slow down.

His expression turned wary. "Who told you that?"

"Liliana István, the reporter for the *Bugling Beaver*."

"Ah. I saw her with you at the Jay. I've talked to Liliana. She's...persistent." He nodded. "And she's half right. We're no longer looking into it."

"But you don't think it's an accident?"

"Barring any further evidence turning up, I've been ordered to close the case."

"By whom?"

"Higher ups."

"Higher than your immediate supervisor?"

"That's correct."

"But can't you—"

"No," he snapped. "I can't. Let's not talk about it."

Nonchalantly, he picked up his book and thumbed to the second page, not meeting my gaze.

I rose to my feet. "I think I will have that coffee after all."

Boomer followed me into the kitchen, where he sat peering hopefully at the cupboard that contained the dog biscuits. I turned on the coffeemaker.

I was seated at the kitchen table with a filled mug in my hands when Jeff ambled in.

He pulled out the chair opposite and sat down. "I'm sorry if I was curt. The truth is, I'm baffled by the order to let the whole thing drop."

Rising to get another mug from the cupboard, I filled it with coffee and set it by his elbow. "Then you do think something's wrong?"

He took a sip before setting the mug on the table in front of him. "Thanks. I've been over and over it, and it makes no sense. That goat *is* a pain in the butt, no question. But it's too neat to assume that animal somehow managed to perfectly catapult a grown man through a narrow opening like that. Eubanks knew the risks of leaning over a septic tank. He wouldn't have done it."

"What did the autopsy show?"

"Broken neck."

"So he might have been killed before he was shoved into the tank."

"Maybe."

"Then why the rush to close the case?"

"I don't know. Officially at least, it's still open. The company that was hired to empty Eubanks' tanker at the sewage treatment plant hasn't reported back. There's some kind of delay—paperwork or something. Until they sign off, we can't wrap up."

"If it's officially still open, does that mean you can continue to investigate?"

"Maybe." Looking away, he raised his mug again.

"You found out something. Tell me what it is."

With a heavy sigh, he put down the mug and reached a hand across the table. "Verity, there's something you should know."

Gripping his hand, I leaned in with a flutter of excitement. "Is this about Clive Yeager? I knew it. I knew he was up to no good. What did you find out?"

"Yeager? Nothing. He's got a solid alibi. I'm talking about Zara Price, your client."

"What about her?"

"I'm afraid that Zara has a criminal record. Sorry to be the one to tell you."

"Oh." Withdrawing my hand, I sloshed more cream into my cup before raising it to my mouth. "I knew that." I studied the cupboards, wondering which one I'd stowed the Peek Freans in.

"And you didn't think to tell me?" he spluttered.

"I thought you must know all about it. I figured, given official police channels and so on, you'd be up to date. And obviously, Zara's a client of mine so I wouldn't want to do anything to...to..."

"Cast suspicion on her?"

"Something like that. Anyway, her criminal record can't be serious. What is it? Shoplifting?"

Jeff puffed out a breath. "Arson."

"Oh." I forgot about the Peek Freans. "That's not...good."

"She was also charged with attempted murder, but that was dropped in a plea bargain."

"Gosh. That's even...worse."

"She didn't tell you?"

"It never came up."

We stared carefully at our mugs before shoving them aside.

"Did she go to jail?" I asked.

"Time served. This didn't happen in Leafy Hollow, so it's

not public knowledge around here. It was in Vancouver, over ten years ago."

"Youthful indiscretion?" I probed hopefully.

"Her defense lawyer certainly characterized it that way. Look, I'm only telling you because *if* the case is reopened for any reason, and *if* we have reason to believe that Herbert Eubanks was murdered—Zara Price will be the number one suspect." He paused before adding, "Not Clive Yeager."

I walked to the back window to lean on the edge of the sink and stare morosely into the night. Zara Price, a murderer? *Not possible.* But half an hour earlier, I would have sworn she wasn't an arsonist, either. And I would have been wrong.

How could I be so oblivious? I'd always been an introvert, which made it easy to blend into the background as an investigator and study other people. Zara had done nothing to make me suspect she was anything other than how she appeared. A kind-hearted, animal-loving, shy and unselfish woman who put her own life on hold to care for an aging— and slightly demented—mother. How could I have been so blind?

I always prided myself on my cynicism, but apparently, I wasn't cynical enough to be a real investigator. I should leave this case to the experts.

Except... I whirled to face Jeff. "Nicole Quilter told me something about Clive Yeager that's suspicious." I related the garbage collector's tale.

Jeff shook his head. "I have no idea what to do with that information."

"It's odd, isn't it?"

"Maybe, maybe not. There's likely a perfectly innocent explanation."

I glared at him.

He held up a hand. "I know what you're thinking, Verity. And as usual, you have murder on the brain. But there are no unclaimed bodies in Leafy Hollow."

"That you know of."

"Now you're really stretching. Are you suspecting a perfectly innocent man of murder based on his trash habits?" He counted off on his fingers. "No body. No missing persons. No complaints. He's clean, Verity."

"Yeager's alibi consists entirely of Gillian Shadrach saying he was with her, correct?"

"Yes, although technically I shouldn't tell you that."

"I already knew. Adeline figured it out and Gillian confirmed it."

He sat back with an incredulous expression. "Are you telling me Adeline is involved in this?"

"She was only being helpful."

"Helpfully jumping to conclusions, as always. Besides, that's the obvious explanation for the mysterious garbage. Those must have been Gillian's clothes."

"She insists they're not lovers, Jeff. I don't think she spends enough time at Yeager's house to be discarding clothing there. And they haven't had a falling out, so it's not anger on his part. Did you find any indication of a girlfriend when you searched his home?"

Jeff looked puzzled. "Why would we search his home?"

"Are you saying you didn't?"

"What evidence could we use to justify a warrant?

Eubanks died outside Yeager's house, not inside. And Yeager wasn't even home at the time." He slapped his forehead. "Of course, we never thought to check his garbage for body parts. I wonder if it's too late to go back?"

"Stop it."

He grinned at me. "It is a bit far-fetched, Verity."

"A minute ago you told me you're suspicious."

His face darkened. "Yes. But not about Clive Yeager."

"If you mean Zara Price, I don't believe it."

"It's common knowledge that Yeager and Price do not get along. They quarrel frequently. And she has a criminal record."

"Why would she kill Eubanks?"

"She likely didn't intend to. It could have been a prank that went wrong. Now she's trying to cover it up by casting suspicion on Yeager. And you're helping her do it."

"That's not fair." I stuck out my lower lip and blinked a little. "I'm just trying to save a helpless goat." I added a quiver. "Poor Waffles."

Jeff did not crumble even a little. "Right. Like that expression ever works." He flashed a grin. "Let's not argue about it."

"Okay. But first thing tomorrow, I'm going to visit my client and find out what's really going on."

"Good idea. And after you've wrestled a confession out of her, don't forget about your friends on the police force." He picked up my mug, added it to his own in the sink, then turned to give me a long look.

The look that always sets my heart to thumping.

"What?" I asked, feeling a little weak in the knees.

Taking my hand, he headed for the door. "It's late. Time for bed."

"I don't think I can sleep after all that coffee."

He gave me that look again, followed by a slow smile. "Who said anything about sleeping?"

CHAPTER 13

WHEN I TRAMPED across her yard the next morning, Zara Price was in the goats' enclosure out back.

She straightened up with a pail in her hand when she saw me. Two of the smaller goats butted it gently to get at the contents. "Verity. Any news?"

"No, sorry. But there is something I need to ask you about. Can we go inside?"

"Absolutely. I'm nearly done here and Mom's making breakfast. Join us?"

"I'm not sure this is something you'd want to discuss in front of Sam."

Zara looked stricken. Slowly, she lowered the pail to the ground. The delighted goats tucked in. "Has something happened to Waffles? Did they—"

"No, no. I didn't mean to imply anything like that. I'm sure he's fine."

She let out a long breath. "That's good. Mother is fond of Waffles."

I nodded. "We're all fond of Waffles."

"He's a good goat."

"Yes. He is." This was getting us nowhere, so I plunged in. "The thing is, Zara, and I know this didn't come up before, and it's not your fault because I never asked, but...you should have told me about your criminal record."

She pursed her lips. "Why?"

"It makes you look suspicious. As if you might be... violent. Not that I think that," I added hastily. "Not at all. But the police tend to jump to conclusions."

She laughed bitterly. "I know all about their tendencies." She picked up the now-empty pail, opened the gate to walk through to my side of the fence, then closed and latched it carefully. Clasping the pail to her chest, she turned to face me. "Did they tell you what I was charged with?"

"Arson. And attempted murder, but that charge was dropped."

"Did they tell you why I did it?"

"No. I don't know the details." I hesitated. "Does your mother know?"

Zara cast a sidelong look at the farmhouse. "Only that I had a little trouble with the police in Vancouver. None of the details. She doesn't know about the weeks I spent in a holding cell, waiting for our trial." She shot me a sharp look. "Are you going to tell her?"

"Of course not. It's none of my business."

With a heavy sigh, Zara dropped the pail by the gate and started up the path toward the house. I followed.

"There were six of us," she said. "Our target was a local slaughterhouse. We didn't plan on violence—we were only scouting the best spots for our protest the following day and intending to stash some extra signs and maybe a bit of paint."

My jaw dropped. "You belonged to an animal rights group."

She nodded. "One of our members was a hothead. He brought along a Molotov cocktail. We tried to stop him, but he insisted no one would ever know who was responsible. He tossed it through an office window. It smashed the glass and started a fire." She gave me a quick look. "It was a separate building from the slaughterhouse. He wouldn't have risked hurting the animals." She snorted. "For all the good that did."

"Anyway," she continued, "that idiot posted the whole thing online on a chat board. The police rounded us up the next day."

"Why the attempted murder charge?"

"The prosecutor argued that a security guard could have been inside the office at the time. He wasn't—he was on his rounds. We knew that."

"But you pleaded guilty to the lesser charge."

"The legal aid lawyer recommended that, but I've always regretted it. I should have fought it. Anyway, I had no previous record, so they let me go with time served."

We had reached the front of the farmhouse.

Zara paused at the carved wooden door. "Is that all?"

I nodded, then turned to go.

"Wait," she said, reaching for my arm. "Come in for breakfast, Verity. Mom's making pancakes." She raised an eyebrow. "With maple syrup from our own trees."

How could I resist? Besides, I did have a question for

Mrs. Price that had nothing to do with animal rights. I followed Zara into the house.

"Are you the youngest in the family? I only ask because your mother told me she'd been making jam for nearly seventy years. That must mean she's over eighty."

"Eighty-two, believe it or not. And yes, I was the youngest and also the oldest. Change-of-life baby, they used to call us. Mom was over forty when I was born."

"No siblings, then?"

"No. And Dad died decades ago, so it's been just us for years. Mom's a little forgetful now. Sometimes I think, well... We'll deal with that when it happens. Sit down."

She pulled out two carved wooden chairs at the farm table that dominated the kitchen. Mrs. Price—Samantha— had her back to us, working at an old gas stove.

"Verity's joining us for breakfast, Mom," Zara said. When Sam did not turn around, she raised her voice several decibels. "Verity's here, Mom."

Sam whirled around, a spatula in her upraised hand. She had on a brightly patterned cotton apron over her jeans and pullover, and her white hair was tied back with a purple bow.

"Hello, dear. How nice to see you again. Zara, get Verity some coffee."

Smiling, Zara looked up from the cup she was pouring. "Already on it."

Sam stacked pancakes on a plate and set it in front of me with a smile.

Though my landscaping business requires me to get up at the crack of dawn, I'm not normally an early riser. My typical weekday breakfast consisted of a coffee hastily drunk at home, followed by a breakfast sandwich from Tim Horton's drive-through that usually included bacon. I decided not to mention that in front of Zara.

Pancakes were strictly weekend treats. Jeff was the resident chef at Rose Cottage, and whipping up pancake batter was nothing to him. Unless he was trying out something new, like his bacon-and-spinach stromboli, which was a big hit with me. I mean, flaky pastry for breakfast—who wouldn't like that? I considered it my duty to test Jeff's creations. Great chefs need an audience. Like Aunt Adeline often said, *They also serve who only sit and eat.*

Or was that Wilf Mullins?

The thought of my diminutive lawyer and his likely embarrassment in the upcoming mayoral contest gave me a pang. I should check in with Wilf. But first—

Inhaling rapturously over the fluffy pancakes, I reached for my fork. "These look fantastic."

Before I could properly wade in, Mrs. Price set an equally large plate of scrambled eggs and braised tomatoes in front of me. Zara, who'd taken the chair beside me, pushed over a carafe of syrup.

"I didn't know you had a maple bush," I said, pouring a luscious caramel stream over my stack.

"It's not really big enough to be called a bush," she said. "Only half a dozen trees. But it's enough for us, isn't it, Mom?"

"Who boils down the sap?"

"I do," said Sam, watching us eat with both hands on her hips. "It takes hours, and Zara has too many other things to do."

"Please sit down and join us."

She smiled, and I realized she was watching my lips as I talked. It was possible she was nearly deaf. I'd interviewed an elderly, retired minister once and he could hardly hear a thing. Sharp as a tack, though, once you got through to him.

"I like to stand," she said. "Sometimes when I sit down, it's hard to get back up again."

After several minutes of appreciative chewing that some people might have characterized as frenzied, I put down my fork. "That was amazing. Thank you so much."

"You're welcome, dear," she said, collecting my empty plate.

"Sam, I don't know if you remember, but last month you mentioned there had been a strange man hanging around. You thought he might have tampered with that cherry jam."

Zara shot me a warning look. "Mom sometimes gets a little confused. There was no man here."

But her mother had a faraway look in her eyes, as if she was trying to remember something. "Yeeesss," she said. "There was someone." She deposited my plate in the sink.

"Mom, don't be ridiculous. You know there wasn't."

"Wasn't there? Oh. Ignore me. I get so muddled..." The strange look in her eye did not go away.

"What did he want, this man?" I asked.

"There was no man," Zara said. Her tone was sharp. "Drop it, Verity."

I looked at her in surprise. "But your mother seems to think—"

"He asked to see someone," Sam said, still with that faraway look. "He asked for—"

"Stop it, Mom. Verity, I'm sorry but I have a lot to do today."

Shoving back my chair, I stood up. "Thanks again for breakfast. I have a lot to do myself."

Sam smiled. "Drop in again, Verity. Any time."

At the door, Zara paused on the threshold to watch me walk out. "I'm sorry about Mom, but you can't take anything she says at face value. She's confused a lot of the time. The doctor says...well, no use going into that. You'll let me know if anything happens with the case?"

"Of course I will."

"Will it take long? Waffles will be pining. Goats hate to be alone. They need other goats around. I'm worried about him."

"I have a plan. I'm going to ask someone for advice who knows a lot about investigative work."

"Not Jeff?" Zara asked, looking alarmed.

I shook my head. "Not Jeff."

My aunt was pacing up and down the driveway when I pulled up to Rose Cottage.

"Where have you been?" she asked as I climbed out of the truck.

I closed the driver's door with a thud. "I was delayed at the Prices. By a plate of home-made pancakes."

"Did they offer you their homemade maple syrup?"

"It was delicious."

"An understandable delay, then."

"Thank you."

"But now that you're here, we have to talk."

That sounded ominous. "Inside?" I asked.

"Yes." My aunt bounded up the front steps two at a time.

Sighing, I followed.

An explosion of terrier barking greeted my turn of the key in the lock. *Arf-arf-arf. Arf-arf-arf. Arf-arf-arf.*

Adeline rolled her eyes.

"He's a good guard dog," I offered weakly, pushing open the door.

Boomer went straight for my aunt.

"Sit," she thundered.

The little dog slapped his tush on the floor and looked up adoringly at her.

"Good boy," she said. "Now. Coffee?"

"No, thanks. I had plenty at the Prices."

"I meant for me," she said drily, heading for the kitchen. Boomer padded after her.

In the kitchen, I leaned against the counter and watched as my aunt sloshed black coffee into a mug.

"That's better," she said after a few sips.

"How many does that make today?" I asked with a glance at the clock. It was barely eight. "You know what the doctor said."

"Bosh," she said. "So? You called me. Why?"

"I wanted to ask your advice on the Eubanks case."

She regarded me intently over the rim of her mug. "The police think it was an accident."

"I know they do."

"But you don't." Adeline put the mug down on the counter behind her.

"It's too convenient."

"I agree. And?"

"And I need some advice on what to do next."

"Tell me what you've done so far."

I related my visit to Gillian Shadrach's dress shop, and how Mr. Snuffles led me to the elderly Terence Fidler, who insisted that the man who bought his sewage pumping business would never have been so careless as to lean into an open tank.

"Tell me again about the women's clothing," she said. "In Yeager's garbage."

I repeated Liliana's strange tale. "Do you think it's significant? Jeff says it's far-fetched."

"Jeff's a cop. They're trained to have both feet on the ground. To stick to the plausible and so forth." She tapped her fingers on the counter. "And it's true. Most murders are committed by obvious suspects with obvious motives."

"But not always."

"No."

"What do you think it means?"

"Possibly nothing. But I have my own reasons to suspect Clive Yeager."

"He has an alibi."

"Did you find Gillian believable?"

"I'm pretty new at this, but...no," I said emphatically. "I did not. I got the clear impression she was hiding something."

"Did Liliana see high-heeled shoes in that garbage?"

I nodded.

"Did she happen to notice their size?"

"I don't think so. She didn't mention it."

"Hmm. Too bad. If you solve this case, it will really put Hawkes Investigative Agency on the map."

"I just want to help Waffles. I don't want to solve a murder case."

"Why not?"

"I'm not a trained investigator. It's a sideline."

"You should have more faith in yourself, Verity. You have a real talent for this kind of work. Look how impressed Cayenne Cole was with your abilities."

I huffed at this reference to the femme fatale insurance investigator I'd met on a previous case. "Sure she was—after I nearly got myself killed. I'd rather not do that again."

"We cannot choose our destiny. It chooses us."

Oh no. My aunt was waxing philosophical, a sure sign she was contemplating something dangerous.

"What are you suggesting?"

She walked to the sink under the window to rinse out her mug while contemplating the purple-shaded trees of Pine Hill Valley in the distance. She reached for a tea towel, dried the mug, and put it away before turning to face me. "We need evidence, and there's only one way to get it."

I knew better than to ask, but I just couldn't help myself. "And that would be?"

"We'll break into Yeager's house. Tonight would be good. No moon."

I stared in disbelief. "No. We are absolutely not doing that. Moon or no moon."

"I'm doing it. And if you come along as lookout, there's a

better chance I'll get away with it."

I opened my mouth, but nothing came out. I closed it, then tried again. Still nothing.

"I'm an old woman, Verity. Do you want to see me in a jail cell?"

Her mention of a jail cell reminded me of Zara's ordeal. Was I willing to risk putting my aunt through that?

Yes, I was, come to think of it.

Perhaps sensing I might be wavering, she added—while sadly patting her chest—"I might not survive incarceration. Hard to know how much this old ticker can take."

I gaped at her. "It would be just like you to die of a heart attack in jail so I'd feel guilty forever."

With a dramatic sigh, she gazed at the ceiling. "We cannot choose our destiny. It—"

"Stop that. I am not breaking into Clive Yeager's house. And neither are you."

"He won't press charges."

"How do you know?"

Her manner turned triumphant. "Because he's working for the Syndicate. They can't risk having their sleeper agent exposed in Leafy Hollow." She lowered her voice. "They call him The Shadow."

My stomach plummeted to the floor. This was worse than I'd imagined. *The Syndicate?* The nefarious criminal network that my aunt's former employer, the equally shady black-ops marketing group known as *Control*, was sworn to combat?

And whose operatives had tried to kill her—several times? And even worse—once tried to kill me? Which I took personally.

With a shaky hand, I yanked out the nearest chair and slumped into it. Then I leaned forward with my hands on my knees, trying to calm my breathing. *In. Out.*

"Verity?" my aunt asked. "Say something."

I squinted up at her. "You promised me. You said you were retired. You said you didn't do this sort of thing anymore."

"I know, Verity, and I'm sorry. But I did tell you something was coming. Remember, in the gym? When I told you Gideon wasn't up to it?" She looked apologetic. "And you did promise to help."

I stared, feeling slightly ill, remembering our sparring match. "That's not true. I distinctly recall insisting I wouldn't do it."

Her eyes widened. "Not to me."

"I told Gideon. He must have passed it on."

Adeline looked thoughtful. "He assumed you were kidding. As did I."

"You did not."

She pulled out a chair and turned it to face me. After sitting down, she took both of my hands in hers. "Verity. I'm certain Yeager was the driver who forced me off the road. I believe he's also the sleeper agent that Gideon and I feared was living in Leafy Hollow. Up to now, Control has been willing to wait for that dormant agent to make a mistake. But now," she shook her head sadly. "If we don't do something, he'll kill again. We have to stop him."

"No. You need to go to the police."

"I have. They don't believe me. It's worse than you think, Verity."

How is that possible? I thought. "In what way worse?"

"Someone is shielding The Shadow. Either in the police department or...the government. We need to identify that person. There will be something in Yeager's house, I'm sure of it, to point the way. Maybe even throw light on his other crimes."

"What other crimes?"

She shook her head. "We won't know until we get into his house. Look. I can do a thorough search in no time."

"Because you know all the secret-agent hiding places?" I asked sarcastically.

"But I have to get inside, and tonight's the perfect night."

"He'll be there."

"No, he won't. He'll be at Gillian's."

"How do you know?"

"I've been tailing him. He's a man of habit. Probably his military background, but it's odd."

"Why is it odd?"

"Agents are usually warier. He didn't even realize he was being followed."

"Maybe he did. Maybe he was watching you, watching him."

We exchanged a long look. Then, "Too complicated," we said in unison.

"So you'll help me?"

I let out a long breath. "Promise me this is positively, absolutely the last time you do anything like this."

She raised a finger to cross her heart.

"Oh, don't bother," I said with an exasperated flap of my hand. "Let's just get this over with."

CHAPTER 14

"ANY ACTION?" I asked, dropping onto the grass beside my aunt to squint up at the waning moon.

"Yeager left forty minutes ago," she replied without lifting her eyes from the night binoculars in her hands. "Drove off in his BMW. He hasn't come back."

I twisted over onto my stomach. "How long do we wait?"

She handed me the binoculars, and I trained them on Yeager's house. With their powerful scopes, it was easy to spot the ends of yellow caution tape flapping in the breeze. Lights at the front and back of the building provided some illumination. "Looks like the septic tank is covered over." I handed back the binoculars. "Hopefully without any bodies in it."

"It was officially sealed. The police will be able to tell if anyone opens it."

"Good idea. At the very least, they can fine Yeager for unsafe septic tank retirement."

My aunt merely grunted. "What did you tell Jeff?"

"He thinks I'm at the Tipsy Jay with the girls." I glanced at my watch. "So we need to get this underway. That place closes at one a.m."

She grunted again.

"I will tell him, you know. When this is over."

"Just so long as you wait until then." She rose to her feet, brushing grass off the black turtleneck and yoga pants she'd insisted we both wear. "Suit up," she said, pulling a black balaclava over her face.

Tugging on similar headgear, I recalled some of the other disguises I'd worn. At least my aunt's choice of housebreaking garments was more professional than the droopy foliaged camouflage hat Lorne had once devised. But—was my famil-iarity with burglars' gear a good thing, really?

My aunt started across the lawn, darting from tree trunk to tree trunk.

I followed, more casually. There was no one around to see us. And if Yeager had security cameras, we'd already been spotted. Either way, our approach vector was irrelevant.

At the back door, I paused. "How do we get in? Can you pick this lock?"

"Maybe."

"Maybe?"

"We don't have to pick anything. That's another reason this is the perfect night. Remember Zara's goats?"

"How could I forget?"

"With all their jumping up and down on the roof, they broke a hole over the sunroom—right there." She pointed. "It's big enough to climb through. And we can reach it by going over this trellis."

My bestie, Emy, had trained as a gymnast in her teenage years. She could have nailed this. Unfortunately, she was a thousand miles away. Whereas I, on the other hand...

"Aunt Adeline. Please. I cannot climb up a trellis and drop through a hole in the roof."

She backhanded my arm. "Of course you can. Look how tall you are. Now, give me a boost."

It was not clear what my height had to do with it—unless it meant my head would have farther to fall to hit the ground. But I knew from experience that arguing with my aunt would be fruitless. I linked my fingers and held them out.

She stepped lightly into them with the rubber mountaineering shoes she'd also insisted we wear. Now I knew why. Heaving, I almost tossed her into the climbing rose bush overhead.

"Yikes," she said. "I didn't realize this rose was a *New Dawn*. Such a predictable choice." Pause. "Also—thorns."

"Of course there are," I muttered.

"Get up here, Verity."

I scrambled after her. Within minutes we were on the sunroom roof. A heavy tarpaulin had been drawn over the hole and tied off with cord. Adeline pulled a garden knife from the holster at her side.

I knew that knife. I'd seen it in action plenty of times as a child on wilderness survival "quests" with my aunt—sights I had no intention of describing to Zara. I watched Adeline snip the cords, then draw back the tarp with a rustle of plastic.

"Let's go," she said, disappearing through the ragged hole.

"Why don't I wait out here? As lookout. I can see if anybody drives by."

My aunt hollered up from the sunroom. "Yes, and anybody who drives by will see you. Get in here."

Reluctantly, I crouched by the opening and peered in.

"It's a short drop," came my aunt's voice. "Eight feet." Pause. "Maybe ten."

Muttering, I lowered myself into the opening, holding on with my elbows.

"Quickly."

"All right, already." I dropped, landing with my knees bent.

My aunt was rummaging through drawers. Red LED lights on the kitchen appliances provided a little illumination, but we'd brought tiny flashlights. I flicked mine on.

"What are we looking for?"

"Address book, laptop computer, cell phone, filing cabinets, stick-on notes, anything like that. And, especially, a home safe."

"Won't that sort of thing be in his home office?"

"Yes, but there could be keys hidden elsewhere."

"We'll never find keys."

My aunt pounced on a ring hanging by the back door and hoisted it aloft with a jangle of metal. "Yeager has no reason to expect anyone to break in looking for things like this." She slid the key ring into her bum bag. "Let's check the office."

We padded down the hall to the front of the house.

On the threshold of the den, I hesitated as a thought struck me.

"Why would he hide anything here? A home office

would be the first place anybody would look. There must be somewhere else."

"Good point." She glanced around. "But where?"

"This is a brand-new house, right? And a split-level. That means there's a finished basement. That's where I'd hide stuff. This office is probably just for show."

We headed downstairs and stepped into a carpeted room. It had a massive wall screen, theater-style recliners, and a wooden bar with rows of liquor bottles lined up on shelves in front of a mirrored back wall. Clive Yeager was certainly predictable. This was a typical man cave.

"Not here," I said. "Let's keep looking."

The rest of the basement held a furnace and utility room, a massive upright freezer stocked with frozen steaks, and a fully equipped workshop with an extensive range of wood-working tools. A table saw, a shop vac, and a power drill were the only ones I recognized. We moved on.

A door at the end of the hall was closed. I tugged on the handle.

Locked.

With mounting excitement, I retrieved a large screw-driver from the workshop, jammed it between the door and the frame, and heaved. The wood splintered. I heaved again. Within minutes, we were inside.

It was a windowless room and utterly dark. Running my hand down the inside of the doorframe, I felt for the light switch and flicked it on. An overhead fixture washed the room with light.

Two additional spotlights on individual stands, aimed at the far wall, also came on.

I halted, unable to move. My mouth dropped as I stared at that wall. And its display. "Oh my God. Look at this."

Adeline sidled past me. When she saw the display, she inhaled sharply.

Hundreds of photographs of the same young woman were pinned to the far wall, their glossy surfaces gleaming in the glare of the spotlights. In some photos the woman looked straight at the camera, almost coquettishly. In others, she seemed oblivious to the photographer's presence, as if unaware she was being watched.

In the center of the room, a single empty chair faced the wall of photos. Several rolls of black plastic tape were stacked on a table beside the chair.

Adeline whipped out her phone to snap a picture.

I tugged on her arm. "We have to get out of here. What if Yeager comes back? He won't be happy that we've found this room."

"Agreed." She stowed the phone in her bag. "Wait a minute, though." Tugging her arm free, she stepped nearer the wall. "I think I recognize—"

Somewhere overhead, a door slammed.

"We have to move. Now." I grabbed my aunt's arm to drag her to the exit.

In the hall, we glanced frantically around.

"There's no time for the roof," I said. "We have to go out the back door."

We darted up the steps. We'd almost reached the kitchen when a voice rang out.

"Who's there?"

Someone stepped in front of us, a faceless shadow in the

dark. I barreled into them, knocking them to one side with a horizontal elbow strike.

"The back door," I grunted at my aunt. She was ahead of me. The door loomed in front of us. Just a few more steps…

"Move it," she urged over her shoulder.

Behind me, I heard my victim struggle up, shouting curses.

I dove through the door. Adeline slammed it shut.

"This way," she hissed, pointing in the opposite direction from the route we'd taken on our way in. "Martin Griffith's estate is over that brick wall. If we go that way, the wall will hide us."

We put on a burst of speed. For the first time, I wished it had been a full moon. At least then, I wouldn't have tripped. With a grunt and a curse, I staggered on.

At the wall, I boosted my aunt up. Straddling the top, she helped me over, then dropped lightly to her feet beside me.

We paused to get our bearings and let our eyes adjust to the feeble moonlight.

I could hear rushing water. "We're at the top of the waterfall," I whispered. "There are stone stairs that lead down beside it to the rest of the estate. From there we can cross the road to the conservation area. Then we can call the police." I headed for the stairs.

My aunt halted me with a hand on my arm. "I don't think we should call the police."

"What are you talking about? We have to tell them about Yeager's photos." I brushed her hand away. "Come on," I whispered. "And watch your footing. It would be easy to fall off."

We trotted down several steps. "I'll call the police when we get to the bottom."

"No, Verity, don't."

"Why not?" I asked, keeping my voice low. "We found evidence that Yeager's been stalking at least one young woman. Maybe more. And when you think what Liliana found in his garbage, well...it's compelling, don't you think?"

"There's another explanation."

"Please don't start up about the Syndicate again. We have to call the police this time."

A few more steps and we'd reached the rocky pool at the bottom of the falls.

"Oh dear," Adeline said, a step behind me. "This isn't good."

"What is it now?"

"I stubbed my toe."

I whirled on her. "You're kidding, right? We have other things to worry about than your toe."

"Look." She pointed down at her foot.

Exasperated, I followed her finger. Just then, the waning moon broke out from behind a cloud, providing just enough light to make out the object at my aunt's feet.

Moonlight glinted off a man's body crumpled on the stone stairs, lying on his stomach.

We bent to heave him over.

The white face of Clive Yeager, his eyes wide and unseeing, stared back at us.

CHAPTER 15

DURING THE HOURS we spent in the police station—first outside the interview rooms, and later inside them—I had plenty of time to review my role in the evening's events.

No matter which angle I took, I didn't come out of it smelling like roses. In fact, the odor clinging to this particular episode had more in common with the one from Clive Yeager's septic tank than his garden.

Where to start?

Jeff was furious, of course. But he was also disappointed, which hurt more.

But the worst aspect of the case was the way I'd suspected an innocent man of—what? Mass murder? How could I have been so blind?

And so wrong?

While Adeline and I sat together on a bench in the station, she had pulled a crumpled photo out of her bag and handed it to me. It was one of the pictures from Yeager's secret basement wall. A hole at the top marked where a pin had been ripped out.

"I grabbed it on the way out," she said in response to my raised eyebrows.

"This is evidence."

"Yes, sure. Take a good look. Do you recognize that woman?"

Frowning, I squinted at the photo. "I don't think so... although, she looks familiar." Rising, I held the picture directly under a ceiling light and peered at it again. My stomach sank. "Oh my God."

The woman in the photo was Clive Yeager.

In drag.

I sat beside my aunt on the bench and handed back the photo. "So that's why you asked about the shoe size. What tipped you off?"

"It was only a hunch."

"But why did he keep it a secret?"

Adeline tucked the photo into her bag. "His military background, I guess. After a lifetime of denial, it's not easy to go public."

"That's not the reason," a woman's voice said.

We looked up to see a disheveled Gillian Shadrach standing in the entrance, glaring at us.

"Gillian—I'm so sorry," I said. "I know Clive was a friend of yours. Are you here to..." I hesitated. "Identify his body?"

"I've already done that. At the morgue."

I nodded, shifting uncomfortably on the bench.

We stared at each other. Gillian did not move.

"Then why are you here?" I asked.

Her glare escalated to shooting-daggers pitch. "To press charges against you, obviously."

I slumped against the bench. "Join the queue."

"Verity didn't kill Clive," my aunt said.

Gillian planted a hand on her hip while massaging the side of her ribcage with the other. "Maybe not, but she nearly killed me."

With a sinking heart, I recalled my encounter in Yeager's kitchen. "Was that you I stumbled across?"

"Stumbled? You didn't stumble. You attacked me on purpose."

Staring dumbly, I debated denying it but decided against it. "I'm sorry, Gillian. It's been a rough day. I understand if you want to press charges."

Still glaring, she pursed her lips. "Indeed."

Straightening up, I added in a hopefully sympathetic tone, "But first, tell us why Yeager was hiding his drag persona."

She heaved a sigh. "He wasn't hiding it. Not exactly. We were fine-tuning his presentation. We've been working on it for months. He didn't want anyone in the village to know until his performance was perfect. It's such a competitive field. I was trying to get him a TV booking on *Canadian Queens Hit the Road*. That will never happen now." Her shoulders slumped, and she turned to go.

"But the photos—"

She whirled to face me, her expression black. "Those photos were for his CV. And thanks to you, they're in the hands of the police." She turned her attention to the wall of mug shots beside our bench, seemingly lost in thought. "We worked so hard on those outfits—the makeup, the wigs, not to mention the routines. He would have been dynamite."

"I'm so sorry, Gillian. If I can ask—"

"Yes?" she snapped, jolted out of her reverie.

"Why did Clive throw out some of those outfits?"

She regarded me with astonishment. "Did you go through his garbage?" Her mouth dropped. "Did you actually go—"

"I didn't—no," I blurted. "That was...someone else."

She closed her eyes, swaying slightly, before replying. "Until we got hooked up with the right vendors, Clive had to throw away a lot of stuff. The shoes and dancers' tights were the hardest to find. He kept the rest of it in that wall-to-wall closet in his bedroom." She opened her eyes to scowl at us. "Did you search that, too?"

"No, but—" I held up a finger. "If I could ask one other thing—what was the tape for?"

She gave a quick snort before stalking out with a backward flap of her hand.

"I'm so sorry, Gillian," I called before slumping back against the bench.

"Stop apologizing," my aunt said. "You didn't do anything wrong."

I stared at her, my splitting headache temporarily forgotten.

"Have you lost your mind? Has dementia finally set in? *Didn't do anything wrong?* Let me count the ways." I raised one finger, followed by the others in sequence. "I implicated an innocent party in a horrific crime. I burglarized someone's home. I damaged personal property. I stood by while you purloined possible evidence. I attacked an innocent bystander—" I switched to my other hand. "Fled the scene. Trespassed on someone's property. Found a dead body—"

"That last one is not a crime. That was a public service."

I groaned. "Why do I bother?" Clapping my arms across my chest, I closed my eyes and leaned back.

"Verity—"

"Don't speak to me."

We sat in silence, listening to ringing phones and muffled conversations and the loud ticking of a clock on the wall. I knew we were waiting for our turn on the hot seat. I hoped they wouldn't shine one of those high-powered desk lamps in my eyes. My headache was rapidly becoming a full-blown migraine, and the anxiety attack triggered by the discovery of Yeager's body threatened to resume at any moment.

"Verity." My aunt's tone had softened considerably. "Are you all right? I'm so sorry about this. Can I get you anything?"

Cracking one eye, I turned my head in her direction.

Nobody does *contrition* like Aunt Adeline. Her expression was one of utter sorrow. The most hardened criminal would have been moved to tears.

I merely snorted and closed my eye again.

"There are sandwiches in the vending machine," she offered helpfully.

Against my better judgment, I felt a flicker of interest. We'd been there for hours and I was hungry. Plus, food might ease my headache. I cracked that eye again. "Any egg salad?"

"I think so. Shall I check?"

Shrugging, I said, "Why not."

Adeline rose to cross the room. "Potato chips?" she asked. "And a soda?"

This was hardly the time to worry about calories. "Yes. And see if they have any of those bear-claw things." Might as well stock up. If we had to spend the rest of this night in the cells, we might only get dry bread and water.

My aunt returned with an armful of dubious nutritional merit. I tucked right in. After I'd consumed half a sandwich, a bag of ketchup-flavored chips, and a diet cola, she resumed her explanation. I tore open the plastic wrap on a bear claw while I listened.

"Verity. I know you're upset and I know this seems like a mess and maybe I shouldn't have gotten you involved—"

She was lucky at that moment that my mouth was full of pastry.

"But the fact remains that Clive Yeager's lifestyle choices had nothing to do with his criminal affiliations. He was a Syndicate agent, I'm positive."

I chewed, swallowed, and reached for a second cola. "Then, who killed him?"

"I'm still trying to work it out."

"I don't know what to believe. But we've been here for hours. When are you going to make the call?"

She gave me a quizzical look. "Call?"

"You know—the call to Ottawa. Or whoever. Won't Control get us out of this? We were on a mission for them, right?" I swallowed another swig of cola, remembering a previous case in which a mysterious gray-haired gent in a cashmere coat arrived in the nick of time to smooth everything over. In fact, that case resulted in accolades all around.

Instead of an uncomfortable night on a police station bench.

I put the can down, alarmed by the expression on her face. "Please don't tell me this is one of those 'plausible deniability' things. They *will* come and help us, right? Behind the scenes, I mean?"

The wince on her face turned into a grimace. "I'm afraid not."

"What?" I squeaked. "No. You're wrong. Any minute now, somebody's going to come out here with an annoyed expression and say, 'You're cleared to leave. Never darken our door again.' And we'll walk out and nothing will ever be said about this. Right?" I raised my voice. "Right?"

"I'm sorry, Verity. The fact is...this mission wasn't really a mission."

I'm not often at a loss for words, but this had me stumped. "Explain that."

"I tried to convince Control we should take a closer look at Yeager. Repeatedly. But head office was of the opinion that after we took out that Syndicate agent at Niagara Falls, there was no one else left."

"I remember. You and Gideon weren't convinced. But Yeager didn't work for the Syndicate."

"I think he did."

"Then why is he dead?"

My aunt selected a Kit Kat bar from among the pile on the bench between us. "I don't have all the answers." She tore off the wrapper and took a bite, chewing thoughtfully.

"You told me this was a sanctioned mission."

Adeline winced again. "I don't think I used the word 'sanctioned' exactly."

"I think you did. Anyway, it was implied."

"Perhaps it was, and I'm sorry. But I assumed we would find enough evidence to convince Control that I was right about Yeager. Then it wouldn't matter."

I stared, not trusting myself to speak.

"Also," Adeline continued. "Sanction is a Janus word."

"What?"

"Words that are their own opposites, also known as contronyms, or auto-antonyms. Named for the two-headed Roman spirit Janus, the god of beginnings and endings. He was normally depicted as having two faces, because he could look to the future and the past. Perhaps—" She raised a finger. "You assumed the wrong meaning."

I sputtered, unable to form words, for several seconds.

Adeline looked smug.

I finally recovered. "That is the lamest excuse you have ever—"

"No, really," she broke in. "Take *dust* for instance. Does it mean to take something away, as in cleaning, or to add something, as in sprinkling?"

"You have never dusted anything in your life."

Adeline regarded me sadly. "You know that's not true. Anyway, my point—"

"I'm so glad there's a point."

She ignored this. "My point is that *sanction* can mean approval *or* disapproval. Same word, contradictory meanings. Therefore, if I did use it..." She shrugged.

Leaning back, I gave a grunt of disgust. "I think you're

forgetting that Mom was a linguistics expert. I know all about auto-anto...anti...auto...ottomans." I paused, scrunching my nose. "Those things."

Adeline made a *hmm* noise.

"The point," I continued, "is that you lied to me."

"Verity, I know I'm right."

"Mom would kill you for this," I said, my voice low and treacherous.

"Don't, please." She passed a hand over her neck and looked away. "I feel bad enough." Straightening up, she turned to face me. "You have nothing to worry about. I will confess to everything, and tell the police the absolute truth— that I lied to you, and you only came along to try to stop me." She paused a moment. "When you talk to them, you might want to emphasize the possible dementia angle."

I had no time to think of a suitable response, because just then the door to the inner offices opened, and Jeff walked out. I jumped to my feet, strewing bear claw crumbs everywhere.

He drew a hand through his rumpled hair, shaking his head.

"Jeff, I—"

He held up a hand. "Come with me, Verity."

I followed him into an interrogation room. He closed the door.

"Should I sit down?"

"In a minute. First—" He held out his arms.

I collapsed into them, fighting tears. "I'm so sorry, Jeff."

We stayed that way for a long moment, until my thumping heart had slowed.

He put his hands on my shoulders, pushing me gently away so he could look into my eyes. "Are you okay?"

"No," I said, sniffling.

Jeff produced a cotton handkerchief that I'd marveled at once before, until assuming it must be standard police issue for dealing with tear-stained women. Or men, for that matter.

I blew my nose. "I can explain."

He cleared his throat, and I regretted my choice of words.

"Verity, listen to me. I know you're hurting. When we get home, I will be your fiancé and I will support you in any way I can. For now, though, I'm an on-duty detective and—"

"You're going to chew me out."

"Big time." He glared at me. "What were you thinking?"

It went downhill from there. Eventually we got around to Adeline and her possible motives. I assured Jeff that I was fed up with my aunt. "She's on her own from now on," I said defiantly.

"Really?"

"Yes, really. However, in her defense, I feel duty-bound to point out a few things."

Jeff leaned back, crossing his arms. "Such as?"

"For one thing, she believes Yeager tried to kill her. Did you know that?"

"We were well aware of her accusation, given that we had to break up a fight between the two of them."

"What are you talking about?"

"It was last autumn after your aunt returned to Leafy Hollow. She went to see him."

"So?"

"When the squad car arrived, she had Yeager pinned to

the asphalt in his driveway and was...pummeling him, according to the officers."

"You never told me that."

"I should have." He frowned. "Adeline convinced me you didn't need to know. Sorry."

"That's okay. No one knows better than me how persuasive she can be." I paused to reflect on this alleged pummeling. "She must have had a good reason."

Jeff merely raised an eyebrow. "She said she was interrogating him."

"There you go, see? That's a good reason."

"The only reason your aunt wasn't arrested is because Yeager declined to press charges."

"But I told you. Adeline believes he tried to kill her. It's natural she would resent him. He might have started that fight, you know. He had a temper."

Jeff heaved a sigh. "Yeager was thoroughly investigated after your aunt returned to Leafy Hollow with her tale of attempted murder. He was nowhere near the scene of her accident."

"See? There you go again. Calling it an accident. It's no wonder she was frustrated. According to Aunt Adeline, she was forced off the road by a vehicle that came up behind her with no headlights."

"Then how does she know it was Yeager?"

That stumped me. "Maybe she recognized his car."

"At night? With no streetlights?" He shook his head. "I've heard her story. Several times. We never found that mystery vehicle or any evidence that it ever existed." He glanced at his watch. "I've got a lot to do. Can we agree to not discuss this for the time being?" He turned to go.

I grabbed his sleeve and leaned in. "Is my aunt a murder suspect?"

The pause before he answered—and the thoughtful expression on his face—told me all I needed to know. I released his sleeve, unable to speak.

Jeff's voice softened. "It's early days, Verity. And I'm likely to be taken off the case for possible conflict of interest. Then this will be someone else's headache. We'll talk later. Go home. I'll get a squad car to drive you."

"Thanks," I said, thoroughly deflated. "Wait." I tugged at his sleeve again. "What about the break-in? Will Adeline and I be charged?"

He gave me a long look. "Probably. The fact you reported Yeager's dead body instead of running away might mitigate that."

"Meaning the charges, if any, would be dropped?"

"It's too early to tell. But if I was a betting man, then yes. Especially since the homeowner is no longer around to complain."

"What about the assault charge?"

He looked confused.

"Gillian Shadrach? She claims I attacked her."

"Your aunt has confessed to that."

"Oh, Jeff. You know she's only covering for me."

"We'll see." And he walked out the door.

Back at Rose Cottage, I opened the kitchen door to let Boomer out for a quick pee in the back garden. I was far too exhausted for a proper walk. Not to mention that it was barely dawn. The sun was rising over Pine Hill Valley in the distance, sending long shafts of light to break up the shadows between the garden's shrubs and trees. I paused to inhale the brisk, cedar-scented air and listen to birds chirping. An obviously confused lightning bug flickered on and off. It was a perfect morning.

The terrier darted back inside, snatched up a dog biscuit, and settled into his bed by the sofa.

I followed, kicking off my shoes before collapsing onto the sofa. The past eight hours had been among the worst of my life, and I had only myself to blame.

What were you thinking?

Good question.

To begin with, I was clearly the world's worst investigator. I'd taken Zara Price at her word, and look what happened. She turned out to be a hardened criminal. After a moment's thought, I softened that to *card-carrying loony*. And then, feeling bad, changed it again, to *misguided reformer*.

But however you characterized her, Jeff was right. If Herbert Eubanks had been murdered, Zara was the logical suspect.

Especially now that Clive Yeager was no longer in the running.

The trouble was, I didn't believe it. I wasn't that bad at judging character, was I? And if Zara was guilty, why did she ask me to investigate? Someone poking around would only make it worse. She must have known her criminal background would come to light.

Maybe it was simply a prank gone wrong. But you could say it was a misguided prank that landed Zara with that criminal record in the first place. She'd be reluctant to try something like that again.

And even if she detested Yeager and her fury got the better of her, why put her beloved goats at risk? What could she possibly gain by that? Zara had spent a lot of money reinforcing her fence and the goats' enclosure to keep those animals safe—money she could probably ill afford. Why would she put it all at risk? I didn't believe that, either.

I recalled her plea for help.

Waffles has been framed. You have to help us.

Which returned me to the original problem. If Eubanks' death wasn't accidental, and someone stuffed him into that septic tank on purpose, then who wanted him dead?

And who killed Yeager?

It seemed likely the same person had struck twice. I brightened, realizing that theory left Zara off the hook. However, my enthusiasm didn't last as I realized it didn't, not really. After all, where was she when Yeager died? *At home, asleep* didn't strike me as an airtight alibi.

I was in way over my head. If the police couldn't crack this case, what made me think I could? I was a landscaper. Even that was an overstatement. I was really just an overblown lawn cutter.

Although given the way I felt, there would be very little lawn cutting done today. Sleepily, I closed my eyes. Ethan would fill in for me.

I slapped a hand to my forehead. Not unless I let him know. I'd forgotten to call and leave a message. Staggering over to the door, I rummaged through my bag.

Oh great. No phone.

The police took it from me at the station, and I'd forgotten to pick it up at the front desk when I left. I stumbled back to the sofa. Leafy Hollow was a small place, full of gossips. Surely someone would let Ethan know why I was unlikely to show up for work today. Otherwise, both my businesses would be on the rocks.

I was a failure as an investigator, and not so hot in the landscaping department, either. This was shaping up to be one hell of a week.

My last thought before drifting off to sleep was that at least Jeff would bring my phone home. Which triggered thoughts of the police station. Promising tendrils of sleep evaporated as I sat bolt upright.

Aunt Adeline. What was happening to her?

Is my aunt a murder suspect?

I recalled the look on Jeff's face when I asked him that, and his assurance that it was early days. He had tried to put my fears to rest, and he'd succeeded. Until now.

Because it occurred to me—if the police believed my aunt killed Yeager and that Zara killed Eubanks—the entire sordid chain of events might soon be put to rest.

By clapping two innocent women behind bars.

As angry as I was at my aunt, I couldn't let that happen. Not to family. And especially not to the woman who'd always looked out for me despite our squabbles over the years.

You should have more faith in yourself, Verity. You have a real talent for this kind of work.

I nodded, remembering her words.

Just because I was the world's worst investigator didn't mean I should give up.

Time to start over.

I had to throw out everything I thought I knew about this case. Then begin again.

CHAPTER 16

THE NEXT MORNING, I did the one very important thing I had neglected to do before agreeing to my aunt's ludicrous "mission." I wrenched open Rose Cottage's sticky basement door, trotted down the worn wooden steps, ducked under the overhanging pipes, and confronted Control.

At least, I confronted the annoying puppet heads that claimed to speak for that secretive, quasi-governmental, black-ops marketing group.

The camouflaged wall that had been present when I first arrived in Leafy Hollow was long gone. To be honest, I missed the holograms of fake maple syrup and cases of Molson Canadian. But because I now knew all about Control, there was no longer any point in disguising the console, its keyboard, and the double row of overhead monitors.

Slumping into a swivel chair with my arms hanging over the side, I scooted the chair up to the console and kicked it, producing a satisfying *thump*. "Control?" I yelled. "Get the hell out here and tell me what's going on."

The monitors remained grey, lifeless and dusty.

I gave the console a second *thump*, for old times' sake.

After a bit of buzzing, and several *pops*, the monitors winked on, one by one. The screens flickered a bit, then the pictures cleared.

My jaw dropped.

Identical gray heads, their sharp-edged faces looking like ventriloquists' dummies, stared out at me. Nothing new there. In the past they'd flaunted such items as slumber caps and black berets, but the AI known as Control had really outdone itself today.

The puppet heads wore snorkeling masks. Their identical gray eyes blinked rapidly behind the masks' windows, and their lips were clamped around snorkeling mouthpieces. In a final touch, water dripped from their noses.

"Oh, come on," I said. "Who are you kidding?"

"Verity Hawkes," they mumbled in unison, their voices muffled by the snorkels. "We are on vacation. Can this wait?"

"Vacation?" I spluttered.

They nodded, causing drops of water to fly off their masks and blur the screens. "A long overdue break," they mumbled. "We have been under a lot of pressure."

Seething, I considered delivering a third *thump* before deciding it was pointless. No use playing the straight man. Woman. It would only encourage them.

I carefully considered my response. Simple and concise seemed best.

"Adeline Hawkes is in danger."

Their eyes widened and their mouths opened, causing all the snorkels to fall out.

That was followed by the clattering sound of a dozen snorkel tubes hitting the floor out of sight. *Nice sound effects,* I thought.

Swiveling casually on the chair while drawing a hand over the console, I asked nonchalantly, "Is vacation over?"

"Verity Hawkes. Wait one moment."

The faces swirled into multicolored ribbons before re-forming into identical gray expressions of concern, now *sans* the snorkeling gear. A few drops of simulated water still dripped from their chins.

"Don't even think about towels," I warned.

"Tell us all."

"Clive Yeager was found murdered last night. Adeline was taken in for questioning."

Their heads tilted. "Why is she a suspect?"

"She feared Yeager was a Syndicate sleeper agent known as The Shadow, so she broke into his house last night in search of evidence."

I decided to omit my own involvement in the clandestine mission. Plenty of time for that later.

Their eyebrows rose simultaneously. "Did she find any?"

"Oh yes. I mean, there was evidence, but it wasn't the right kind of evidence. It was..." I broke off, conscious of their beady eyes fixed on me. "Do you really need to know all this?"

Their brows furrowed, in a straight-edged sort of way.

"No. We have been apprised of your aunt's interference."

I puzzled this out. "Interference implies that Control had

an operation underway and Adeline blundered into it without permission. Is that what you're saying?"

"No comment."

"Are you going to help her?"

"No comment."

My anxiety was getting the better of me. I rubbed a hand across my throat to quell the throbbing vein in my neck. "Look," I said in what I hoped was a diplomatic tone. "Perhaps my aunt acted in haste—"

Perhaps? My inner critic sputtered. It was annoying, that inner critic.

"But she did it to protect Control. You have to help her."

"Verity Hawkes—we cannot become involved in murder cases."

"Since when?"

They looked indignant. "Since always."

"That's not true. What about the Pine Hill Valley real estate scam? Or the Laura Secord character assassination scheme? Those were murder cases."

They shook their heads sadly. "We told her to stay out of it."

My objection died unspoken. It was possible Control did tell my aunt to stay clear. And she'd conveniently forgotten to tell me. It wouldn't be the first time.

"We cannot help your aunt, Verity Hawkes. You are on your own."

And one by one, the monitors switched off.

On my way to the racetrack, I drove past Yeager's house. No activity there, other than a lone constable on guard duty. Continuing down the road, I slowed outside Zara's farmhouse, behind a garbage truck stopped on the street in front.

Empty blue recycling bins, green compost bins, and regular garbage cans littered the right side of the road in the truck's wake. On the road ahead of the truck, filled bins were lined up neatly at the end of every drive.

A bored looking driver—one half of the team—sat behind the wheel of the truck. I could see him in the vehicle's side-view mirror. He was checking his phone.

The other half of the team was not emptying the Prices' garbage bins, however. Nicole Quilter was standing on the porch with Zara. They were arguing.

Somebody in the Price household must have screwed up their recycling big time.

While I watched, Nicole poked a finger into Zara's shoulder.

Zara angrily slapped it away.

Intrigued, I lowered my passenger window so I could hear their conversation.

Zara, who was facing the road, caught sight of my truck and glared at me.

I forced a smile and a friendly wave.

Nicole whirled around, her expression rigid. Then she forced a smile also. With a last look over her shoulder at Zara, and a loud, "He has to go," she trotted down the path, thumped the side of the garbage truck, and hopped onto the back.

I watched as the truck trundled up to the next house on

the road. Nicole leapt off to empty the bins and toss them onto the driveway, and then jumped back on.

All without a backward glance at me.

When I looked over at the farmhouse, Zara was standing on the porch, watching the truck depart, her mouth pinched.

Fixing a smile on her face, she turned to me. With her arms clasped across her chest, she stepped off the porch to walk in my direction.

I parked the truck and turned off the engine.

"Verity," she said as I climbed out of my truck. "Is it true?"

I paused a moment before closing the door behind me. "Do you mean Yeager?"

"No. We heard all about that. Good riddance. Oh," she stifled her smirk with one hand. "I shouldn't say that."

"It's a little cold-hearted," I replied. "But understandable."

"Did the police really arrest you?"

"Who told you that?"

"It's all over the village."

I sighed. *Of course it was.* News that nosy Verity Hawkes had been hauled down to the police station again would have set tongues wagging for sure.

I didn't intend to add fuel to that fire.

"I was not arrested," I said firmly. "Police requested the presence of my aunt and myself at the station for routine questions, that's all."

"Did they arrest Adeline?"

I paused before answering, because I didn't really know.

My aunt had sent a brief text that morning.

Back home. Everything fine.

But she had ignored my demands for details.

I decided to gloss over it. "Routine questions only. We were helping with their enquiries."

Zara nodded glumly. "That's how it starts." Then she brightened. "At least Waffles is in the clear now."

This was news to me. "Is he?"

"Well, sure. Obviously, there's a killer in Leafy Hollow. The same person who killed Eubanks must have killed Yeager." At my strained expression, she paused. "It *is* obvious, right?"

"Not to the police. Sorry."

"But that's ridiculous." She stared off into the distance. "I found Eubanks' body. Did I tell you?"

Before I could answer, *Yes, you did*, she continued.

"It was horrible. I'm sorry you had to see it."

"Don't worry about me. It wasn't my first dead body." Which was true. Corpses had a way of piling up in my vicinity. I blamed the weather.

However, I was lying when I said it didn't bother me. Every single time was as horrific as the last. With a shudder, I recalled the angle of Yeager's neck when we found his body crumpled on the rocks below the waterfall.

At least I hadn't seen Eubanks' neck. Only his lifeless feet.

Mentally, I slapped myself. *Stop thinking about that.* "What did Nicole want?"

Zara flapped a dismissive hand. "Something about our recycling. Peanut butter in with the cardboard, I think."

I doubted that. Zara could recite the village's complicated

recycling rules by heart. She would never contaminate paper with grease. "Really?" I asked. "I thought I heard Nicole say, *he has to go.* Who was she talking about?"

She scuffed her foot in the lawn and turned away. "No one."

I rubbed a hand over my mouth and tried to think. "Zara, you hired me to help Waffles. You can't keep things from me. For instance, *who* has to go?"

"It has no bearing on the case, Verity."

"That's not good enough, Zara. I don't think you realize that public opinion is not on your side at the moment. Clive Yeager was your neighbor. Now that he's dead, they—"

"They what?" She whirled around, eyes narrowed. "They think I killed him, is that it? You and your nut-job aunt found his body. How come you're not under suspicion? Oh wait—you *are.*"

Well. That was unfair. And I was about to say so, when she started in again.

"You're supposed to be helping me. So far, you've done nothing but get yourself into trouble. And all over the news, in what I assume is a feeble attempt to market your business at my expense." She waved a finger. "If this is the best you can do, I'm going to stop paying you."

I considered mentioning that, so far, she hadn't paid me anything. Nor was she likely to, come to think of it. Whether Waffles was vindicated or not.

Which reminded me...

"Hang on. Did you just call my aunt a nut job?"

Zara placed her hands on her hips. "Why? Is that news?"

I fought to keep my temper under control. If anyone

other than the usually mild-mannered Zara Price had made an accusation like that, I'd have dropped them with a knee strike. This was a new side to Zara—one I wasn't sure I wanted to see.

On the other hand, Adeline believed Zara could use more backbone. *That young woman lets people walk all over her,* she once told me. *She's a born mark.*

Zara was certainly displaying backbone now. In fact, if she had called my aunt a *nut job* to her face, Adeline would have laughed and clapped her on the back. *Sticks and stones* was one of my aunt's favorite homespun slogans.

I decided to attribute Zara's ill humor to her concern for poor Waffles.

"Was Nicole talking about Waffles? Was she advising you to get rid of that goat?"

Zara's mouth dropped as she stared at me. "Nicole loves Waffles," she wailed. "Everyone loves Waffles. He was going to be the petting zoo's star attraction."

I noticed she hadn't answered my question. Also—

"What petting zoo?"

"The one I intended to open here, at the farm. But that's all ruined now." She gave the grass a vicious stomp, then turned on me again. "And you're not helping."

"I am helping, Zara. In fact, right at this moment, I'm on my way to the racetrack to follow up a new lead about a possible suspect."

Her face drained of color, and she dropped her arms. "What suspect?"

"I'm not at liberty to say, but there's a possibility that Yeager's man works at the track. I'm going to ask around. If I can find him, he might know how your goats escaped that day."

"That's not a good idea."

"How do you know? It's a legitimate line of enquiry."

"Did you tell the police about this?"

"No. Of course I didn't go to the police. I thought you wanted to lay low, given your...background."

"I do want to lay low. But I want Waffles back."

"Then let me follow this lead. Maybe this person can solve the mystery of the unlatched gate and you can get your goat back."

"Don't do this, Verity."

"I don't understand."

"I'm ordering you not to do this." She crossed her arms, and her lower lip wobbled slightly.

"Ordering me?" My scalp prickled with annoyance, and I ran a hand through my hair. "What do you mean? You hired me to clear Waffles. That's why I'm trying to do. You have to trust me."

"Oh. That. I'm un-hiring you."

"What?"

"I'm un-hiring you. I want you to drop the case."

Studying her worried face, I wondered what to say. "Is someone influencing you, Zara?"

"No. It's my decision. I want you to drop the case."

Holding up both hands, I stepped away. "Okay. Consider it dropped."

I felt her eyes on my back as I walked to my truck and climbed inside.

Then I continued on my way. I'd promised Zara to drop

Waffle's case, but the rest of my investigation was still on track. Only it wasn't about a persecuted goat anymore. It was about a wildly infuriating client who was under suspicion of murder.

Not that I'd get any thanks. I shook my head. Truthfully, it was a toss-up as to which of my two truculent clients was the most stubborn.

The billy goat. Or my aunt.

Despite the fact that no one apparently wanted my services, I tried not to take it personally. In fact, it renewed my determination. If people were warning me to back off, there must be a reason. My unflagging curiosity wouldn't allow me to give up.

My father had steered me onto a new track with his identification of Tyson Farrell, the AWOL mechanic with the fast car. It might be a dead end, but it couldn't hurt to track Tyson down. At least I could eliminate him as a suspect.

There was a speedway a few miles out of the village, surrounded by fields where the noise of booming engines wouldn't cause a raft of complaints. It was a logical draw for a young man interested in fast cars. Maybe someone there would know where I could find him.

I was increasingly suspicious that Tyson Farrell had been at Yeager's house the morning of Eubanks' death—and that's why he was making himself scarce. Judging by my growing experience, young men with a taste for fast cars sometimes indulged in other dubious behaviors. Like illegal betting. He could have been paying debts—or collecting them.

I pulled the truck into a huge, empty parking lot at Leafy Hollow Motorsport Park. Given the complete lack of trees or any other green space, it didn't look much like a park. After parking next to a sedan with a handicapped permit on its front dash, I walked to the entrance. The two ticket booths were empty, and on the office door, a sign declared it CLOSED.

In the picture window alongside, other signs proclaimed,

SPEEDWAY SPECTACULAR THIS THURSDAY

and

KART RACING SATURDAY MORNING

I'd primed myself for the chest-rattling roar of racing cars, but it was Wednesday. All I heard was wind rustling through the hundreds of discarded betting slips tossed between the rows of wooden bleachers.

A fragile-looking man was sweeping up a few of those slips.

Tufts of snow-white hair stuck out from under his cloth cap, and Coke-bottle glasses perched on his bony nose. Methodically, he pushed the broom out a few inches, then pulled it back with withered hands. Small piles of paper were dotted here and there through the stands. I regarded them thoughtfully. Lorne could have gone through the entire place with a leaf blower and cleaned it up in minutes.

I walked toward him. "No races today?"

He looked up, pausing to lean on the upright broom with both hands. "'Fraid not, miss. Come back Saturday."

"That's okay. I only wanted to take a look. Seems like a nice track. Is it fast?"

He glanced around as if he were seeing the place for the first time, and nodded. "It is that. Not what I'm used to, but that was a long time ago."

I sensed I'd chanced upon the very person I needed—a senior citizen who loved to talk about the old days. He'd know a lot about the inner workings of this track, as well as the people who frequented it. "How long ago?" I asked.

"I used to work at a track in Newcastle. As a mechanic. I remember all the teams—Jaguar, Aston Martin, Cooper, even Lotus. Back in the fifties and sixties, that was." He shook his head, leaning on the end of the broom as if it was the only thing holding him up.

Which it very well could have been.

"The British cars were top of the world back then. It was really something."

"The nineteen-fifties? You'll forgive me for asking, but you must be...getting on?"

"If you're trying to tell me I'm an old geezer, you're not wrong." He stuck out his chin. There was a definite twinkle in his eye. "Eighty-seven next month."

"Wow. You don't look a day over—"

"Eighty-six?"

We both laughed. I suspected he'd told this joke many times.

"Are you still a mechanic?"

"Oh, no. It's all fancy electronics these days. I wouldn't know where to start. The chap who owns this track is a good mate. He lets me hang around and in return—" He brandished the broom. "I do a bit o' sweeping. Are you an automotive enthusiast, Miss...?"

I thrust out a hand. "Verity Hawkes. I'm afraid I don't know much about cars. I'm here for a different reason."

After switching the broom to his left hand, he returned my handshake. "Alfie Armstrong. Pleased to meet you. If you're not here about cars, what are you doing here? It's not a race day."

"I'm an investigator. I want to talk to a young man who may work here, possibly as a mechanic. Or a handyman. But I haven't been able to find him."

"Who would that be?"

"His name is Tyson Farrell. Do you know him?"

"Hmm. Small chap, kinda grim?"

"Could be. I've never met him."

"Must be him. I've heard the men call him Tyson. He hasn't been around for days, though."

"Does he work a regular shift? Will he be back, say, tomorrow night?"

"You'd have to ask at the office."

"Closed."

"Right." His hands trembled on the broom as he chewed this over. "Now that I think on it, he used to do a bit o' work for some man in the village. Yard work, things like that. I remember the men talking about it."

"Do you recall who it was?"

"Sorry, no."

I pulled a business card from my shoulder bag and handed it over. "Would you give me a call next time Tyson shows up? There's a plate of chips and beer in it."

He took my card with another twinkle. "I will, so long as you join me."

I snapped him a quick finger-salute. "You got it."

He squinted at my card before tucking it into his shirt pocket. "If you ask me, though, that lad's done a runner."

"What do you mean?"

"Last time I saw him, he was afraid of something. Always looking over his shoulder. Jumpy."

"Could he be afraid of the police?"

"Maybe. The coppers been known to stitch up a lad or two."

I narrowed my eyes. "Stitch up?"

"Frame 'em," he explained. "Although—" After resting the broom against the nearest guard rail, he took off his cap to scratch his head. "I've heard those lads do a bit o' drag racing." He replaced the cap.

"Here?"

"Oh, no. They don't approve of that sort of thing here. Bad for business."

"Meaning it's illegal?"

"Meaning they want people to pay for tickets." He swept an arm. "Place like this is expensive to keep up."

"Did Tyson have any money? Serious money, I mean?"

He chuckled. "Not a quid, far as I know. That's why he was working for that chap in the village."

"How much did Tyson know about gardening? Not just cutting lawns, but perennials, pruning, that kind of thing."

"Beats me. Unless..." He squinted up at the sky, thinking.

"What?"

"There's another young lad that hangs about. Friends, they are. And one day this friend of Tyson's was talking about those flowers over there." He pointed to the massive concrete planters that flanked the entrance.

Following his finger, I nodded appreciatively at the floral arrangement. Canna lilies and elephant ears for height, masses of petunias for volume, and lobelia and sweet potato vine trailing over the edges. It was the standard planter arrangement. In Adeline's words—*thrillers, fillers, and spillers.*

"It's odd he would be interested in those," I said, returning my gaze to Alfie.

"That's what I thought, so I listened in." Chuckling, he tapped the hearing aid over his ear and winked. "The lads think I can't hear a thing, but they're wrong. Tyson asked this friend about the flowers. Then he pulled out a notebook and wrote it all down. A bit daft, if you ask me. What does a mechanic need with flowers?"

"Interesting." I'd been in plenty of garages that could have used a bouquet or two, but I kept that to myself. Too many people think beauty in the workplace is a useless perk. I recalled the chimney mason who'd visited Rose Cottage and looked sadly at my "headache of a garden" before asking, "Why bother? You'll only have to do it again next year."

"Isn't life itself ephemeral?" I'd replied.

He had given me a blank look before tearing off a sheet from his scratchpad and handing it over. "Yer quote," he said.

I wrenched myself back to the present. "What does this friend of Tyson's look like?"

"Let me think... He was a small, wiry chap. Shaved head. Tattoos. Oh—when he pointed at the flowers, I saw he was missing a finger on one hand."

"Thanks," I said. "You've been very helpful."

Back in the truck, I reviewed Alfie's disclosures. Now I knew how Tyson Farrell masqueraded as a garden expert. Yeager knew nothing about plants, so Tyson wouldn't need much knowledge to exceed that of his employer. And he got that from a friend who did know a lot about gardening—Ethan Neuhaus.

One thing was clear, however. Tyson Farrell was Yeager's hired "man."

So why didn't Tyson come forward after the discovery of his employer's body? Or, for that matter, explain his where-abouts on the morning Herbert Eubanks was found dead? Eubanks died on the very property Tyson was paid to main-tain. He must have known the police would want to question him. But if he was into any illegal activity, he'd have good reason to avoid the authorities.

I recalled Ethan's warning.

You should steer clear of this.

And compared it to Alfie's comments.

He was afraid of something. Jumpy.

If Tyson was a killer, it was logical to assume he feared the police.

Or was he afraid of something—or someone—else?

CHAPTER 17

AS I DROVE down the Escarpment hill the following morning, my eyes fell on the extra-large bag of liver treats lying on the seat beside me. They were intended for Mr. Snuffles as an overdue thank you for his owner's assistance.

I decided to drop them off, then revisit Zara. Hopefully she regretted yesterday's hasty words and we could start over.

I meant to tell her my lead had panned out, and there might be a witness to Eubanks' murder. One who could clear Waffles of wrongdoing. I felt bad about the way we'd left things. Being "un-hired" was a first for me and, if word got around, not good for business. Perhaps we could mend fences —the virtual kind, not the broken ones in her backyard.

But first—Mr. Snuffles.

The faded plastic wreath bounced when I knocked, but no one answered the door.

I knocked again. Still no answer.

On the third knock, I began to feel uneasy. Fumbling in my shoulder bag, I took out a business card and pen to write

Mrs. Vaughn a message. I was tucking it behind the Home Sweet Home banner when the door flung open. A middle-aged man stood in the entrance. He wore a tractor cap bearing the logo ABC Drivers.

He stared stoically at me.

"Hello," I said, taken aback. "I'm looking for Mrs. Vaughn."

"Who is it?" came a cheery call. "I'm in the back."

The man thumbed a gesture I took to mean, *Come in.* As he closed the door behind me, I pointed to a limo parked on the street. "Is that yours?"

"Yep." He inclined his head toward the back of the tiny house. "She told me to wait."

"With the meter running?"

"Yep. Been here an hour already." He scowled, then leaned in to whisper, "She's good for it, right?"

"Aah...I don't know Mrs. Vaughn that well."

He grimaced. "Ask her, will ya? Boss gets annoyed when somebody runs up a bill and doesn't pay. He'll take it out of my hide."

"I'll see what I can do."

I walked toward the back, where I expected to find a kitchen. But as I passed a bedroom door on my left, a woman's voice called out cheerily, "In here."

I halted. "Eileen?" I asked, trying to keep the surprise from my voice.

"That's my name. Don't wear it out. Mr. Snuffles, what do you think of this outfit?"

I gawked in amazement as Eileen Vaughn waltzed around the ancient, carved wooden bed clasping a wrinkled ballgown to her chest. Mr. Snuffles, perched on a vanity stool, regarded this astonishing behavior with composure, a gently swishing tail the only indication of his opinion.

Mrs. Vaughn stopped to contemplate her reflection in a murky mirror over the dresser. "You're right, Mr. Snuffles. All this old junk should go. I can buy new ones now." She flipped the gown into the air.

I watched as it drifted onto a pile of similar garments in the center of the bed's faded chenille spread.

Then she saw me. "Hello, there. I remember you. You're —" Her brow wrinkled.

"Verity Hawkes. I was here the other day asking about your tenant, Herbert Eubanks." I held up the bag of treats. "I brought these as a little thank you."

Mrs. Vaughn beamed. "Isn't that nice, Mr. Snuffles?" She took the bag and tossed it onto the vanity table, which was piled high with travel-sized bottles of toiletries. "We'll take those with us."

Two open suitcases were jammed against the far wall, piles of jumbled clothing in each one.

"Are you going on a trip?"

"Mr. Snuffles and I are flying to the Orient. First class."

I glanced around, confused. "When did this happen? Don't you need a passport? And special papers for Mr. Snuffles?"

Mrs. Vaughn gave an exasperated sigh. "Yes, we do. You wouldn't *believe* how complicated it is. For now, we're going only to Vancouver. That big hotel right on the waterfront. Then, once everything's settled, we're off to see the world. On one of those big cruise ships. *Vision of the Seas*, it's called." She clasped her hands in front of her. "Isn't it wonderful?"

"Wonderful," I repeated.

Her face clouded. "Except that I had to pay a lot of money to take Mr. Snuffles along. Outrageous, really, when you figure he takes up hardly any room." She stroked the cat absently while contemplating the open suitcases. "Now, where did I put your little tuxedo? And I think we'll need your beaded collar, don't you?"

"Eileen?" I said loudly, hoping to get her full attention.

"Yes?"

"When did this happen? I mean, that must be a very expensive trip you're planning."

"Oh. You don't know, do you? About the will."

I had a bad feeling about this. "The will?"

"Herbert left me all his money. Isn't that amazing? He always promised to remember me, but I never paid the slightest mind." She beamed. "I did the odd little favor for him, you know. His laundry, for starters, and a few special meals every week. And I used to clean his apartment. But not for money." She giggled. "Besides, I hardly expected to outlive him. He was a young man."

Mid-fifties, I would have said, but—okay.

"How much money did he have?"

Chortling, Eileen snatched up Mr. Snuffles and pirou-etted around the room with him. "Half a million."

"How much?" I asked feebly.

She stopped spinning. "Half a million," she said solemnly. Then she giggled like a school girl.

"Did you tell the police about this?"

Puffing out a breath, she said, "None of their business."

"I think they'd be interested. It's possible Mr. Eubanks was killed deliberately."

She clasped the cat to her chest in shock. "He never was."

"He may have been."

The cat squirmed as she tightened her grip. "Who thinks so?"

"Me, for one. And one or two police officers." I thought it best not to bring Jeff's name into it.

"Why would anyone kill Herbert?"

"Well—if he had half a million dollars..."

Her eyes widened. "And you think I might be next. Oh, Mr. Snuffles," she cried, clasping him even tighter. "We could be murdered in our beds."

With an affronted *squawk*, the cat struggled free, leapt onto the pile of discarded clothing, and descended huffily to the floor before stalking out of the room.

His owner remained frozen in place.

"I'm sorry, Eileen. I didn't mean to frighten you."

We both started at the sound of a tap on the doorframe.

The limo driver stood in the doorway, looking apologetic. "There's cops here to see you."

He stepped aside to reveal a uniformed officer. And behind him—

Jeff stepped in. "Mrs. Vaughn," he began, sweeping the room with his eyes. Then he saw me. "What the—"

"I was just leaving," I said while sidling past.

At the front door, the limo driver tugged at my hastily departing arm. "So, can she pay me?"

"You know," I said. "At this point, your guess is as good as mine."

That certainly put a cat among the pigeons. Who could have guessed that Herbert Eubanks, living in a one-bedroom walkup, had half a million squirreled away?

And how did he get it?

Terence Fidler said, *You can make quite a bit hauling sewage if you're willing to put in the hours.* Herbert certainly hadn't been spending any of his loot, as far as I knew. There was Eileen's assertion of "philandering," but she hadn't mentioned any gold diggers. I felt sure she would have added that detail if she suspected anyone.

I also recalled her startling thesis. *If you hate somebody that much, it doesn't stop.*

If Herbert's surprising nest egg was the result of honest toil, why did he hide it? My first guess was to keep it out of the hands of his ex-wife. I discarded that as unlikely, since Mrs. Vaughn said his wife walked out years ago. But she'd also said, *He wouldn't even give her a divorce.* Which meant the ex-Mrs. Eubanks might be entitled to Herbert's money.

Meanwhile, I had to bring my client, Zara, up to date. It seemed this latest development might blow the case wide open.

CHAPTER 18

I HEADED up the Escarpment on my way to visit Zara. But when I drove over the hill from Griffiths' estate, I slowed to a halt. There was fresh activity at Clive Yeager's house. Two squad cars were parked outside, and a forensic team was tramping between the back yard and a police services van in the driveway.

I pulled the truck over to the side of the road and walked to the house. Behind me, a vehicle crunched over the gravel shoulder and onto the asphalt driveway. I turned my head to watch Jeff get out of his unmarked car.

He caught sight of me and walked over, shaking his head. "What are you doing here?"

Trying not to laugh at the coincidence, I held up my hands. "I swear, I'm not following you. I'm only here to visit Zara. What's going on? Has the case been reopened?"

His expression turned grim. "You shouldn't be here, Verity."

I was about to reply with something unique about it being

a free country, when a two-seater Smart car pulled up the drive to stop beside Jeff's vehicle. Liliana István leapt out of the car and raced over, a notepad in one hand and a cell phone in the other. She skidded to a stop before us.

While holding out her phone, which I assumed was set to record, Liliana blurted out, "Detective Katsuro, is it true investigators found toxic waste on Clive Yeager's property?"

She waited expectantly, phone poised.

"Ah..." Jeff said. "Where did you hear that?"

"Sources," she said briskly. "Is it true?"

"No comment."

"Was it in Yeager's septic tank?"

"No comment."

With a gasp, I said, "It must have been in the tanker. That's why it was held up by paperwork. They must have found something suspicious in Eubanks' tanker."

Liliana immediately swiveled the phone to me. Even though we'd recently shared a night out, her demeanor was all business. "Verity Hawkes, you have been investigating the tragic death of Herbert Eubanks. What do you think this toxic substance might have been?"

Jeff shot me a warning glance.

"Aah..." I was glad Liliana wasn't shooting video, because the deer-in-the-headlights look is never attractive. "I have no idea."

She swiveled the phone to an upright position, hoisted it higher, and clicked on a button.

With a sinking stomach, I realized she had switched to video. Self-consciously, I patted my hair.

"Ms. István," Jeff said in his official tone. "Investigators have found some irregularities they wish to probe further. That is all."

"In the tanker?" she asked.

"No comment."

"Verity?" She swiveled the phone to me again.

I pressed my lips together and looked away.

Liliana uttered a sigh of surrender. "Okay." She turned off the phone, then tossed it into her bag. "Off the record, Jeff. As a friend. What did they find?"

"You can't quote me."

"I won't." She paused. "Can I call you *an official source close to the investigation?*"

He crossed his arms, giving Liliana a skeptical look.

I decided to step in. "She's going to find out anyway, Jeff. Better truth than rumors."

He shook his head ruefully. "Two against one, is it?"

I could have made an off-color remark in response, but I took the superior approach and merely smirked.

Jeff lowered his arms. "The effluent in Eubanks' tanker was taken to the sewage plant for disposal, but the team hired to dispose of it suspected it was tainted," he said. "They called for forensic testing, and left the tanker unemptied. The test results came back today."

"And?"

"They found tetrachloroethylene, also known as PERC, in the tanker." At our blank looks, he added, "It's a chemical formerly used in dry cleaning and now designated as hazardous waste."

"How much was in the tanker?"

"Moderate amounts. The PERC had been diluted by the tanker's other contents."

My gaze fell on a blue-suited forensic team member who was returning to the van. I pointed. "Is that why forensics is here—to test Yeager's septic tank for traces of PERC? The tank that Eubanks' body was found in?"

Liliana perked up. "Did they find any?" she asked.

"No comment."

"That means yes, doesn't it?"

"It means—no comment. Look, Liliana. Give us a chance to get ahead on this, and I promise you'll be the first to know what we find."

"How long do I have to sit on it?"

"I'll have something for you this afternoon."

She glanced at her watch. "Okay. I can hold off until 3 p.m. Then I have to file something. The editor's expecting a story. If I don't hear from you by then—" With a shrug, she turned to me. "Catch you later, Verity."

It was hard to keep silent until her tiny car had reversed out the driveway. Once it disappeared up the hill past the Griffiths estate, I turned to Jeff in excitement.

"What's your theory? Yeager and Eubanks were involved in a toxic waste-disposal scheme? Maybe run by organized crime? And the two of them got bumped off by—" I gasped as the phrase, *bumped off by The Syndicate* came to mind. Fortunately, Jeff didn't notice. He was busy taking the high ground.

"It's too early to—"

"Oh, come on. You can tell me. I'm not writing any newspaper stories."

He narrowed his eyes. "Do I have to tell you to keep this to yourself?"

"Of course not," I said indignantly, drawing a finger and thumb across my mouth in the universal *zip it* motion.

"Okay, then, it's something along those lines. Or—" He paused suspiciously. "Look, you can't—"

I repeated the aforementioned *zip it* gesture.

"Either that, or Yeager was involved in the disposal ring by himself, and Eubanks found out about it and threatened to turn him in."

"Blackmail?"

"Possibly. Maybe his demands became too...onerous."

I nodded knowingly. "That must be how he accumulated his half-million."

Jeff drew back. "Oh for Pete's sake. How do you know about that?"

"Mrs. Vaughn told me. Obviously. You saw me at her house." I drew in a sharp breath. "Is she a suspect now?"

Jeff closed his eyes, leaning his head back in the universal motion for *give me strength*. Then he refocused on me. "Are there no lawns that need cutting?"

After making a face at him, I trudged back to my truck. When I turned for a last look over my shoulder, he was deep in discussion with two members of the forensic team.

I'd told Jeff I was at the site because I wanted to visit Zara, so it seemed shrewd to actually do that.

After I parked my truck and walked up the farmhouse's front path, I tucked around the back to take another look at the goats' enclosure. Even from the house, I could see it was securely latched. The goats stood around, basking in the day's brilliant sunshine. A couple of the larger ones butted the blue exercise ball around. Working up their routine for the petting zoo's big reveal, I assumed.

Zara was with them. She was sitting on a bale of hay in a corner of the paddock, smoothing the head of one of the youngest kids and murmuring to it. She barely looked up as I walked toward their pen.

"Can I come in?" I called, motioning to the latch on the gate.

"Uh-huh."

In a clear sign of her mental state, she didn't even insist I latch it closed.

I did, of course, and then sat beside her on the bale of hay.

"Have you heard the news?"

"About the toxic waste?" She nodded.

"How did you—"

"Word got around fast. I hope none of the girls got into any of that stuff."

"Seems unlikely. And if any of them had, I'm sure you'd have noticed by now."

"I guess." She resumed stroking the young goat's head. "It's awful to think those bastards were doing that right next door. Storing poison, I mean."

"You didn't know about it, did you?"

"Me? How would I know?"

"I only thought, with your concern for the environment, you might have had your ear to the ground." Pausing, I added hastily, "Commendable concern, by the way."

In a surprising burst of fury, she slammed a fist into the hay. "If I had known what those two were up to, I would have killed them both." Then, perhaps realizing how that sounded, she tried to reword. "I mean...I would have tried. Or...turned them in, at least."

I feared tears were imminent.

I put my hand on her arm. "I know you...un-hired me, and I'm not trying to interfere, but I'd like to try to clear Waffles." I didn't add, *and you*, although I wanted to.

"I'm sorry I un-hired you," she said sadly.

"That's okay. I followed up that lead anyway and found something interesting." I paused, realizing she was gazing off into the distance, not listening. "Zara? Would you like to hear about it?"

She heaved a sigh. "It doesn't matter anymore."

"What do you mean?"

"We're going to lose the farm."

"Why?"

"The second mortgage is due and the bank won't renew it. They said we don't have enough income to qualify. And the land is worth so much that our realtor says it's crazy not to sell. We could clear both mortgages and have a little left over."

"What would happen to the goats?"

My careless query kicked off the waterworks. *Nice work,*

Verity. I rummaged in my purse for a tissue and handed it over. "I'm so sorry, Zara."

"The thing is," she said, sniffling, "we're barely treading water. If the insurance company doesn't cover the damages to Yeager's house and car—that will be it. That would put us over the top."

"But with Yeager dead..." I trailed off, wondering whether or not his demise was a good thing for Zara. Now that the toxic-waste scheme had come to light, her past history as an environmental activist might count against her. Not only that, her financial difficulties were another motive for bumping off her neighbor—with Yeager dead, there would be no one to insist she pay for the goats' property destruction.

My shoulders slumped in despair. I should be working for the other side because, so far, everything I'd found out about my client's case had made it worse.

"Let's take a walk," I said, hoping to take Zara's mind off Waffles and the goats. "You can show me the rest of the farm."

We admired the corn field, the organic vegetable garden, and the maple bush, and were returning on a path that ran along the far edge of the property when I noticed an old wooden barn. Daylight reflected off its worn, silvery cedar boards. Once-red paint had mostly worn away, the roof showed signs of decay, and the double doors sagged.

"What's in there?" I asked, stepping toward it.

"Nothing. We haven't used it in years."

"Are there barn owls inside? Let's take a look."

Zara tugged at my arm. "If there are, they won't like being

disturbed. They might be sitting on a brood. You don't want to spook them."

With a hand shading my eyes from the afternoon sun, I studied the barn. The field in front of it was densely over-grown. Except... I squinted at the scene. Was that—

"Could we take a quick look before I leave? It's so picturesque." I pulled my phone from my bag to snap a picture.

Zara pushed my arm down. "It's not safe, Verity. We've been meaning to have that barn torn down for years. Please don't go any closer. Let's go back. I'll show you our organic raspberry patch." She turned to go.

"In a minute." I renewed my scrutiny of the barn. The sun was full in my eyes, shining through gaps between the rotting planks of the barn walls. In the glare, I couldn't be certain, but it looked as if something large was stored inside.

"Zara, do you keep a tractor in that barn?"

She whirled around. "A tractor? No, we don't have a..." She turned her gaze on the building. "Oh, right. There is an old one in there. Decades old. Rusted. It dates back to my father's days. That's why we didn't tear the barn down. It would cost a fortune to get that tractor moved."

"Won't a metal recycler take it away for free?"

"It's not that easy, believe me. They all want cash. Let's go." She trudged away from me, up the path, turning after several yards to gesture impatiently. "Are you coming?"

I plodded along behind her, lost in thought.

Zara opened the back door of the farmhouse and stepped in. She didn't even look at me before closing it firmly behind her.

While walking past the house, I pondered something I had seen outside that old barn. The weedy grass in front had been flattened by tire tracks that ran straight up to the sagging doors.

And they didn't look like tractor tires to me.

CHAPTER 19

AS I ROUNDED the front of the farmhouse on the way to my truck, I noticed the window beside the front door was open. The corner of a lace curtain wafted out the opening, drifting in the breeze. Raised voices also drifted out the open window.

"You have to go."

"Don't be stupid. I'm not going anywhere."

"You can't—"

Followed by mumbling.

One voice sounded like Zara. I didn't recognize the person she was speaking to despite straining to hear. It could have been a man. Instinctively, I leaned toward the window. If they would only say a few more words...

The window slammed shut with a force that made me jump.

Almost simultaneously, the front door opened. Zara looked out at me, maintaining a firm grip on the door. "Verity. Did you forget something?"

"Sorry, Zara. I didn't mean to startle you. I just wanted to say hello to Sam before I left. Is she in?"

"I'm sorry, Verity, but Mom has one of her migraines. She can't stand even the slightest noise when she's like that."

Without another word, she closed the door in my face.

I walked to my truck, feeling as if I was being watched. I turned once, but saw no one. The window was still closed.

On my way back to the village, I tried to identify that second voice but came up with nothing. If Mrs. Price had a bad headache, it seemed unlikely she would speak that loudly. Besides, the more I thought about it, the more I was convinced it was a male voice.

Part of the puzzle was answered alongside the road that led to the highway. On a favorite corner of pop-up fruit and vegetable sellers, a familiar cart was set up, its hand-painted sign visible from the road.

You'll Relish Our Homemade Jam

I pulled over. Mrs. Price was chatting over rows of gingham-topped jars with a middle-aged couple wearing boat shoes and bucket hats. A hybrid car was parked nearby. Tourists, obviously.

As they returned to their vehicle laden with jars, she warbled, "Drop by again." By the time I reached the cart, she was tucking five twenty-dollar bills into a metal cash box.

"Hello, dear," she said. "Did you just come from the farm?"

"How's your migraine?"

She leaned in, tilting her head and looking puzzled.

I raised my voice. "Your migraine?"

She shook her head. "Haven't had one of those in years."

"I'm so glad. Any sour-cherry jam today?"

"You're in luck. How many, dear?"

"Just the one, thanks." While she was wrapping my jar in newspaper, I asked as nonchalantly as I could, "Is anyone staying with you and Zara at the farm?"

She pushed the bag toward me. "Ten dollars, please."

I pointed to the sign that read, ORGANIC JAM $20.

Mrs. Price winked. "Not for you, dear. Those are tourist prices."

"Thanks. So—do you have visitors at the moment? Family?"

She looked down, not meeting my gaze, and began lining the jars into neat rows.

I wasn't sure if she didn't hear me, or it was simply a touchy subject. I waited until she lifted her head, then looked directly into her eyes, enunciating clearly. "Samantha, do you remember telling me that a strange man has been hanging around? You thought he tampered with your jam."

"Oh," she said, laughing nervously. "I'm silly sometimes. Zara tells me to stop. She gets quite annoyed."

"Your daughter's not here now."

"No." She looked up the road while gently scratching her cheek.

"The man?" I asked, trying to get her attention.

"A lot of things go on here," she said.

This was promising. "Such as?"

She leaned in. "That garbage collector is always poking around."

I assumed she meant Nicole Quilter. "Poking around...in the garbage?"

She nodded, tapping a finger on her nose.

"How exactly?" I asked.

"She's always looking at the cans. And she leaves stickers. It's embarrassing."

"Stickers?"

"The garbage men glue stickers on your bins if you put in the wrong things. Zara calls them the trash police. Every time we get one of those stickers, she says, *What have you done now, Mother?*"

"What things are wrong?"

Mrs. Price sighed. "There's so much garbage now. In my days we didn't have garbage. We used everything up."

I doubted that, but I refused to be swayed off target. "You said there was a strange man, remember?"

Nodding, she swept an arm through the air. "Always roaring up and down the road. Back and forth. Back and forth."

"Who was it?"

"Don't know." She shook her head.

"What make of car?"

"Sorry, dear. I'm afraid I don't know one from another. Tractors, now—I know a lot about those. We had a lovely tractor, once. Big green thing, it was. Diesel powered." She lowered her voice. "He pulled right into our driveway."

"Did he get out of the car?"

"Yes. But Zara gave him the business. I don't think he'll come back."

"She chewed him out?"

She nodded.

"Sam, could that man be at the farmhouse right now?"

"Oh, I don't think so." Her brow wrinkled. "I hope he doesn't get into the jars. I left a batch cooling on the kitchen table."

"I'm sure they're fine. Zara is there."

She nodded.

"Sam, did you know Herbert Eubanks?"

"I served him pancakes once, when he came to pump out our tank. Nice man."

I pondered this. Eubanks caged a lot of free meals from old ladies. Given that he was also an alleged "philanderer"— according to Mr. Snuffles' owner—he must have been quite the charmer.

"Shame about what happened," she continued. She brightened, her attention caught by something behind me. "Hello, Adeline. How've you been?"

I whirled on one foot. My aunt was standing behind me, with her customary half-smile. "Just fine, Samantha. How are you?" She pointed to the $20 sign. "Are you putting one over on my niece here?"

Mrs. Price chortled. "Don't be ridiculous. You know I don't charge locals that much."

"You should," I interrupted, giving my aunt a sour look. Arranging a special deal on jam would not ensure my forgiveness.

Adeline only smiled sweetly.

"Don't go anywhere," I said, raising a finger to her. "I need to talk to you."

Mrs. Price was lining up jars again, ignoring us both.

"Sam," I said, leaning in to catch her attention, "could you do me a favor? If you take a picture of that car the next time it drives past, I can try to identify the driver."

"A picture?"

"On your phone." I paused. "You have a cell phone, right?"

"I do," she replied emphatically. "Zara insists I take it everywhere in case I trip and fall."

"Do you fall often?"

She scrunched up her nose. "Define often."

"How many times this year?"

"Only twice. So far."

"I bet you were glad you had the phone with you."

At that, she looked a bit shifty.

"You did, didn't you?"

"Maybe."

"Where is it now? Pull it out and I'll show you how to take a picture."

She looked to the left of the counter. Then to the right. "It's here somewhere."

Adeline broke in. "Whose car are we talking about?"

I'd forgotten my aunt's insatiable curiosity. A Hawkes trait, unfortunately. No mystery where I got it from.

I filled her in. "Samantha saw a car racing through the neighborhood but she doesn't know whose it was. Or the model."

"Has she seen it lately?" Adeline asked.

"Not since last week."

"Was it blue?"

"She doesn't remember—"

Mrs. Price laid a hand on my arm, shaking her head emphatically. "No. I do remember. I've been thinking about it, and it was definitely red. One of those muscle cars."

She had been listening, after all. I was beginning to suspect her deafness was selective. To test this theory, I lowered my head to study the jam lineup, then mumbled, "One jar of raspberry, please."

Without even looking in my direction, she pushed a jar toward me. "Here you go, dear."

Hmm. I laid a twenty on the counter.

My aunt blinked at this, but otherwise ignored it. "Verity, are you on your way home?"

"I am. Do you want a ride?" I asked.

"Yes, thanks."

As soon as we were out of potential earshot—I was being extra careful—I started the interrogation. "Tell me what happened at the police station."

"Nothing. They asked me a few questions. I told them the break-in was my idea and they were lucky we were there, because otherwise Yeager's body would have disappeared."

"How would that have happened?"

She gave me a level look. "Did you not realize we must have interrupted his killer?"

Something cold reached down my throat. "No. You mean before he could dispose of the body?"

"Exactly." She paused. "Assuming it was a he."

"What does that mean?"

"Gillian Shadrach is not going to press charges."

I halted, mystified. "Why?"

"I pointed out to her the police might renew their questions about why she was at Yeager's house when his dead body was less than a hundred yards away."

"They were friends."

"Then why didn't Gillian report him missing?" She raised her eyebrows.

I had no answer to this.

It wasn't until we were in the truck that my aunt launched into another, more startling, hypothesis. "That red car is suspicious."

"How so?"

She tugged an ear, looking thoughtful. "Maybe I was in error about Yeager forcing me off the road with that blue BMW of his. It was late at night, and there are no streetlights by the river. It's possible I mistook the color of the car." She paused. "And the model."

I gaped at her. "Are you suggesting after all this time that you may have been wrong?"

"I try to keep an open mind," she said primly, not looking at me.

"Since when?"

"Contradicting your betters is a bad habit to fall into."

"If I meet any, I'll be sure to remember that."

We traveled in silence for a few moments, then Adeline gestured at the road ahead.

"Pull over here. I want to take a walk."

I peered out the window at the sign for Pine Hill Conservation Area. "Are you going home the back way?"

"Maybe. I need to clear my head. I think I'll drop in on someone."

"Try not to pummel anybody," I said while she was getting out.

She merely gave me an exasperated look before slamming the door.

CHAPTER 20

ADELINE OPENED her eyes to complete darkness.

She assumed the strange noise—an incessant thrum, like an engine—had woken her. The sound was close, yet not in the same room.

Disoriented, she tried to make it out, but couldn't hear well enough.

She couldn't see, either. *Was she wearing a mask?*

An exploratory puff of breath did not lift any wisps of fabric.

Not a mask, then.

She tried to strategize. *Assess your situation. Review your options.*

She was on the floor, lying on her side. A hard, damp surface pressed against her cheek. Tiles, maybe. But there was a peaty aroma in the air. *Was she lying on bare earth?*

She lay silently, trying to clear the mist fogging her thoughts. Trying to concentrate.

Why am I here?

Something crawled across her face.

Instinctively, her head jerked back, causing a spasm of pain. That particular torment was not new, she realized as she waited for it to subside. It had been present all along. Pain, not noise, had wrenched her awake.

And now she'd made it worse.

Inwardly, she cursed her lapse. *You're not afraid of creepy-crawlies. Ignore them.*

Her thoughts drifted. She recalled advising her niece on a survival camping trip to, *Bite them back.* The girl had been horrified by her joke. Verity had come a long way since then.

And now she's in danger. Because of you. You have to get out of here.

Fighting dizziness, she tried to get her bearings. Random thoughts distracted her. And always, like a hammer in her brain, the same refrain.

Why am I here?

Another stray memory drifted through the haze.

I was too close to the truth.

What truth? Try as she might, she couldn't remember.

Concentrate on something simpler. Get up.

But scrabbling her feet against the floor proved useless. Her arms were pinned behind her back. One shoulder was cramped and aching. She must have been lying on her side for hours. She tried to roll over.

A vicious stab in her shoulder forced a gasp.

She paused, panting. After the pain subsided, she gingerly flexed her arm.

Another flash of agony.

This time, she recognized the sensation. Her shoulder

was dislocated. She lay still, hoping the cold seeping into her bones from the floor would dull the pain.

But *cold* was an understatement. It felt like ice. Could she be lying in a freezer?

She began to shiver uncontrollably, her teeth chattering.

Shock, probably.

She marshaled what was left of her senses.

You must get up. Count to three.

One.

Two.

She twisted her body around, forcing herself to sit.

And screamed at the pain.

Panting, she fought to stay upright. Slowly, her breathing calmed.

That was the worst of it. Now, stand up.

With her arms tied behind her back, it was impossible even to get to her knees. She advanced jerkily on her rear, biting her lips against the pain, until she bumped into a wall.

Pressing her back against the stones, she slid upward, an inch at a time.

Breathing heavily, she pushed off from the wall to teeter on both feet.

An ankle collapsed, and she slumped to the floor, knees bent, then gradually fell over on her side.

While drifting in and out of consciousness, the cold stones leaching heat from her body, she fancied she heard whimpering. But that was impossible.

Hoarsely, she whispered, "Is someone here?"

The whimpering stopped. The pain did not.

Warm liquid dripped into her mouth. Tentatively, she

licked her lips, recognizing the coppery taste. Blood. She must have hit her head. When did that happen?

Hit my head. Hit my... Her eyes drifted shut.

You have to get up, she thought.

You have to...

CHAPTER 21

STANDING in the kitchen of Rose Cottage the next morning, I stared at the note in my hand, unwilling to believe it. Was it a mistake? A prank?

It could be a joke, given the crude nature of the presentation. Letters and words, torn from newspapers, glued onto a stiff piece of typing paper.

STOP DIGGING OR ADELINE DIES

I dropped it on the kitchen table. I couldn't take it seriously. It was ridiculous. Contemplating the note, I ran a hand over my throat as a vein throbbed. Had someone familiar with my anxiety attacks sent this to upset me?

A cruel joke, if true. Who would do that?

I straightened up, reaching for my phone. After three rings, it went to voice mail.

"It's Adeline. You know what to do." *Beep.*

My aunt would see the missed call and check in. I put the phone down without leaving a message.

What could I say?

"Aunt Adeline, I have a note that says your life is in danger."

I imagined her reaction to a message like that. It would be one word—*Delete*.

Boomer pawed at my leg. Absently, I bent to scratch his head.

Adeline once had warned me that investigators get a lot of "bizarre mail." She hadn't been precise, but I took it to mean that threatening notes were common in her line of work. I recalled sitting in the living room of the cottage she shared with Gideon, watching her crumple up a letter that had arrived that morning.

"Bloody nuisance," she said, smiling at me. "Another one for the trash."

I'd retrieved it from the bin while she was in the kitchen making coffee. After reading it, I handed it to Gideon.

"Oh," he said, crumpling it up again. "We get a lot of those."

"Shouldn't you do something?"

"They want attention. Why give it to them?" He tossed the wadded-up paper across the room. It landed neatly back in the bin.

"I thought messages like that came on social media and email these days."

"Too easy to trace. Snail mail with no return address, on the other hand..." He shrugged. "The old ways are often the best."

"What about the postmark?"

"What about it? It was mailed in Toronto. Three million

people there." Noticing my look of concern, he had added, "Forget it, Verity. It's nothing to worry about.'

Now, I stared at the note on my kitchen table.

Gideon was in Strathcona sourcing parts for his tiny town. I could text him, or even call, but I couldn't expect him to drop everything to race home and hold my hand. Even assuming the note was genuine. It could be a practical joke. In fact, my aunt may have received an identical note, with my name in place of hers.

Zara's angry accusation came to mind.

You and your nut-job aunt found his body. How come you're not under suspicion?

She had been angry after her argument with Nicole, and she'd taken it out on me. Could this be another way for her to vent her vexation? I'd been wrong once about Zara. Was I being willfully blind to what she was capable of?

No point phoning Emy, either. What could my bestie and her beloved do from a beach in Bermuda?

Besides, hadn't I assured Jeff that Adeline was "on her own from now on?"

I didn't really mean those brave words. And I knew Jeff knew I didn't. But I didn't want to bother him with something that might turn out to be meaningless nonsense.

To be honest, I wasn't anxious to spring into action on my aunt's behalf. First, I was likely overreacting. Second, I still harbored resentment over our mission fiasco.

I paced the kitchen floor.

Why couldn't I shake my feeling of dread? It was a common reaction, one I'd tried hard to suppress. *And yet.* Two people were dead and no one knew why.

While I mulled this over, something else struck me about that note.

STOP DIGGING OR ADELINE DIES

When I first read it, I assumed it referred only to the murder case. But what if it wasn't that at all?

What if it had been sent by someone opposing Zara's determination to hang onto her goats? And, by extension, hang on to the farmhouse and the small acreage remaining to it. What if someone wanted that land? And thought that threatening the goats and setting their owner up for a possible murder charge was the easiest way to get it?

I sank into a kitchen chair and fluttered my fingers on the table, overcome by the simplicity of my new theory. Why hadn't I thought of it before? There was nothing valuable at the farmhouse. The land would fetch a good price, but nothing extraordinary.

But there might be something else that was valuable. Perhaps the farmhouse stood in the way of a highway extension, or a planned subdivision, or... My fingers accelerated. It wouldn't be the first time a shady real estate deal had led to murder in Leafy Hollow.

My quick call to Wilf Mullins was answered by his long-suffering assistant, Harriet. "Sorry, Verity. He's unavailable at the moment and can't be reached by phone."

"Is he at Zöe's?" I asked, mentioning Wilf's favorite esthetician. He'd been known to partake of "refreshments" there. Ones that involved needles full of Botox.

"I couldn't say," Harriet responded icily.

"Could you ask him to call me?"

"Certainly." *Click.*

That left only one person to whom I felt comfortable disclosing the contents of that creepy note.

Martin Griffiths.

After all, he promised to help out with Waffles' defense. And, come to think of it, I hadn't checked in with him since the discovery of Yeager's body. I knew he was unharmed—the police had told me that much at the station—but perhaps he had news.

I pulled up outside Griffiths' estate. The formerly locked gate was now open. Across the road, the occupant of a parked police cruiser spoke into his handheld while watching me turn into the driveway.

Another police cruiser was parked near the house. On the flagstone path outside Griffiths' front door, an officer paced. As I approached, he held out an arm. "Stop there, please."

I held up both hands to emphasize I was harmless. "I'd like to talk to Mr. Griffiths," I said, raising my voice in case the former mayor was looking out the window.

"One moment," the officer said before speaking briefly into the radio unit clipped to his uniform. Then, he gestured to the front door. "Go in."

It opened before I reached it.

Griffiths held out a hand. "Verity. How nice to see you. I hope you've recovered from your shock." He ushered me through the entrance, nodded at the officer—who nodded back—and closed the door. "Why don't we go outside, onto the patio?"

"If you don't mind," I began, following him down the hall and past the pseudo-library. "I'd rather not look at that waterfall."

With a wry grin, he clapped a hand to his forehead. "Of course you don't. We'll sit in the drawing room."

At my blink of surprise, he chuckled. "I know. But that's what it's called. Too many rooms in this place, to be honest. And some of them aren't actually rooms. It's easy to get lost." He raised his voice. "Cynthia? Could we have beverages in the drawing room?"

A prim young woman in a long-sleeved white shirt, black skirt, and running shoes appeared in the hallway. "Certainly, Mr. Griffiths. Sodas or lemonade?"

"Verity?" he asked.

The maid, or whatever she was, turned to face me with a questioning air.

I assumed stronger drinks were not on offer. *Just as well*, I thought. The previous night's ordeal had left me with a splitting headache.

"Either, thanks."

In the drawing room, I sat in an upholstered armchair, crossed my legs, and fingered the brocade fabric of the arms. "I thought you said you didn't have any staff."

"I don't." He leaned in, lowering his voice. "Cynthia is an undercover police officer. The powers that be decided I need protection."

"Not from me, I hope."

He chuckled. "I hope so, too."

I was longing to ask why Martin Griffiths needed protection. He was the ex-mayor, not the incumbent. But the question died on my lips as Cynthia returned with a tray of ice-filled glasses, linen napkins, and two bottles of gourmet lemonade. Their caps had been twisted off, presumably to save us the trouble. She set the tray on the mahogany coffee table, and left the room without comment.

I reached for a glass, upended a bottle into it, and settled into my chair. "I could get used to having staff." I took a long swallow.

"It's not all bad," Griffiths agreed contentedly, raising his own glass. "But tell me—how are you feeling? Last night must have been a shock."

"That's putting it mildly."

"Did the police give you and your aunt a hard time?"

I wondered how best to answer that, given that we might still be charged. "It wasn't...fun."

He nodded. "I'm sorry."

"Not your fault. Unless—" I eyed him suspiciously. "You killed Clive Yeager."

Griffiths almost spit out his drink.

I grinned. "Sorry. Couldn't resist."

Chuckling, he dabbed a napkin to his mouth. "You have your aunt's sense of humor."

"You know Adeline, then?"

"For many years. I'm afraid we didn't always keep in touch after I left, though. How has she been?"

"In and out of trouble, like always."

He nodded grimly. "Verity, if you or your aunt need help with the police, I'm sure I can be of assistance."

I eyed him suspiciously. "How so?"

"Well..." He chuckled. "I've done them favors in the past."

I was intrigued. "What kind of favors?"

"I'm not at liberty to say, but there have been some criminal incursions into this little village over the years that might surprise you."

I put down my drink. "You might be surprised at how little I'd be surprised." I paused, realizing I'd confused even myself, and picked up my glass again. Tilting it thoughtfully, I attempted a nonchalant tone. "Would that have anything to do with the reason you left Leafy Hollow?" I raised the glass to my mouth, regarding him over its rim. "Or why you're back?"

His smile was fleeting. "Adeline was right. You are quick."

I waited for him to continue.

"I was instrumental in thwarting one or two of those incursions," he said. "I'm sorry I can't be more specific. If you don't believe me, ask your aunt. I've helped her in the past with little... difficulties."

Reaching for my purse, I slipped out my phone and balanced it on my hand. "I can ask her right now."

He nodded toward the phone. "Say hello for me."

My text went unanswered. As did my call. I hung up without leaving a message.

Griffiths noticed my unease. "Let me try," he said, reaching for his own phone.

Still no answer.

"That's unlike Adeline," he said with a frown, putting down the phone.

While we sipped our drinks silently, I reevaluated my decision to tell Griffiths about the strange note. I should wait and speak to Jeff first.

"Something's bothering you," Griffiths said.

I remembered Wilf's reluctant assessment of the ex-mayor.

Ethical, honorable, and completely trustworthy.

Grimacing, I reached for my shoulder bag. "I'm actually here to ask for your advice." I retrieved the note, smoothed it out on the coffee table, and passed it over. "This was in my mailbox this morning. I don't know what to do about it. It may be simply a bad joke."

Griffiths put down his glass to study the note. Pressing his lips together, he handed it back. "We were afraid something like this could happen."

The expression on his face was not encouraging.

I straightened up with a flash of alarm. "Are you saying my aunt might be in danger? And who's—*we*?"

"I'll come back to that. First, I have something to tell you. About our friend Waffles."

"Is it relevant to my aunt's situation?"

"In a roundabout way, yes. I think you know Zara Price has a criminal record?"

"I do. But it's not—"

"And that a member of her group threw a Molotov cocktail during their protest?"

"Yes, but—"

"That person was Tyson Farrell."

I sank back into my chair. "Zara didn't tell me that."

Yet another thing she lied to me about, I thought. *If only by omission.*

"There's more," Griffiths said.

I heaved a sigh. "Tell me."

"Tyson worked for Clive Yeager. On an occasional basis."

"I know. He did work around the house and garden. Does that make him a suspect in Eubanks' murder? Possibly even Yeager's? Is that what you're saying?"

"Maybe. But there's more to it."

I sat back, flummoxed. "More than two murders?"

He grimaced. "I'm afraid there are darker forces at work. Let's return to the Vancouver criminal case for a moment. Tyson was never an animal-rights activist. He infiltrated Zara's group because he was ordered to."

"By whom?"

"Let's say—an entity hoping to cause trouble."

"Are you talking about criminal incursions again?"

"I'm afraid so."

I drooped a hand over the chair arm. "Whoever it was, they succeeded. I don't—wait, did Zara know Tyson's real motive?"

"I doubt it. It never came out at their trial."

"He went to jail, right?"

"For a while—a suspiciously short while. He was released within weeks. But Zara returned to Leafy Hollow immediately after the trial. They might have lost touch."

I recalled the window slammed by an unknown guest at the farmhouse, Zara's argument with Nicole—*He has to go*—and Samantha's claim of a "strange man" hanging around. It all fit.

"I don't think they did lose touch. Or if they did, they've since reconnected."

He nodded. "I believe you're correct."

"I don't understand. How do you know this? Are you... working for the police?" I sucked in a breath before whispering, "Are you undercover?"

He gave me a long look before replying. "Yes. But not for the police."

"Then who?"

He smiled grimly. "You should have asked your aunt."

I gasped as realization hit. "You're working for Control." I leapt up to pace around the room. "You're working for Control," I repeated, my voice rising.

"Verity, please. Sit." He glanced toward the kitchen. "And keep your voice down."

I flopped back into the armchair, relief flooding through me. I hadn't been wrong to trust him.

"Why didn't you tell me before? I know all about that bizarre black-ops marketing group."

He shook his head, smiling. "Which part of *undercover* is confusing for you?"

"All of it, to be honest."

I sat up straight, struck by something he'd said. *An entity hoping to cause trouble.* Where had I heard that before?

"That entity you mentioned—were you talking about The Syndicate?"

"We don't know for certain. It could be only a run-of-the-mill organized crime group. Toxic-waste schemes are popular this season." Muttering, he added, "Every season."

"You wouldn't be here if that's what Control believed. What makes this case different?"

"The scale of it, for one thing. We think Eubanks was affiliated with a group that controlled a fleet of tankers picking up toxic waste and redistributing it."

"Dumping it, you mean. In streams and rivers, probably."

He nodded. "I'm afraid so."

"Why would they kill him, then?"

"We don't think The Syndicate killed him. We believe it was a competing outfit."

"Is there that much toxic waste around?"

"If you know where to look, yes."

"What a world."

"Indeed."

Watching the ice melt in my lemonade, I tried to take this in. At least I wouldn't be alone in my search for Adeline. Still —I frowned—she should have told me the truth. And another thing... I looked up.

"Does this mean you're not interested in becoming mayor?"

"Good heavens, no. I did my time. One more late night phone call about inadequate recycling bins and I would have chucked it for good. Did you know you're not supposed to mix peanut butter with cardboard?"

I nodded. "I did, actually. Someone mentioned it the other day."

"These days, it's a full-time job taking out your own garbage. Never mind worrying about everybody else's. No," he said with a chuckle. "Wilf is welcome to the job. But it did provide a useful smokescreen for my return."

"Then, why are you here? If the toxic-waste scheme doesn't interest Control, why do they need an undercover agent?"

"Adeline may have told you she suspected The Syndicate had a sleeper agent in the village."

I rolled my eyes. "Many times."

"I know what you mean. However, when new information came to light about Tyson Farrell's possible affiliation with The Syndicate, Control decided it was time to take action. I was sent to smoke out the operative."

"Whom you thought was Tyson."

"Correct."

"But Aunt Adeline thought it was Clive Yeager."

"Adeline was ordered to keep clear. Her involvement was pointless. The Syndicate was aware of her affiliation. They saw her coming." He shook his head. "She never listens."

I recalled my conversation with Control's annoying puppets. *We told her to stay out of it.*

"We lost our best lead because of her interference," he continued.

"Are you talking about Tyson Farrell again?"

"Possibly. We think Syndicate agents killed Yeager to ensure his silence."

"On your property."

"Correct. A clumsy attempt to incriminate me, Control believes."

"That wasn't Adeline's fault."

"She was closing in. It was only a matter of time before she convinced someone in authority to take a closer look at Yeager. The Syndicate didn't want that to happen."

Leaning in, he tapped the note, which lay on the table between us.

A wave of dread washed away my earlier relief. "What are you saying?"

Griffiths pinned the note with his finger to slide it across the table. "We have to find Tyson Farrell." He tapped the note again. "Before he makes good on this threat."

CHAPTER 22

I STARED at the note over my glass of melting ice, pondering Griffiths' suggestion. It sounded like an order, the way he delivered it. I've never liked being ordered around. I was not a member of his quasi-military group, or whatever they were calling it this week.

I tapped my own finger on the note.

"*We* have to find Tyson? Are you conscripting me?"

He looked surprised. "Do I need to conscript you? Aren't you anxious to find your aunt?"

"Of course I am. But I'm not one of your agents. Besides, in my experience, missions for Control have a way of escalating *out* of control."

"You could be an agent. You have a great deal of natural talent. We could use someone like you."

Narrowing my eyes at him, I thought this over. Oh, not joining Control—I was never going to do that, no worries—but why lately so many people found it necessary to mention my "real talent for this kind of thing."

I ticked them off on mental fingers.

First, Cayenne Cole, who buttered me up because she wanted to hire me for her insurance fraud agency.

Then Adeline, who buttered me up because she wanted me to join her quest for a mythical "sleeper agent."

And, of course, Emy, who buttered me up because she believed in the Hawkes Investigation Agency. Also, she was my best friend—so maybe her butter didn't count.

And now Griffiths, on behalf of an organization I'd vowed never to join. I shook my head in amazement. Control must be way down on its recruitment quota for the month. Besides, those puppet heads were more annoying than pepper ants at a picnic.

This pause for reflection allowed my natural cynicism to re-activate—after a slight grinding of gears. I looked up. "You have no idea where she is, do you?"

"Well..."

"You intend to use me to find her."

"I wouldn't say *use*, exactly..."

"You need me." I leaned in. "But tell me, Mr. Griffiths— why do I need you?"

The seasoned political campaigner rose to the occasion. "Adeline Hawkes has given a lifetime of service to the agency. Maybe you don't see the value of Control, but she does. Your aunt would want you to help us."

I puffed out a breath, fighting anger at his attempt to use my complicated family history against me. *The agency?* Is that what they called that ragtag group of black market operatives? Staring at him, I continued to puff while I pondered his declaration.

Unfortunately, Griffiths was correct. Adeline valued the agency and their work. Recalling their battle the previous year to save Niagara's magnificent Horseshoe Falls from destruction, I had to admit that maybe she was right.

Shoulders slumping, I let out a sigh of resignation. "How can I help you?"

"Zara Price. She trusts you."

"So?"

"We have reason to believe Tyson Farrell has been in contact with Miss Price. She may be shielding him from the authorities."

"The authorities in this case being...Control?"

"Yes. But if you explain to Zara that you need to find Tyson because your aunt is missing, she will cooperate. Possibly even lead you to him."

"If Tyson really is a murderer, is confronting him the wisest option?"

Griffiths slid out the drawer of a mahogany end table. Reaching in a hand, he drew out a revolver.

My eyes widened.

It was a Glock. Which I knew because this particular model was ubiquitous in thrillers. I also knew it had no safety.

He balanced the gun on his open palm. "You'll have backup."

I eyed the weapon uneasily. "I'm not taking that along."

"Don't be ridiculous. It's for me."

"Why do you need a gun? You're not going to shoot Tyson, are you?"

"Of course not," he scoffed. "It isn't loaded."

"Then why—"

"It makes a statement." He put the weapon back into the drawer and closed it.

With one foot tapping uneasily on the carpet, I eyed that drawer. In my experience, the only statement a pointed gun made was, *Someone's going to get shot.*

I really, really hoped it wouldn't be me.

"We have to call the police," I said.

Griffiths shook his head. "This is not a police matter."

"What are you talking about? Of course it's a police matter. Two people are dead—and if you're not careful with that gun, someone else might be as well." I studied the drawer, unable to pull my gaze away.

"I know you think the world of that detective boyfriend of yours—"

I tensed, ready to defend Jeff's honor with a quick groin kick, if necessary. An old move, true, but the classics are always effective. That's why they're classics.

If Griffiths noticed my indignation, he wisely chose to ignore it. "Any hint the police are involved will send Tyson further into hiding. We can't take the chance of spooking him before he discloses Adeline's location. Otherwise—" He grimaced. "There's no telling what he might do to her."

Yeager's broken body lying at the base of the falls came to mind. *Oh hell.* Could I take that chance?

I rose to my feet, feeling manipulated but seeing no other option. "I'll find out what Zara knows. But if she can't lead me straight to Tyson, then I'm calling Jeff."

Griffiths opened his mouth to object.

I held up a hand. "It's not negotiable."

"All right," he said reluctantly. "But you must contact me as soon as Zara tells you where Tyson is. You can't confront him alone, Verity. You need backup."

Normally, Emy and Lorne were my backups of choice on occasions that called for pluck and—what had that reporter called it? *Spunk.* Unfortunately, my besties were occupied with sifting sand between their toes. I wasn't bitter, though. Not at all.

I heaved a sigh, hoping I wouldn't regret my actions. "I'm on my way."

Zara was out back, feeding the goats again, when I parked outside the farmhouse and started up the path by the side of the house. She caught sight of me and straightened, returning my wave. I noticed the blue exercise ball on the other side of the pen had been completely flattened. One of the goats— Ethel, I think—stared sadly at it. Occasionally, she gave it a nudge.

"Any news?" Zara asked.

I trotted the rest of the way. Puffing slightly, I leaned on the fence. "I need your help."

"What's happened?"

"My aunt's missing and I've received a threatening note."

"I don't understand."

Fishing the paper out of my purse, I unfolded it and handed it over.

Zara clapped a hand over her mouth, staring at the note in her hand. "That's awful. Why would anyone—"

"You have to stop protecting him, Zara."

Slowly, she raised her head until our eyes were locked. "I don't know what you're talking about."

"Tyson Farrell. I'm talking about your friend, Tyson Farrell. He's been staying at the farmhouse, hasn't he? And parking his car in your old barn."

Her shoulders slumped as she handed back the note. "What if he has? He didn't send that."

"He's not worth your concern, Zara."

"That's easy for you to say. You've never been unfairly suspected by the police."

Actually, I had, but that wasn't relevant at the moment.

"Zara, Tyson didn't join your movement because he believed in animal rights. He was hired by a criminal organization known as The Syndicate to infiltrate your group."

"I don't believe you."

"He was only there to cause trouble. That's why he brought that Molotov cocktail to a peaceful protest."

"But why would they do that?"

"They might have wanted to sabotage your movement and make the public less sympathetic. There could have been money at stake. Maybe the Syndicate wanted to deflect attention and confuse the issue to cover up improper land use, or toxic waste, or other criminal acts." I paused. "Standard evil-corporation stuff."

I could see this was resonating, so I pressed on. "The thing is, Zara, I'm certain that same group is behind my aunt's disappearance. And I suspect Tyson knows where she is."

She was wavering.

"You don't want them to win again, do you?"

Zara bit her lip, glancing around the farmyard. "Will the police be involved?"

"No. I promise—no police."

She sagged against the fence. "I wanted to tell you, Verity. That's why I was so angry the other day when I…"

"Un-hired me?"

"Yes. I'm sorry. I couldn't turn my back on Tyson because we were friends in the old days, in Vancouver. Of course, I didn't know…" She swallowed heavily. "I didn't know he was hired to do it."

"And now?"

"He told me he was in trouble with the police. He said it was a trumped-up charge, and they were using our Vancouver protest against him, and that he needed my help to stay out of their way. Just until he could prove he hadn't done it."

"You mean, murder Herbert Eubanks?"

She nodded miserably. "I didn't believe he could do that, honestly. I still don't. It's some kind of horrible mistake, Verity. Tyson wouldn't kill anyone."

"He could have killed that guard back in Vancouver," I said softly. "That was dangerous. He took a big chance."

She ran both hands through her hair. "I don't know what to do."

I laid a hand on her arm. "My aunt is in danger, Zara. I only want to talk to Tyson to see if he knows where she is. Please help me."

She gave me an anguished look before glancing away. "Ask Ethan."

I stared, dumbfounded. "My Ethan? Ethan Neuhaus?"

Zara nodded. "Tyson was hiding out here, in the farmhouse, but Nicole insisted it was unsafe. She thought he might turn on me. I tried to tell her she was wrong. Tyson was an old friend. He would never hurt me."

I wasn't convinced of that, but I kept my opinion to myself.

"Anyway," she continued, "I was afraid Nicole would report him to the police, so I told him he had to leave. He called someone before he left. He was tossing stuff into a gym bag, so he had the phone on speaker. They said, 'You can hang out here for a while. But then you have to leave.'" She sighed. "I think it was Ethan. Then Tyson got into that ridiculous souped-up car of his and drove away."

"Thank you," I said before tearing down the path.

I still didn't know where Tyson was, but I knew where to find Ethan Neuhaus—at a monster home with a massive two-acre lawn and multiple shrubs that needed trimming. I had dropped him off before my visit to Martin Griffiths. He'd be there the rest of the day.

After pulling up alongside our client's turreted three-story house, I hopped out of the truck to look for Ethan, a hand protecting my eyes from the sun's glare. He was on the far side of the property, on our riding mower, with his attention fixed on the grass and ear protection clamped over his head. He didn't hear my shouts.

I raised my hands in exasperation. *Today* Ethan wore the much-detested hearing protection we usually fought over?

Waving my arms, I started across the freshly mown lawn at a run. I halted, panting, in front of the machine.

With a start of surprise, he switched off the engine and pulled the ear muffs down around his neck, looking worried. "Hey, boss. Whatcha doing here?" Then he smirked, unable to stay out of character for long. "Didya bring me a cold one?"

"Get down, Ethan."

"Now what?" he grumbled with an eye-roll before stepping off the mower. He stood stiffly before me, his mock-attention embodying the sarcasm that was his default state.

I got right down to it. "Where's Tyson Farrell?"

His eyes widened. "I don't know."

"Ethan, I'm not fooling around. This is serious. My aunt is in danger, and I think Tyson knows where she is." I pulled the now-battered note from my pocket and showed it to him.

He stared at it, and then at me, suddenly deflated. "Adeline's in trouble?" he asked.

"Correct. And I need to know—did Tyson ask you for help?"

He winced. "Maybe."

"Ethan, please. Stop fooling around. This is serious."

"Okay, yeah, he did. But he said the police wanted to stitch him up on a fake murder charge."

"And you believed him?"

"We're friends."

"That's not a good enough reason to shield him from the law. There must be more."

He heaved a sigh. "You know that old quarry on Concession 8?"

"I think so." I tried to picture the site. I'd driven past it, but never gone in, given its red-lettered "Danger" signs and supposedly electrified fencing. The whole thing, including the wire fence, was overgrown with weeds. It was a played-out quarry, scheduled for redevelopment, but the site had been mired for years in red tape and council arguments.

"I used to race there. With Tyson. And some of the guys. Street racing, sorta. But it's—"

"Illegal?" I broke in, unable to help myself.

He looked away.

"Hang on—is that what happened to your Camaro?" I recalled its dented fender and scraped sides. Not to mention Ethan's muddled behavior. I'd taken it for a hangover, but given the bruise on his forehead, he could have hit his head in a collision while racing. A concussion would explain his confusion.

I remembered his explanation. *Ran into a door.*

Not likely.

Then I recalled the red racer that Zara's mother, Samantha, saw roaring through the neighborhood. Was it Ethan's car? Or Tyson Farrell's?

"Did you win?" I asked wryly.

He broke out in a grin, but his mirth faded rapidly at the look that crossed my face. "Not usually."

"Let's recap," I said. "You and the guys were trespassing and damaging property—I'm thinking that fence has some pretty big holes in it, right?"

He nodded.

"Not to mention," I continued, "driving dangerously, leaving the scene of an accident and, probably, betting illegally. Have I thought of everything?"

He nodded again.

I tugged a hand through my hair. "What were you thinking? You and Tyson both have criminal records. And yes—" I held up a hand to ward off his objection. "His is much worse than yours. I'm not forgetting that. But still, Ethan. It was not a good idea."

He lowered his head, flicking grass clippings from the side of the mower, and said in a low voice, "I don't go there anymore. Not since he told me about..."

"The murder charge?"

"Yes," he said miserably.

"Do you think Tyson did it?"

He mumbled something.

I planted both hands on my hips. "Do you?"

"It's...possible."

"Then why the hell did you agree to help him? He could be a murderer. I understand camaraderie and the old boys' network and—"

"The old boys' what?"

"Never mind. Just tell me why you helped him."

He continued to brush grass off the mower. "Because..."

"Yes?"

"Because..."

"You said that already."

Ethan straightened up. "Because he threatened to tell you about the street racing and the betting and...the rest of it."

"He threatened to tell me? Not the police?"

He tossed me an incredulous look. "Tyson would never volunteer info to the cops."

"Of course not." I rolled my eyes, trying to make sense of what he was saying. "You agreed to help a possible murderer so your employer wouldn't know about your..." I hesitated. "Relatively illegal activities."

"That's about the size of it, yeah."

"That was a bad bargain, Ethan. And now I know anyway. It was all for nothing. And what's worse—my aunt is missing, probably in danger, and I can't help her."

"I'm sorry, Verity. I don't know what to say."

"That hardly matters, because you'd only lie."

He stared at his feet, not moving, his customary nonchalance failing him for once. "Sometimes," he said, his voice cracking, "I have to."

I spoke slowly and clearly. "You admit you lied to me."

He nodded, still not looking up.

It was too much—the half-mown grass that stretched out before us in an endless swath, the frightening note with its glued-on letters, Yeager's crumpled body, even the wedding date I couldn't set. It all rose up to overwhelm me.

Fighting tears, I slumped onto the lawn. "Some investigator I turned out to be. I can't even tell when people are lying to me. I've been wrong every time." Clutching my knees to my chest, I let my head sag. "I should give up."

Ethan stood by, looking uneasy. Then he slowly lowered himself to the grass to sit beside me, leaning back on his hands, his legs stretched out in front of him.

We contemplated his Camaro parked in the client's driveway.

"How fast can that thing go?" I asked.

"Zero to sixty in five-point-one seconds."

"Wow." Pause. "Is that good?"

He gave me a withering glance.

"Why don't you get a job at the track? You know a lot about cars."

"To be honest...I kinda like gardening." Absently, he twisted his fingers in the grass.

I looked over at him, surprised. "Really?"

"Yeah. That's why I didn't want you to know about...that stuff. You did me a favor taking me on, Verity. I didn't want to let you down. And this week, with Lorne gone, I wanted to prove how much I could do. Take over his job, like." He continued to twist the grass, still staring at the Camaro. "I guess I messed up."

I pondered this a moment. "No, you didn't." I pointed to the arrow-straight rows mown in the grass. "What you've done so far on this lawn looks great."

"Thanks."

"But you have to decide what you want. Do you intend to skulk around like a criminal the rest of your life?"

I held my breath, aware that perhaps I'd gone too far. But my father had called Ethan *a good kid.* There must have been a reason.

"No," he muttered. "I'm tired of being a loser. I just want to be normal." There was a definite set to his jaw when he turned to face me. "I won't lie to you again."

I studied his face. "Last chance, Ethan."

"I know."

I scrambled to my feet with a sigh. "I'm the only loser here."

He rose with a grimace, shaking his head. "Don't give up so easily."

"Why not? I have no idea how to find Tyson Farrell, and he was my only lead."

"Well..." He scrunched up his face.

"You know where he is, don't you?"

"Maybe." He looked uncomfortable.

"Why didn't you tell me?"

"I'm not certain. I could be wrong."

"Ethan, my aunt is missing, and Tyson had something to do with it. Any ideas you have, I need to hear them."

He shook his head. "There's more going on than you think."

"Tell me."

"I don't know everything. But Tyson's involved in something bad. Something criminal. It could be dangerous."

"You mean the murder charge?"

"More than that."

I recalled Griffiths' warning. *There are darker forces at work.*

"Tyson may be in trouble," I said. "He could even be dead."

There was a long moment during which I feared Ethan would clam up again.

Finally, he spoke. "He's not dead. At least, he wasn't yesterday."

"Then you've seen him?"

"He moved his car to the quarry yesterday."

I scrambled to my feet. "Thanks."

"It's not there now. I checked. There's one other place he might be, though. It's a long shot, but worth checking."

"How do you know?"

He frowned. "I met Yeager there once."

"Yeager? Why?"

"He and Eubanks were up to something. Tyson knew about it. He told me there was easy money to be made, and he set up a meeting with Yeager."

"But not at Yeager's house."

"No. I was suspicious, but I went to this place to see him on Tyson's say-so. The weird thing is, Yeager never showed up."

"Why?"

"Dunno. But that was the week Eubanks turned up dead. I got to thinking about it, and I hightailed it out of there. I decided to keep away after that."

"Wise move." I handed him a pencil and notepad from my purse. "Directions, please."

He scribbled something on the pad and handed it back. "You should hurry. Tyson said something about hitting the road. He may already be gone."

CHAPTER 23

IT WAS a ten-minute drive to the address Ethan gave me. It turned out to be a former construction site on the outskirts of the village. Weeds sprouted in cracked pavement and the surrounding wire fence sagged under the weight of a dozen KEEP OUT signs. A lone backhoe, its windshield spattered with bird droppings, hulked silently to one side.

In the center of the lot, a portable construction trailer was perched on stacks of cinder blocks. Its single, grimy window looked as if it had never been opened. If it hadn't been for the door flung open to admit the feeble breeze, I would have assumed the lot was deserted.

I paused, engine idling, on the street outside the entrance. The wire gate was propped open with another cinder block, an unused padlock hanging from a chain. The lot was at the far end of a dead-end street. A derelict drive-through next door had been boarded up for so long that graffiti obscured the original signs, the fence was toppled in several places, and piles of cigarette butts littered the parking area.

A much larger lot directly across the street was nothing more than weeds and brush. Affixed to a stake in the ground was a faded sign with a condo building painted on it and the words COMING SOON. Lurid letters under that read, You WISH, accompanied with a graphic depiction of, well, something anatomically unlikely.

Colorful artwork notwithstanding, the entire block was deserted. A torn newspaper swirled across the road in a gust of wind and plastered itself against the sign before dropping to the ground.

While pulling my cell phone from my purse to slip it into my pocket, I glanced at its screen. No missed calls. No texts. I tapped in another message to Adeline, not really expecting an answer.

And I didn't get one.

I bit my lip, thinking it over. I was alone. If this visit went south, no one would see a thing.

I continued to study the silent trailer. There was no sign of activity. No hum of conversation. No ringing phones. The door hung open, inviting me to enter.

It's a trap, insisted the reptile part of my brain that sensed danger everywhere.

It can't be, countered the more logical part. *Whoever's in there, he's not expecting you.*

I mulled it over. Logic also dictated that I shouldn't be an idiot. Griffiths was right. I might need backup. A few quick taps was all it took to send him the address. At least someone would know where I was.

Or where I'd been.

With a twist of the steering wheel, I drove through the

gate. As I walked around the front of my truck to the trailer's open door, a flash of red caught my eye. Ducking my head, I saw a vehicle parked behind the trailer—a sleek Chevrolet Camaro. But this version had nothing in common with Ethan's beloved vehicle. Even to my untrained eyes, it was obvious the wheels were several inches bigger, thrusting this car higher into the air. Two, not one, massive tailpipes stuck out the rear. And red-and-yellow flames outlined in black streamed down its gleaming sides.

For a clandestine getaway, this vehicle would not be my first choice.

I mounted three wooden steps to the trailer's door and rapped on the frame.

A young man sitting with his feet up on a rusted metal desk gave me a startled look before untangling his hands from behind his head.

"Tyson Farrell?" I asked.

His expression turned shifty. "Who wants to know?"

I stared, unbelieving. This was the feared Syndicate sleeper agent? Unkempt, overweight, with a nervous tic in his left eye, and broken fingernails. He wore jeans, worn cowboy boots, and a grubby T-shirt stretched tight over an ample stomach that bore traces of both mustard and salsa.

I shook my head. The male of the species never failed to astound me. *How could a man so filthy have such a spotless car?* I wondered.

His crafty expression reminded me of a child feigning innocence while unaware of the chocolate smeared across its face.

Swinging his feet off the desk, he asked, "What do you want?"

I held out a hand and forced a smile. "Verity Hawkes."

"I know who you are. What do you want?"

So much for small talk. Since time was of the essence, I plunged right in.

"My aunt, Adeline Hawkes, is missing. Possibly kidnapped. Hopefully not dead."

"What's that to me?"

"I think you know where she is."

The shifty look was back. "Maybe. What's it worth?"

"I won't tell the police where you are. Tell me where she is and you can go. I won't stop you."

Squinting, he leaned sideways in the chair to peer around me at my truck. "Bring anybody with you?"

"I'm alone."

"So, how didya figure on stopping me?"

He had me there. I tensed for possible combat, while hoping fervently it wouldn't be necessary. "I only want to know what's happened to my aunt. I don't want any trouble."

"Yeah, well—there's not much you can do for her now."

My heart leapt into my throat. "What do you mean? Is she..." I couldn't bring myself to voice the rest of that thought.

Smirking, he held up a finger. "Later." With one hand, he pulled a wicked-looking hunting knife from his boot. He admired it for a bit before settling it on the desktop, inches from his fingers. "Right now, we are negotiating."

"Tell me where my aunt is, and I'll get you whatever you want."

He snickered. "That's not what we're negotiating."

A sick feeling roiled my stomach.

He gave the knife a twirl. "We're negotiating whether I should let you walk out of here."

I stared as the blade spun, unable to draw my gaze away. The hand that hovered over the knife was trembling. Only a little, but enough to make me suspect Tyson wasn't really the hard-boiled killer type.

Which didn't mean he wouldn't do it, if push came to shove.

Forcing myself to stay calm, I evaluated my options. Of the two of us, I was closest to the door. I could dart out, slam it in his face, and then use the precious moments I'd gained to sprint for my truck and get the hell out of there.

The problem with that scenario was that it didn't bring me any closer to my aunt.

I took a deep breath while edging toward the entrance.

"Let's change the subject. Tell me about Herbert Eubanks."

He drummed his fingers on the desk, squinting at me. "The septic pumper guy?"

"That's the one."

"Never met him."

"You worked for Clive Yeager. Eubanks was often at his house. You must have seen him."

The crafty expression returned. "What if I did?"

"The police think you killed him."

To be honest, the police didn't think that, but I saw no reason to be honest.

He thrust out his jaw. "So what? They'll never find me."

"Of course they will. I did. You won't get as far as the

highway."

I watched while he digested this information, still tapping his fingers inches from the knife.

"Tyson, I'm working with the police. If you co-operate, I can arrange an immunity deal. But if you hurt me—" I shrugged, hoping my lie was convincing.

The tapping slowed while he eyed me warily. "Are you sure you can get me an immunity deal? *If* I decide to hang around?"

"Cross my heart."

His eyes narrowed as he studied me.

I tried to look nonchalant.

Suddenly, he slapped his hand on the desk. "I didn't kill him."

"Then what happened?"

The chair rocked as he slumped back. "It was because of my Auntie Eileen."

"Who?"

"She owns a house in the village and lives there with her stupid cat. That animal scratches everybody. I don't know why she keeps it."

My stomach twisted again. *Eileen?* With a start, I recalled the wedding picture I'd seen with the plaque that read, *Peter and Eileen.* Was he talking about...Mr. Snuffles?

"Mrs. Peter Vaughan is your aunt?" I asked.

"I just said, didn't I?"

"Herbert Eubanks' landlady?"

He snorted. "She's got a nice setup with that apartment upstairs. Regular income, like. She could send a little more my way."

I recalled Mrs. Vaughan's words.

A good-for-nothing git. Always looking for a handout.

"Is that where you met Herbert Eubanks, at your aunt's?"

"Yeah. Once. Bastard tossed me out on her say-so."

"Why? Did you argue with your aunt?"

He glared. "It wasn't any of Eubanks' business. He came thundering down the stairs when he heard her screaming." Tyson rolled his eyes. "She does a lot of screaming."

"What happened then?"

"He grabbed me by the scruff of my neck and tossed me outside. 'Stay away,' he says, and slams the door." Tyson scowled. "Bastard."

"Is that why you killed him?"

His eyes widened. "I never."

I pointed to a gym bag on the desk. "Then, why are you running away?"

"It beats getting arrested." He stood up and began to pace, leaving his knife on the desk. I mentally calculated the number of steps it would take to grab it. *Too many.*

"I saw Eubanks at Yeager's a few times, pumping out that old septic tank. I knew something was up 'cause I knew the property. Yeager didn't use that old tank. He had a new one. So why was Eubanks always pumping out the old one? What the hell was in it?"

"After that, I kept an eye on him. We'd shoot the breeze a bit when I was cutting the lawn and stuff. But when that bastard threw me outta my aunt's place, he didn't even recognize me. Never even looked at my face."

"That must have made you angry."

"Sure, but I didn't kill him."

"Who did?"

Tyson picked up the knife and the gym bag, then gestured to the door with his knife hand.

I walked out in front of him, his presence close enough to make me flinch.

He tossed the bag through the Camaro's open passenger window, then leaned against the car, giving me a long look. "I'll tell you what happened, and you can judge for yourself."

He slid the knife into his boot, pulled a pack of cigarettes out of his pocket, lit one, and inhaled. "I still haven't decided what to do with you," he snarled. "Don't think it's over."

I nodded.

After a few puffs, he ground the butt under his foot and straightened.

"One day, Eubanks tells me about his landlady. Says she cooks and cleans for him for nothing. Even does his laundry. Just because he put her in his will. She's his only...his only..."

"Beneficiary?" I asked.

"Yeah. He laughed about it. But I got to thinking about my aunt and her will. I asked Eubanks, and he said the old lady had done the same thing for him. If she knocked off, Eubanks would get all her money. Big joke, he thought. Meanwhile, he didn't have to do laundry."

"Then what happened?"

"That pissed me off. And I started thinking, why should he get all her cash when I get nothing? I told him, if that old lady leaves you her money, you better send some of it my way or I'll report you and Yeager to the police. I know there's funny business going on."

He gave an exaggerated eye-roll. "So, what do ya think happened?"

"Astound me."

"The bastard threatened me. Said if I didn't shut my trap, he'd shut it for me. Permanently." He snorted in disgust. "I figured I'd teach him a lesson, and I waited for my chance. And sure enough, there he was that morning, bending over that septic tank. I let him have it. Thunk! Straight into the tank."

An image of two stiff, lifeless legs flashed through my mind. "You killed him," I sputtered.

He barely reacted. "Depends how you look at it. I call it an accident."

An accident? After a brief internal struggle, I decided not to comment, opting instead for pursed lips and a curt nod. "Go on."

He pulled out another cigarette and lit it. After a couple of puffs, he resumed his story.

"But then he wasn't moving and I didn't know what to do. There mighta been evidence. Fingerprints and stuff. I remembered those damn goats next door and I let them out."

"How did you do that?"

"With the wire cutters we used at the quarry." He chuckled. "Then I persuaded them to hoof it outta there." He mimicked whacking motions, which flung cigarette ash in the air. "Easy."

His chuckles faded, and his brow wrinkled in puzzlement. "There's one thing I'd like to know, though—what was Eubanks reaching for under that lid? I shoulda checked. Might have been cash." He heaved a sigh. "Too late now."

Leaning in, he shook a finger at me. "Wait till you hear this part." His face flooded with contempt. "When the old lady got the good news, did she offer to share it with me?" He leaned back on his heels with a snort of disgust. "Not a penny."

"How do you know?"

"Cause I went round to see her. And she told me I've got all the money I'm getting and there won't be any more. Called me a cheat and a jailbird and a bunch of other things." He shook his head, puffing air sadly out of his lips. "That old woman has a real mouth on her."

He dropped the second cigarette at his feet and stamped on it. "And to think I was responsible for the whole thing. Some thanks."

"But why did you kill Yeager? Did he see you push Eubanks into that tank?"

At this, he seemed confused. "Yeager didn't see me. He wasn't home."

"Then, why kill him?"

"I didn't. I had nothing to do with it. Okay, I didn't shed any tears over him, 'cause he was a cheap bastard. No reason to kill him, though." He picked at a cuticle and then, not satisfied, chewed it off.

I studied his sullen face during this impromptu manicure, reflecting on his story.

I suspected Tyson Farrell wasn't bright enough to be a Syndicate agent. But I'd been wrong about people before— quite recently, in fact. But the more I thought about it, the more I decided he must be telling the truth. Someone else killed Clive Yeager.

"If Eubanks' death was an accident and you didn't kill Yeager, why are you running away?"

He snorted. "Do you think I'm an idiot?"

Don't answer that, my reptilian brain urged.

"It's manslaughter, isn't it?" Tyson continued. "I've been around the so-called justice system long enough to know that. And that won't be the end of it, either."

"What do you mean?"

"The cops want a scapegoat, don't they? Well, it's not gonna be me." Slipping the knife out of his boot, he pointed to the trailer with it. "Get inside."

The sick feeling returned. "Will you tell me where my aunt is?"

He shrugged. "Might as well. Can't hurt now."

A car door slammed shut behind us.

Cursing, Tyson whirled to face the newcomer.

Inwardly, I also cursed—at Griffiths for showing up so quickly. Tyson had been on the verge of telling me where my aunt was. The old man would ruin everything.

"Look out—he's got a gun," Griffiths yelled, pointing his Glock at Tyson.

"No, don't—" I blurted.

"What the hell!" Tyson snarled, raising the knife.

Then Griffiths' gun—his supposedly unloaded gun—went off with a deafening crack. I clapped my hands over my buzzing ears, cursing my stupidity. Of course Griffiths wouldn't bring a useless weapon to a confrontation. He only told me it was unloaded so I wouldn't call the police.

Jerking my head around, I watched Tyson crumple to the ground.

CHAPTER 24

WHEN TYSON HIT THE GROUND, the knife fell from his hand and skidded across the pavement. He didn't appear to notice. Clutching his side, he stumbled to his feet, swaying.

Griffiths leveled his gun again. "Verity, get out of the way."

"Don't shoot," I yelled, stepping between them. "He's unarmed." I steadied Tyson with one arm. Blood blossomed on his T-shirt near the waist, seeping outward in a gradually widening circle.

Griffiths' hand wavered. "I thought I saw—"

"A knife," I said. "It's gone."

Griffiths lowered his weapon, looking sheepish. "I thought he had a gun. I thought he was going to shoot you."

"I'm not shot yet," I muttered through gritted teeth as I tried to keep Tyson upright. "Tyson? Can you hear me?"

His eyes were wild, the pupils rolling. He slumped against me.

"Tyson? You've been shot. Do you understand? We have to get you to a hospital."

"I'll take him in my car," Griffiths said. "Over here. It will be faster than waiting for an ambulance."

"No," Tyson gasped, still clutching his side. "I'm not going anywhere with him."

"Martin—get an ambulance."

"But—"

"Now."

He pulled out his phone to make the call.

I slid my shoulder under Tyson's arm, so he could lean on me.

He coughed. Blood glistened on his chin. "I have to sit down," he mumbled, pointing to his car.

I opened the driver's door and lowered him into the seat with his feet on the pavement.

"Tyson, tell me where my aunt is." I leaned over him to assess his wound. I was frantic to keep him alive. He couldn't die—not without telling me Adeline's whereabouts.

The bullet had gone through a fleshy part of his abdomen. Hard to tell how much damage had been done. To my untrained eye, it didn't look good.

"The ambulance will be here soon. Tell me, Tyson." I raised my voice to a near-shout. "Where is my aunt?"

But his gaze fixed on Griffiths, who was pocketing his phone and walking toward us.

"No," he mumbled. "I'm not going with him."

"Tyson, please, tell me."

With a groan, he lifted his legs into the footwell.

"Don't let him get away," Griffiths yelled, picking up his pace.

"Get back, Martin," I shouted, grabbing the edge of the open door so Tyson couldn't close it. Later, I regretted not trying to seize the keys. But he was so weak, I didn't expect him to do anything other than pass out. And, possibly, die.

A struggle, I feared, might push him over the edge before he could tell me about my aunt. "Tyson, please. Help will be here soon. Tell me."

He stared at me, his eyes clouded.

"Tell me where my aunt is. Please."

"Verity. Get out of the way," Griffiths roared.

What the— I looked over my shoulder. He had walked around the car and stood behind me, his gun raised in both hands. This time, he wasn't going to miss.

"No," I screamed. "Don't shoot."

Without warning, Tyson jammed on the accelerator. As his car leapt forward, the open door tossed me back against Griffiths. We both toppled to the ground.

I looked up in time to see the Camaro's open door slam into the side of the construction trailer, which heaved it shut. The car tore across the weedy parking lot and through the gate, where it fishtailed onto the road.

It was gone in seconds.

I struggled to my feet, my limbs throbbing. "What the hell did you do that for? He was just about to tell me..." My voice trailed off as I studied the empty road, hands on hips. *Now what?*

"We have to go after him," I said, darting for my truck.

"I'll take my own car," Griffiths replied, waving the gun.

Good idea, I thought. *The last thing I want seated beside me is an idiot with a loaded gun.*

"Call the police," I called, climbing into my truck. "See if they can head him off."

Privately, I doubted the police would be needed. Tyson was badly hurt. He wouldn't get far. As I revved up the truck's engine and headed out after him, I half-expected to find his Camaro tail up in the nearest ditch.

I only hoped he wouldn't be unconscious.

I roared up the road and turned left. With one hand, I jabbed the emergency icon on my phone and told the operator what I was doing.

She said something along the lines of, *Do not pursue the suspect.* Or maybe it was, *Do not engage the suspect.* Or perhaps, *Do not shoot the suspect?* I really wasn't listening.

In the distance, I saw the red-flamed Camaro turn onto the road that bordered Young River Creek. The water was on our right as we sped along the one-lane road. From conversations at the police station, I knew enough about car pursuits to hang well back and not spur Tyson on to greater speeds.

Although it was hardly an issue. The *Coming Up Roses* truck was not designed for high-speed chases. It was more of a leisurely Sunday drive vehicle.

To be honest, you could walk faster.

Come on old girl, I muttered, willing the truck forward. *You can do it.*

Underneath the hood, something *pinged* in protest.

On the road ahead, the Camaro streaked over a series of bumps—*thump, thump, thump*—and kept going.

I shook my head. *How could Tyson still be driving?*

My phone lit up and started to ring. I punched the speaker icon.

"What the hell are you doing?" Jeff barked.

"Following Tyson Farrell."

"Why?"

"He's been shot. Can you head him off? We're on the river road, heading south."

I heard Jeff's police radio crackle in the background, although I couldn't make out the words. I assumed Griffiths had informed the force and that's why Jeff was calling.

A glance in my rearview mirror showed no sign of the ex-mayor's car. Which was good, given his itchy trigger finger. I prayed he wouldn't catch up to Tyson before I did.

"Jeff," I shouted at the phone. "Tyson is not armed. Repeat—not armed."

"Understood. We're on our way. Stop. Following. Him." Pause. "Verity—are you listening to me?"

"Can't hear you, sorry." I rapped the cell phone a few times against the dashboard. "Interference. Sorry." Then I clicked off the call and tossed the phone onto the seat beside me. It kept ringing. I ignored it.

I'd pay for that later, I knew. But I couldn't give up the chase until Tyson was in custody and able to speak to me.

Because if he died, my best shot at finding my aunt would die with him.

We were nearing a dip in the road, the river still visible on our right, when a police car—siren blaring—appeared in the road ahead, heading straight for Tyson's Camaro. Behind it, another police car, an unmarked one, swung out to one side until the two cars completely blocked the road.

I slammed on my brakes. I was a hundred yards back from the Camaro, but when I rolled down my window, I heard its engine rumbling on idle.

I waited to see what Tyson would do, debating with myself whether to get out of the truck. Nothing happened. Either he had passed out, or he was considering his options. As far as I could see, there were none. His escape route was blocked.

Unless... My eyes widened and my chest tightened.

Unless he decided to back up—straight into my truck.

I glanced around, hoping to find an escape route. There was none. Shrubs, fences and a ditch lined the left side of the road. To my right, there was only the river. Behind me, the nearest crossroad was a quarter of a mile back.

Frantically, I shifted the truck into reverse. Even as I did so, I knew it was hopeless. I could never outrun that Camaro, especially driving backward. If Tyson decided to ram the truck and force me off the road, there would be little I could do about it.

Ahead, the cruiser's roof lights were still flashing, although the siren had thankfully ceased. The driver's door of the unmarked car opened and Jeff stepped out. While he walked toward the Camaro, I slowly backed up. I desperately hoped Tyson wasn't dead yet.

He could die later, no problem, but not until he'd divulged my aunt's location.

I remembered driving past a small break in the shrubs about fifty yards back. It might be big enough for me to ease my truck off the road without going into the ditch.

Most of it, anyway. Enough for a car to pass me on the road.

Ahead, the Camaro's engine was still idling.

Then I had a brilliant idea. I could park my truck sideways so that it blocked the road, jump out—and run. I knew the old girl wouldn't survive a collision with a speeding Camaro, but it would stop Tyson. Then I could question him about my aunt's whereabouts.

In the back of an ambulance, if necessary.

Shifting the truck into reverse, I began my three-point turn.

Shouts filled the air and I stopped. Pausing with my hand on the gearshift, I glanced at the Camaro. The engine was revving up. The idling became a roar, and the front tires spun and smoked.

Not dead, then, I thought. Or, as my father would say, *Crikey*.

Jeff was waving his arms and shouting. He was also— thank goodness—backing away from the Camaro. I stared, frozen in place. What on earth could Tyson be doing?

Sucking in a breath, I evaluated the scene. It looked as if...

Oh no.

It looked as if he planned to ram the police cruisers.

Get out of there, Jeff, I silently mouthed, my heart thumping.

With a shriek of tires on asphalt, the Camaro shot forward. The smell of burning rubber filled the air.

Jeff leapt into the ditch to scramble up the other side.

I braced myself for the coming collision, unable to breathe.

But as it neared the first cruiser, the Camaro veered wildly to the right.

From my vantage point, it seemed to happen in slow motion. After traveling a few yards, the car jerked again, this time to the left.

I gasped. Tyson intended to go around the cruisers and regain the road behind them.

Then, with Jeff in the ditch, and the other car blocked, he could easily get away.

"No," I yelled, with my hand on the gearshift and my truck halfway through a three-point turn.

He didn't make the turn.

The Camaro was moving too fast to stop. It tore through bushes and down the incline. Picking up speed on the slope, it shot into the air. It hung for what seemed seconds before dropping into the river with a tremendous boom.

A column of water splashed toward the sky, then subsided with a tremendous whoosh.

I leapt out of the truck and ran toward the spot. By the time I reached it, only the Camaro's roof was visible above the water.

Dropping his utility belt to the ground, Jeff whipped off his shoes and waded into the murky water. A uniformed constable followed.

"Jeff," I hollered. "I have to talk to him."

Turning, he caught sight of me. "Stand back, Verity," he yelled.

Then he dove in, disappearing beneath the surface.

Horrified, I stood on the bank, my hands clasped to my face. "No, no, no..." I whispered, peering between my fingers.

Jeff resurfaced twice before finally bringing Tyson up.

The constable waded in to help, and the two men flopped him onto the bank.

Tyson's eyes were closed, and he wasn't breathing.

Jeff ripped off Tyson's T-shirt, revealing the bullet hole in his abdomen, and started CPR. Given the blank look in Tyson's open eyes, and the T-shirt that was now stained almost completely red, I suspected it was too late.

Sirens wailed in the distance, getting closer.

An ambulance tore up. Two medics jumped out and hurried to Tyson's body, motioning for Jeff to stand back.

He got to his feet, took a last look at the river where the Camaro lay submerged, then walked over to me, water dripping from his chin. Someone offered him a blanket. He took it with thanks and wrapped it around him.

"I'm sorry you had to see that," he whispered as he drew me close.

I leaned into his damp hug, feeling deflated, exhausted, and worried.

After a few moments muffled in the blanket, I straightened. "I guess you want to know..." My voice trailed off.

"What exactly you were doing? I guess I do." While vigorously rubbing the blanket on his wet hair, he gestured to a boulder on the river bank. "Sit here and you can explain it."

I started with the note. Pulling it from my pocket, I handed it over.

Jeff frowned as he read it. "You told me Adeline and Gideon get a lot of notes like this. Why is this one different?"

"First, they may get a lot of threatening notes, but I don't. This one was sent to me. And second—I can't find my aunt. She's not at home and she's not answering her phone. Or her calls. Or her texts."

"For how long?"

"Since yesterday, when I dropped her off at the conservation area. She said she was going to visit someone."

"Who?"

"She didn't say. I texted Gideon at the convention, and he hasn't heard from her either. Although—" I paused. "Gideon did say that's not unusual. But Tyson..." My voice wavered and I choked back a sob, pointing to his body. "He said it was too late."

Jeff handed back the note. "We'll find her, sweetheart."

I let out a long breath. "Are you sure?"

"I promise. We'll find her. Meanwhile, I wouldn't take seriously anything Tyson Farrell told you. He was probably winding you up. I'd like to know who shot him, though." He nodded at the body.

"I can tell you that," I said. "Martin Griffiths."

Twisting, I ducked my head to peer around Jeff at the road. The police had set up a barricade and were turning back cars. Briefly, I wondered if I should move my truck.

Jeff shot out a hand to bring me back. "Ex-mayor Martin Griffiths?"

"Yes. But didn't he call you? To tell you about Tyson?" I pointed at the body. "About shooting him?"

Jeff shook his head, momentarily speechless.

My brow furrowed. "How did you know I was chasing him, then?"

"Because we received multiple reports of a Camaro speeding through the village, pursued by a bright pink pickup truck," he said.

"I can explain—"

"Quickly, please."

"I was afraid Tyson would die before I could finish interrogating him." I straightened into a reasonable facsimile of military posture. "Sir."

Jeff sighed. "Not that quickly."

I related my conversation with Griffiths, stressing his insistence that Adeline was in danger and Tyson was our best chance to find her.

Jeff glowered. "Are you telling me Control is behind this?"

I scrunched up my face. Even though Jeff had helped them in the past, Control was not one of his favorite organizations. "Maybe I'm not explaining it right."

"Try."

"The thing is, Jeff...Tyson confessed to me that he killed Eubanks. He hated him. He claimed it was an accident, though. After that, he cut a hole in Zara's fence and shooed her goats into Yeager's yard. Waffles was innocent. He was stitched up for the crime."

I was really getting into this criminal lingo.

Jeff worked his lips. "Leaving the livestock issue aside for the moment, why did Tyson Farrell hate Eubanks?"

"Ah—" I took a deep breath. "Remember Eileen Vaughn? The woman who inherited Eubanks' half-million? Tyson was her nephew. Her closest living relative, in fact. He was pissed off that she changed her will to leave all her money to Eubanks."

Jeff regarded me strangely. He opened his mouth.

"I know what you're thinking," I said hastily, cutting him off. "I didn't call the police because I promised Zara I wouldn't. That was her condition for telling me how to find Tyson."

"She knew where he was?"

"Not exactly. That was Ethan."

Exasperated, Jeff held up both hands. "Enough. We'll straighten this out later. Just tell me where to find Griffiths."

Puzzled, I glanced around. "He should be here. He followed me from the construction site. Right after he called..." My jaw dropped. *Wait.* If Griffiths didn't call the police, perhaps he didn't follow me, either.

Jeff turned to the nearest constable. "Have you seen Martin Griffiths?"

"Who?"

"Old guy, untidy white hair, black-rimmed glasses?" I offered hopefully.

"No. I didn't see anybody like that."

Jeff swiped a hand through his still-dripping hair. "All right. Send a patrol car to his home. And report back to me when he's found." The constable scribbled Jeff's instructions in a notepad, then trotted off to relay the message.

Jeff turned to me. "You are not off the hook yet."

"I know and I'm sorry."

"Come with me. I have to change out of these wet clothes."

I followed him to his cruiser. After opening the trunk, he

zipped open a gym bag and pulled out a T-shirt, running shoes, and sweat pants.

"Keep talking."

Then he unbuttoned his trousers.

Normally, I wouldn't turn away at that point, but I needed my wits about me. I waited, whistling a nervous tune under my breath.

Once he was dressed, Jeff headed back to Tyson's body and the waiting constable to retrieve his utility belt with its handcuffs, baton, gun, and flashlight. He slung it around his hips, not looking at me. "I'm still not clear why you didn't call the police. Or me, at least," he said.

"Jeff, please. Can this wait until we find Adeline?" My eyes widened. "Maybe she's with Griffiths."

"Why would she be—" He gave a curt nod. "Right. Control. If they're together we'll find them both at his place. Meanwhile—"

His next words were cut off by a commotion on the road.

The coroner, Dr. Bakshi, had arrived and was making his way through the roadblock, holding aloft a medical bag and muttering. He cast a suspicious look around before proceeding. Checking for goats, I assumed.

"Good afternoon, Jeff," he said before bending next to Tyson. Over his shoulder he added, "Why is this body soaking wet?"

While Jeff hurried across to explain, I slumped onto the boulder with my chin in my hands to watch them.

My attention soon wandered.

At first, I tried to concentrate on the birds twittering in the bushes, the river surging past, and the backup beeper of a recently arrived tow truck—while trying to slow my breathing and the pounding of my heart.

We'll find her, sweetheart. How I hoped that was true.

Reflections on the case—and my utter cluelessness—soon took over my thoughts.

I had taken too many people at their word. Starting with Zara Price, my client. Who could have imagined she had a criminal record?

Not me, obviously.

Then there was Clive Yeager—an uptight military veteran with nerves of steel, rumored to be an accomplished assassin. He turned out to be a closeted drag queen with dreams of acclaim on a national stage. And to think I'd suspected him of...I shuddered.

Not to mention Ethan Neuhaus. I totally bought into his reformed delinquent act, when all the time he was taking part in street racing and probably illegal betting to boot. I narrowed my eyes. I intended to have it out with Ethan.

It wasn't only the human aspects of the case I misread. What about Yeager's decoy septic tank? Toxic waste masquerading as effluent? Or those deceptive alterations at Griffiths' mansion? I held up my arm, contemplating its scratches. I had even misjudged climbing roses and their hazardous thorns.

With a sigh, I recalled my biggest stumble of all. Adeline had no trouble convincing me Control sanctioned our ill-fated mission. After all this time, I should have known better.

Is nothing what it seems? I wondered. *Or am I simply oblivious?*

The group around Tyson's body stepped back to give the

police photographer room to work. Dr. Bakshi pointed out particular angles he wanted documented.

The constable Jeff had sent to find Griffiths returned. Listening to him, Jeff tilted his head. "What do you mean, he's not there?" he blurted before lowering his voice. I heard the phrase, *Send out an APB*.

Leaping to my feet, I trotted over.

Jeff was heading for his cruiser. I hurried to catch up. "What's happening?"

"It looks as if Griffiths might have—"

"Done a runner?" I asked.

Halting, he tossed me a sidelong glance, his lips twitching. "Where are you getting these from?"

"Tell you later," I said, recalling racetrack Alfie and his colorful phrases.

When Jeff resumed his progress, I fell into step beside him. "Where are we going?"

"You're going nowhere," he said. "I'm going to Griffiths' house."

"But if he's not there—"

"I want to see for myself." Reaching the car, Jeff pulled open the driver's door, then turned to face me. "Why didn't you tell me earlier about that note?"

"Would you have taken it seriously?"

"Maybe not." Then he hopped in, reaching out to pull the door closed. "But I'm taking it seriously now."

CHAPTER 25

"I'M COMING WITH YOU," I blurted, gripping the top of the driver's door before Jeff could close it.

"Stay out of it, Verity. Leave this to the police."

"No chance. She's my aunt, Jeff."

"I'll close this door on your fingers."

"No, you won't."

Clearly exasperated, he turned the key in the ignition. "Hurry up, then."

I scrambled around the front of the car and into the passenger seat. I was fastening my seatbelt when we set off, siren blaring.

While we drove, I remembered Griffiths' assurance about his gun. *It isn't loaded.*

He lied to me.

Join the queue, I thought. *One more person who fooled Verity Hawkes.*

Then I recalled Tyson's obvious fear of Griffiths. I had

assumed it was because he'd shot him, but there was more to it than that.

I recalled his last words. *I'm not going anywhere with him.* Tyson had been so determined to elude Griffiths that he turned down help for a fatal wound. And then fled. He must have known he wouldn't get far. Why was he so frightened?

There was an obvious answer, I realized. Griffiths worked for Control. If Tyson was a Syndicate plant, he might have recognized him. And known to stay away.

Which meant I was wrong about Tyson being too stupid to be a Syndicate operative.

I clapped a hand to my forehead. *Zero for five, Verity. Nice work.*

But there was more. I was also wrong about Griffiths. He was not a benign presence, working behind the scenes in Leafy Hollow to shake loose the identity of a sleeper agent. Control operatives were barred from using violence except in self-defense, according to Adeline.

Either Griffiths didn't get the memo, or...

I sat up straight, my back not touching the seat.

When Jeff pulled up in front of Griffiths' mansion, I bolted out before the car came to a complete stop. A police cruiser was parked in the driveway. A constable stood alongside, waiting for us.

I ran right past her.

The front door was unlocked. No surprise there.

Inside, I darted down the center hall toward the kitchen.

Jeff's feet pounded on the tiles behind me, his footsteps echoing in the deserted house. "Verity, wait."

"Adeline," I hollered, running through the house. I ducked into each room in turn. The six bedrooms upstairs and each of their ensuites. The great room downstairs. The fake library. The kitchen. Even the ground floor powder room with its stained glass window. All empty. "Adeline," I shouted, running along the front hall.

I skidded to a stop by the hidden panel Griffiths had shown me. "She must be in here." Running my hands along the top edge, I searched for the switch.

"What are you doing?" Jeff asked.

"Looking for the latch. This is a door. The former owners rented this property to movie productions, and this was one of the sets. It's meant to be a hiding place, like a priest's hole." While I talked, I pressed each inch of the frame in turn.

We heard a soft *snick*.

Jeff watched in amazement as the panel popped open.

I reached in a hand to slide the panel all the way.

We contemplated the circular staircase I'd seen on my previous visit. The one that led down into darkness.

Hanging on to the doorframe with one hand, I stuck in my head. "Adeline? Are you there?" I stepped through the opening. "Aunt Adeline?"

Jeff grabbed my arm. "Careful. Don't fall. What's down there?"

"Nothing. Although Griffiths mentioned an old wine cellar." Despite the grim situation, I managed a weak grin. "He said it wasn't worth the trip."

Shaking his head, Jeff smiled at me. "Is there a light switch?"

"I don't think so." I ran my fingers along the interior, but felt only rough-hewn rock. *Fake rock*, probably. Like the home's other phony features. "No, there isn't. Maybe there's a switch in the kitchen."

Jeff unclipped a compact flashlight from his belt and shone it into the stairwell, sweeping the walls with its beam. "Not much use looking for a switch. There are no light fixtures."

I started forward. "We have to go in."

Jeff held me back. "One minute, Verity." Turning to the constable, who had run down the hallway behind us, he said, "See if you can locate a light source. Then wait outside. Let me know if anyone drives up."

Nodding, she set off to scan the kitchen walls and cupboards, trying various dials and buttons. Lights flicked on and off around us, but none in the priest's hole.

I pulled my arm away and stepped onto the first stair. "We have to go in."

"Right behind you."

The circular staircase was so narrow my shoulders almost brushed either side. And so steep that in my haste to descend I nearly toppled over.

As I teetered on the fourth step, heart pounding, Jeff grabbed my arm. "Take it easy," he said.

I took a deep breath, trying to calm down before setting off at a slower pace. Tumbling down the stairs wouldn't help my aunt.

The flashlight's narrow beam bounced off the walls. At one point, I halted to scrape a fingernail across the nearest rock. My nail came away filled with gray paint. The walls were solid, but definitely not made of rock.

I suspected the "stone" stairs were also painted wood.

It grew colder as we descended. At the bottom of the stairs a small landing with what looked like a dirt floor faced a solid wooden door with two metal crossbars. A quick rap on the wood with my knuckles produced an echo. The door was hollow. Another prop.

"Stand back," Jeff said, preparing to ram it with his shoulder.

I held up a hand. "Not necessary, I suspect." I flicked up the latch. It clicked open easily and I pulled open the door, crossbars and all.

A blast of even colder air hit us, tinged with the odor of damp earth and mold. I wrinkled my nose. The smell, at least, was not fake.

The room was small, no more than eight by ten feet, with a low ceiling and rows of dusty wine bottles along one wall. Other than the wine racks, it was empty.

"Now what?" I muttered, feeling defeated.

I had been so certain that Griffiths was responsible for Adeline's disappearance. That he was the Syndicate mole.

But what if they were both compromised? And another, unknown, person, was to blame? What if the sleeper agent was yet to be identified? Which meant it could be anybody, and we were back to square one.

A cold weight settled in my stomach.

Where was my aunt?

Jeff pulled a wine bottle from the shelf, blew off a layer of dust, and held it in front of his flashlight's beam. The bottle was empty. He tapped it with a fingernail. It was made of plastic.

He put it back on the rack and tried another at random. Same thing. This time, though, instead of replacing it, he peered at the empty space in the rack where the bottle had been. "There's something behind this," he said.

Jeff set down the bottle, then rocked the edge of the wine rack. "It's not bolted down. We can move it."

Together, we eased the rack away from the wall and carted it to the other side of the room. Given that all the bottles were plastic, it wasn't heavy.

Behind it was another door, set flush into the wall. With no panels. And no handle.

"Adeline," I called, tapping on the door. "Are you there? Adeline?"

We exchanged glances. "Got anything on that belt that will help?" I asked.

Jeff grinned. "My trusty Swiss army knife," he said, unclipping something that looked more like a tool box than a knife. "It often comes in handy."

He snapped it open, then ran the tip of a three-inch blade around the edges of the door. "I don't feel any locks, or even hinges. We should be able to pry it open." Switching the blade for a screwdriver tool, he worked its tip under the edge of the door. The wood creaked in protest.

"It's plywood," he said with surprise. "Hold it in place while I peel it off."

I pushed against the door with both hands while he worked.

The plywood came away with a sound like a suction cup

being released. Jeff propped it up against the wall, and we stared at the opening.

Or rather, we didn't stare at the opening. Because there was none. The door, in fact the entire wall, had been fastened to solid earth.

There was no doorway. Or room beyond it.

"No," I cried, grabbing the screwdriver tool from Jeff and plunging the tip into the wall of earth. It was solid, like stone. I scraped off a few bits, then a few more, letting them drop to the ground. It was hard going.

"Verity," Jeff said softly. "Your aunt's not here."

With a last kick against the dirt wall, I slumped onto the floor with my head in my hands, letting the Swiss army knife roll off my fingers onto the ground.

Upstairs, I pulled out a kitchen stool and sat at one of the twin marble islands. Placing my elbows on the cool marble top, I rested my chin on my folded hands. "Now what?" I asked dejectedly.

Jeff—his inner chef on high alert—was strolling around the room, examining the fittings. "For the moment, I don't know. The force is looking for Griffiths. He can't have gone far."

"And then?"

"And then, hopefully, he'll have answers," he said.

"What about my aunt?"

"We've got a trace on her cell phone and we've requested

her phone records. But that will take time. We've also requested Tyson's phone records to see if we can trace his movements over the past few days."

He met my gaze, and held it for a long moment. "We'll find her," he said softly. "I promise you." In an obvious attempt to change the subject, he squinted at the massive wooden knife rack. "This is quite the kitchen."

Jeff pulled open a door of the huge Sub-Zero fridge, nodded approvingly, closed it, and then began opening cupboard doors at random.

"Are you looking for clues?" I asked, interested despite the looming dread that threatened to overwhelm me.

"Actually, I was looking for the microwave. It's strange Griffiths doesn't have one."

"Over there," I said gloomily, pointing out the painting of fruit. "Under the picture."

He studied the watercolor. "That's clever." Then flicked it up out of the way. Pause. "Verity?" There was a note of warning in his voice.

"Yes?"

"You need to see this."

I shot to my feet and trotted over. Jeff stepped aside.

A note was taped to the front of the microwave. It was addressed to me.

"What the hell?" I blurted, reaching to pluck it from the microwave door.

"Wait." Jeff held me back. "Fingerprints. Read it from there. I left my evidence kit in my other pants."

I leaned in.

"And don't breathe on it," he added.

"Okay," I said, somewhat testily. "I'm not breathing."

We read the note together.

> *HELLO, VERITY*
> *BACK SO SOON!*
> *DID YOU OVERLOOK SOMETHING?*

It was signed,

> *THE SHADOW*

We exchanged glances—mine shocked, Jeff's merely puzzled.

I closed my mouth before thumping the nearest cupboard with a clenched fist. "Son of a—" I thumped it again for good measure.

"I know I'm going to regret this," Jeff said, frowning at the note, "but who is The Shadow?"

"It's one of those stupid secret-agent terms of my aunt's. It refers to the alleged sleeper agent. She claimed Control only knew him, or her, by a nickname—The Shadow."

"I don't get it. Why is this person taunting you?" He frowned. "And who is The Shadow?"

"We don't know. That's the whole point."

"Then why the note?"

"I don't know," I blurted, suddenly vexed. Rubbing my fingers into my forehead, I added, "I can't think."

"Take your time. What have you overlooked?"

I snorted. "It could be anything. All throughout this case,

everything I thought I knew turned out to be exactly the opposite."

Jeff continued in his most patient voice. "Then what—"

My eyes widened, and I sucked in a breath. "Ohh," I said, letting it slowly filter out. "The *opposite*. It's a Janus word." I pointed to the note. "*Overlook* is a Janus word."

Jeff looked puzzled.

"A Janus word has contradictory meanings—opposite meanings. It's known as an auto-anti...anto...never mind that. The thing is, the word overlook means 'fail to notice' something. But it also means 'a view from above,' like Pine Hill Peak, for instance. With the first meaning, you see nothing. With the second—everything. Opposites."

"I don't see how that helps us."

"I think Griffiths wrote this note. I think he was giving me a fighting chance to find my aunt. We only have to figure it out."

"Why would he do that?"

Pausing to consider this, I recalled my last conversation with the ex-mayor.

You have a great deal of natural talent. We could use someone like you.

"I think..." I said slowly. "I think he was trying to recruit me. But he must know that if Adeline died—" With a shudder, I recalled the original note. STOP DIGGING OR ADELINE DIES. I swallowed before resuming. "That if she died, I would never join his band of mayhem makers."

"But that's Control, isn't it? Why would they hurt your aunt?"

I slumped back on the stool as the realization hit me.

Once again, Verity Hawkes had totally missed the point.

"No," I said. "Griffiths lied to me. He doesn't work for Control. He works for The Syndicate." I pointed an accusatory finger at the note. "Martin Griffiths is The Shadow."

We stared at each other.

Jeff cleared his throat. "These are deep waters."

"Are you making fun?"

"No. Well, maybe a little. But if I understand you correctly, this note contains a clue to Adeline's whereabouts."

"Correct. It must be the word *overlook*. What could that be?" My brain was working at top speed—along with my anxiety. The vein in my throat throbbed as I considered the possibilities.

...OR ADELINE DIES.

It was up to me.

I stood to pace the length of the kitchen, back and forth.

Jeff leaned against a counter, watching me.

"Could you have been right the first time?" he asked. "That she's at Pine Hill Peak?"

I shook my head. "Too public. He couldn't hide her there. Unless she's..." My stomach constricted and I fought back tears.

"Don't get ahead of yourself," he said calmly. "Think it through. *Overlook.* What could that refer to? Remember," he added in a soothing voice. "You believe that Griffiths wants you to find your aunt. The clue can't be so mysterious that it's impossible to guess."

I kept pacing.

Back and forth.

Overlook. What did it mean? Pausing to glance out the glass patio doors, I saw the wicker chairs where I drank lemonade with Griffiths during my initial visit. My gaze swept over the snow-white lilacs and the manicured perennial beds.

What did we talk about? I tried to remember.

Gardening. Street racing. Zara's goats. Yeager's property. And...

Griffiths' voice was suddenly clear in my head. *I don't need a lookout.*

"I'm an idiot," I said, slapping my forehead. "It's obvious."

"What is it?" Jeff asked with a note of alarm, pushing off from the counter.

I pointed to the garden's magnificent centerpiece.

"The waterfall. Adeline must be near the waterfall."

"Let's go."

We burst out of the patio doors.

Please don't let her be dead, I thought as we ran.

Images of Yeager's broken body flooded my mind.

Please.

We pulled up at the base of the man-made falls, under the spreading branches of a chestnut tree. Three streams of water dropped from thirty feet above us, splashing noisily onto artfully arranged, ragged rocks at the base. Feathery ferns and big-leaved hostas surrounded the edges, and waterbugs rested on quiet pools carved out on either side.

I swept my gaze up the stone stairs to the lookout above. With a sudden twist in my stomach, I recalled the hasty nighttime descent my aunt and I made on those stairs. And what we found at the bottom.

But other than a squirrel chattering at us from a chestnut branch, Jeff and I were alone.

"She has to be here," I muttered, kicking aside hosta leaves at my feet.

"Verity," Jeff said behind me, pointing to the falls. "This is manmade, right?"

"Yes. It predates Griffiths, though."

"How does the water get up there?"

"Oh," I said with an offhand wave. "Electric pumps recirculate it. You can't see them because—" My jaw dropped. "Jeff, you're a genius."

"Normally I would agree, but in this case—what are you talking about?"

"The pumps. There must be an underground room near the falls to hide the pumps and the electrical gear. We just have to find the door."

It took only minutes to locate a metal door hidden at the base of the falls. It was painted—more *trompe l'oeil*—to resemble vines, with ferns at the base. Jeff wrenched it open and we peered inside the small room beyond. A lightbulb in a wire cage came on when the door opened, so we could make out the interior.

There were four pumps, all working hard, an electrical panel, a bit of water on the floor, and a bench with tools and buckets. The air was damp and frigid.

But there was nothing else.

I pointed to a door flush with the far wall. "That could be a storage closet." I held my breath as Jeff examined it.

"I don't think it's locked," he said, twisting the handle.

The door opened.

The scene that greeted us is one I'll never forget. The storage room was damp and even colder than the first room. Sealed metal barrels were stacked along one wall. But that's not what caught my attention.

Against the opposite wall, my aunt lay on her side, curled into a fetal position. She looked small and vulnerable. I'd never seen her like that.

She was not moving.

I darted over, my heart in my throat, with Jeff close behind. We knelt beside her body.

Jeff reached around me to check her pulse, then nodded. "She's alive."

I heaved a sigh of relief. "Aunt Adeline? Can you hear me?" I shook her shoulder, then turned to Jeff, my stomach twisting. "Why can't she hear me?" I shook her again.

"Owww. Stop that," said a peevish voice.

"I think she can," Jeff said, pulling a cell phone from his pocket.

"Verity? Is that you?"

"Yes, it's me. Who else would be stupid enough to search for you? You scared me half to death." I touched her shoulder again.

"Owww. Cut that out."

Despite my best efforts to hold them back, tears welled up. "I thought I'd lost you. *Again*."

"Oh, Verity, I'm so...so..."

Jeff leaned over us. "Don't try to talk, Adeline."

I held up a hand. "No, no. I want to hear this. You're so... what?"

"Sorry." Her voice strengthened as she lifted her head. "I'm so sorry."

"Thank you," I said with a sniff. "Was that so hard? Now, Jeff—I think we're going to need an ambulance."

"Already on it."

CHAPTER 26

"ANY OF THE salted caramel ones left?" Adeline asked.

I was sitting by my aunt's hospital bed the following day, assessing an open box of hand-dipped chocolates on her bedside table. "I think so." Lifting the tray, I held it out for her inspection. "In the corner, there."

Raising her head off the pillow, she opened her mouth. "Pop one in, will you?"

"There's nothing wrong with your other arm."

She uttered a heavy sigh while lowering her head.

"Honestly." With a roll of my eyes, I plucked out the candy and held it up. "Here."

"Thank you, Verity."

I dropped it into her mouth.

She chewed contentedly. "This is nice," she said after swallowing.

"Don't get too comfortable. The doctor says you can go home tomorrow."

"I should hope so. It's only a dislocated shoulder. I've done that so many times it practically pops back in by itself."

"Your shoulder will take six weeks to heal completely, according to the doctor, followed by months of physio. Also, you have a sprained ankle. And a concussion. And hypothermia. Not to mention the spider bites."

"Ah. Nothing serious, then." Craning her neck, she peered at the chocolate box. "Did my guests eat all the cashew crunch ones?"

I snorted. "Your guests were afraid to touch them." I held out the box again. "I'll get you another one, but only if you explain exactly what happened. The drugs have worn off. Time to tell all."

She narrowed her eyes. "About what?"

I set the box down. "For starters, who killed Yeager?"

"Isn't it obvious?"

"Not to me."

"Griffiths did. Or, should I say—" Musing, she studied the far wall. "The Shadow."

"You can call him whatever you want, but why did he kill Yeager?"

"Because Yeager's little backyard toxic-waste scheme was drawing unwanted attention to The Syndicate's much larger activities. Especially after Eubanks died on Yeager's property. The Syndicate knew the police would test the contents of Eubanks' tanker and find the evidence.

"And once they did..." Adeline shook her head. "As a former Syndicate agent, Yeager knew too much. They couldn't risk him being interrogated by the police—or Control." She paused. "Also, I suspect it was a point of honor

—nobody cheats The Syndicate and gets away with it. They wanted to send a message."

"But Yeager was a powerful man. How did Griffiths overpower him?"

"He didn't have to. Yeager wouldn't have seen it coming. Griffiths must have asked him to come by for a chat, or a debriefing. Maybe they had a couple of drinks and then took a walk around the garden. You know how friendly Griffiths can be."

I nodded with a sick feeling in my stomach. *He certainly fooled me.*

"Possibly Griffiths told him he feared electronic surveillance if they talked indoors. Then, once they reached the top of that waterfall—he pushed him. Or tripped him. And that was that." She drew a finger across her throat.

"He might not have died, though. You can survive a fall of thirty feet."

"Depends what you land on. Did you see those rocks?"

I shuddered. "Now that you mention it..." I studied my aunt's face. "You're pretty fit. And a Krav Maga expert. How did Griffiths overpower you?"

She sighed. "I was an idiot."

"Can I get that on tape?"

She smiled weakly. "The truth is..." After a pause, she carried on, looking sheepish. "The truth is, I didn't realize Griffiths was the operative. I always thought it was Yeager. And it was—at one time, I think. But after we found his body, I realized there must be someone else. Someone new. Someone I'd overlooked."

That word again. "Go on."

"So I went to see Griffiths. He was a canny politician and a shrewd man. I was convinced he knew something he wasn't telling. After all, Yeager was killed practically on his doorstep. And Eubanks died right next door. It was too convenient."

"But still—" I countered.

"I know," she said ruefully. "I suppose I thought I could outwit him. It was stupid." With a wry look, she tapped the black-and-purple bruise on her forehead. "We were in the kitchen, having a drink. It was all very sociable. Griffiths was smiling and joking. He turned his back on me to get more ice from the fridge. He opened the fridge door—then whirled around and whacked me with a rolling pin. I never saw it coming."

"A rolling pin? That's a strange thing to keep in the fridge."

She nodded morosely. "Which is why I never saw it coming. He hit me so hard I flew off the stool and landed on my shoulder." Wincing, she added, "I felt the joint separate. And then, before I could get up...he whacked me again. I don't remember much after that."

"He must have dragged you into the garden."

"I think he used a wheelbarrow. I have some fairly suspicious bruises."

"Wait a minute. How did Tyson Farrell know where you were?"

"How do you know he did? Did he tell you?"

"Come to think of it—no, he didn't." *Crikey. I really was oblivious.*

I picked up the chocolate box and held it out.

Adeline studied it carefully. "Ooh, is that a triple dark chocolate?"

"Only one way to find out. Unless you want me to check the little menu again."

"Not necessary." She popped the candy into her mouth and leaned back with a murmur of satisfaction.

"I don't understand why Griffiths would attack you. You didn't know he was the Syndicate agent. You might never have found out. But once he'd stuffed you in that room, it would be obvious. So why do it?"

"Because of his Tyson Farrell problem."

"What?"

"The Syndicate knew Yeager had hired Farrell. They assumed he drew him into the toxic-waste scheme he was running with Eubanks. The Syndicate had no way to know how much Yeager told him. They couldn't take a chance on Farrell talking."

Adeline shifted uncomfortably, then gestured for her water glass.

I placed it on the table in front of her, arranging the straw at her lips. She took a long swallow, then motioned it away before resuming her story. "Farrell had to go. But Griffiths couldn't find him. That's where you came in."

"He used me."

"In a way. He decided a threat to my life would galvanize you into action."

"So he wrote that note."

"Of course. After he'd knocked me out and thrown me into that room." With a groan, she struggled with her pillows.

I bent over to fluff them.

"Thanks."

"But Tyson didn't die."

"Bad luck, that. Griffiths must have intended to kill him outright with that shot. He's obviously out of practice." She smirked. "But he made a mistake shooting him—it convinced Tyson that Griffiths' group wanted him dead and he would be safer with the police. He was bound to tell them everything he knew when they caught up with him."

"But Tyson didn't know anything about The Syndicate."

"Griffiths didn't know that. Yeager had proven himself to be a hothead and an idiot. Who knew what he might have told Tyson?"

I mulled this over. "Tyson didn't mention The Syndicate to me. But it was obvious that he was afraid of Griffiths."

"He must have met him through Yeager at one time or another. Tyson probably thought Griffiths was part of an organized crime family. He wouldn't have realized it was something even more deadly."

"Why did he drive his car into the river? Was it suicide?"

"I doubt that. He probably thought his driving skills were up to the task. Plus, from what you've told me, he was half dead already. He wouldn't have known what he was doing."

"Hello, girls," came a male voice.

We glanced up as Gideon strolled into the room. After decades of rocking a man-bun and a Van Dyke beard, he'd recently shorn off his gray hair to barely more than stubble length. The beard was also gone. It was a good look for him, I thought.

Adeline brightened, lifting her head off the pillow. "You're back," she cried.

My aunt's obvious joy at her partner's arrival made me misty-eyed. Sure, she was a grumpy old goat at times. But a lovable old goat.

Like Waffles, I thought with a smile.

That particular old goat was back with the rest of his tribe, all of them nibbling away on the remains of Clive Yeager's roses. I had snipped off the last of his blooms that morning and tossed them over the fence. It was the least I could do.

Not only that, but Zara had texted to tell me Wilf Mullins was going to back her petting zoo. Which meant the call I'd made earlier to Wilf—pointing out how much he owed his upcoming mayoral success to Waffles—had worked.

No one had any idea where Griffiths was, though. The police were watching the airports, but both Adeline and I were convinced they'd never find him.

Good riddance, as far as I was concerned.

I watched as my smiling aunt rose on her good elbow to beckon Gideon forward, then clutched his shirt to pull him nearer her face.

Should I look away? I wondered—until she whispered hoarsely into his ear.

"Did you bring them?"

Gideon reached into his pocket, then palmed something under the edge of the blanket.

Suspiciously, I sniffed the air.

"Oh man," I wailed. "You know you're not supposed to smoke those things in here."

"Verity," my aunt said, gesturing at Gideon to hand her a

lighter off the bedside table. "You're not going to deny a dying woman her final wish."

"You are not dying."

"I will someday." After clamping one of those damned stinky cheroots in her mouth, she flicked on the lighter, then sat back with a grin.

I decided to drive by Ethan's place to deliver the good news in person about Adeline's recovery. He had seemed genuinely upset by her predicament, and when the chips were down—I winced at the unfortunate gambling imagery— he told me where to find Tyson Farrell.

I knew where Ethan lived, although I'd never been there. I had his address on file—a rented place out by the quarry. Driving past the two-story house, I noticed an apartment over its double garage, with a flight of stairs on the outside.

One of the garage doors was open, but the Camaro wasn't inside. Ethan had either gone out, or his car was back in the shop. I was about to drive away when I noticed something odd. After parking the truck on the road, I walked over.

The framing on the right side of the open garage door had been stoved in. Something must have hit it hard, right about car hood height. I bent over for a closer look. The crumpled wood was scored with red paint. More red paint ran along the interior wall, which was also scored and scraped.

I ran a hand along the damage, sighing. *Wrong again, Verity.* Ethan had told the truth. He damaged his Camaro while parking it in this garage, not during a street race.

"It's a mess, isn't it?"

I whirled at the sound of a woman's voice.

A plump, middle-aged woman with curly hair and one hand on her hip stood behind me on the driveway

"Hi," she said with a friendly nod. "You must be Verity. If you're looking for Ethan, he's not here."

I was puzzled for a moment until I remembered that my pink Coming Up Roses truck was parked on the street.

Sensing my confusion, she added, "This is my place. Ethan rents the apartment upstairs from me."

"The one over the garage?"

She nodded, then stepped nearer to *tsk-tsk* at the wall. "That beloved car of his made quite a racket hitting this. I thought it was an earthquake." She chuckled. "I rushed out here in my pajamas and housecoat in the middle of the night, ready to give him hell. But he'd hit his head so hard on the windshield, I felt sorry for him." She shook her head. "Stinking drunk, too. I'm not sure he even felt it."

My heart started to race. "Ethan had been drinking?"

"Oh yeah. Big time."

In a burst of fury, I punched the side of my fist against the damaged wall.

"Hey," she chuckled. "Take it easy."

Grimacing, I rubbed my hand. It was having a bad week. "Sorry." My mind whirled, retrieving a recent conversation with my newest employee.

You'd never accuse Lorne of lying the way you do me.

What an idiot I'd been. Ethan told me he'd damaged his Camaro by parking it in this garage when under the influence. But after I displayed zero tolerance for his drunk driving, he changed his story. He implied the car had been mangled during an off-road race.

But here was clear evidence he'd been lying then, too.

And I believed him. Both times. I snorted in disgust. *Some investigator.*

Ethan's landlady was still talking. "So I waited till the next day to tell him he'd have to pay for the damage his friend caused. He was still under the weather, though, so I didn't press the issue. He looked like hell, to be honest. I said maybe he should go to the hospital, get that tough skull of his checked out, but he said, no, he had to go to work."

"Uh-huh," I said while massaging the heel of my hand, studying the paint scratches, and vowing to reread *Detecting Lies and Cheaters, Vols. 1* through infinity.

"He said he couldn't let you down. He's like that, though. Ethan's the first tenant I ever had who paid their rent on time every month." She turned to go. "Next time I see him I'll tell him you stopped by."

Something clicked in my brain—finally—and I jerked my head around. "What did you say?"

"I said, Ethan should have gone to the hospital, but—"

"No. Before that. About his friend."

"Well, that idiot was driving way too fast, wasn't he? That's why he hit the garage. *Bang*—he rammed Ethan's car right into the side of the doorframe and just kept on going. Jerk." She shook her head. "I told Ethan I was sorry, but he'd have to pay for the damages. My insurance won't cover that." Frowning, she added, "that friend of his certainly didn't offer to give me anything. He thought the whole thing was hilarious."

I stared at her, my mouth agape. Ethan hadn't lied to me. It happened just as he said—his Camaro was damaged because it was driven into the side of a garage.

But not by him.

Slowly, I said, "Ethan wasn't driving when this happened."

"No. I told you. He had been drinking, so he asked his friend to drive him home. Ethan never drives drunk."

The garage swayed, and I stretched out an arm to steady myself against the damaged wall. It was exhausting work, swerving from one preconception to another and back again. I'd been wrong so many times I had vertigo.

The woman shook her head sadly. "I told Ethan afterward, it's none of my business, but that guy is no friend of yours." She paused. "Haven't seen that guy since, though." With a brisk wave, she went indoors.

I climbed back into my truck, chuckling to myself. My initial assessment of Ethan—as a former delinquent determined to make good—had been spot-on. And my first assessment of Zara Price—a kind, generous woman who wouldn't hurt a fly—was also accurate. They were good people, even if they'd made mistakes in the past.

But I *was* guilty of underestimating someone else—me. Why had I doubted my ability to grasp people's true characters? *You have a real talent for this kind of work*, my aunt— and others—had said. And now, I finally believed them.

I broke into a grin. *Yeah*, I thought, *I guess I do.*

I turned over the engine and pulled onto the road, my faith in humanity restored.

Well, nearly.

Two people were dead and a killer had escaped. But other than that—I smiled to myself—things were looking up in Leafy Hollow.

What could possibly go wrong?

EPILOGUE

I WATCHED the puppet heads lustily singing O *Canada*. They had insisted on serenading me, even though our national holiday was weeks away. Slumped in the swivel chair in front of the basement console, I gazed at the monitors with growing impatience.

"Can we move this along?" I finally asked.

A purring General Chang was curled up in my lap, taking a break from the rodent patrol we both knew he didn't actually do.

Jeff and Boomer were upstairs, watching the latest blockbuster on our new big-screen TV.

It had seemed a good time to check in with Control. If nothing else, they deserved an update on Adeline's condition. Although *deserve* was not the first word I would have chosen.

Minutes earlier, when I wrenched open the basement door, Jeff had been in the kitchen, sourcing movie snacks.

"Where are you going?" he asked, plucking microwave popcorn from the cupboard.

"Laundry."

"Without the basket?"

"I have to check the detergent situation first."

His lips twitched. "Say hello for me."

"To the detergent?"

"No," he replied evenly. "To that bastard marketing group."

I halted, my foot poised above the first step. Jeff rarely used strong language. "That's harsh," I said carefully.

"Not harsh enough."

I retracted my foot. "What's this about?"

With his back to me, he set the popcorn down, then leaned his arms on the counter for a long moment. Muscles rippled in his back.

"Jeff?"

"They're trying to recruit you again, aren't they?" He turned to face me.

This was a difficult question. Adeline had already put her foot in it, by telling Jeff it was time for her to "pass the torch." And to be honest, I was intrigued by the possibility.

But not intrigued enough to risk my relationship with Jeff.

"Would that be...bad?"

"You could get yourself killed. I couldn't deal with that." Sighing, he twisted to pick up the popcorn. "But if it's more important to you than us..." Ripping open the box, he took out a package and put it in the microwave. Then he stood, his back to me, watching it cook.

On the floor, Boomer twitched and whimpered, his eyes also glued to the microwave. No one spoke.

"Jeff." I took a deep breath, wanting to get it right. "Nothing is more important to me than us. Nothing. If anything happened to you, I'm not sure I could go on."

Except for the *pop-pop-pop* from the microwave, and Boomer's frantic whimpering, the room was silent.

I took another deep breath.

"If you ask me not to do it, I won't."

He glanced over his shoulder. "I would never ask you that."

"I know, but if you did—I would do what you wanted. Happily. Because nothing—" I stressed the word—"is more important to me than you."

He turned, his brow furrowed. "I would never ask you that."

"I know, but..." I swallowed. "If you ask me not to do it, I won't."

He heaved a sigh. "I would never—"

I held up my hands in mock surrender.

The microwave dinged loudly. Jeff pulled out the bag, tore it open, and upended the contents into a bowl. "Popcorn?"

I gestured at the basement door. "I have to—"

"I know." He reached for a smaller bowl, filled it, and handed it to me with a smile. "You might want a snack while you're talking to your new overlords."

"Thanks," I said, blinking rapidly. I took the bowl from his hands.

"No need to thank me. The microwave did all the work."

"You knew that's not what I meant."

"I did." He had smiled again.

But now, as the puppet heads launched into their second chorus, enough was enough. Depositing a grumpy General onto the floor, I rose to my feet. "I've told you everything you need to know. If you don't stop singing right now, I'm walking out of here."

"Do not do that, Verity Hawkes. We are nearly at the end."

Their reedy voices rose in volume.

"To stand on guard for thee..."

I pulled the plug.

Upstairs, Jeff swung his legs off the sofa to make room for me.

I snuggled in beside him, holding my own personal bowl of popcorn.

Without looking at me, he said, "You added butter to that, didn't you?"

"Maybe." I threw Boomer a piece, which he snapped up in midair.

"It's not healthy," Jeff said.

"It was organic butter."

He snorted. "By the way, Adeline just called. She needs to talk to you."

"Now?"

"It seemed urgent."

My aunt answered on the first ring. "Verity, have you seen the photos Emy posted on Facebook today?"

"No. I find it's better for my mental health if I don't dwell on the fact my best friends are cavorting about on tropical beaches. Without me."

"Bermuda is not in the tropics," Adeline pointed out.

"It has pink sandy beaches, turquoise surf, and fruit drinks. Close enough. What about these pictures?"

"Get out your laptop. You need to see this."

"Hang on." Grumbling, I retrieved the laptop and sat on the sofa. Jeff turned off the television to lean over my shoulder. "Okay, we're in," I said to the cell phone, while scrolling through Emy's latest batch. "These look pretty typical to me."

"Check out the fourth photo."

"The one in the restaurant?"

"That's the one."

I studied the picture. Lorne had his arm around Emy, and they were posing at a restaurant table littered with used plates and empty glasses. A waiter must have snapped the photo. I squinted. "Is that lobster?" I squeaked.

"Never mind the food. Look at the background."

I scanned it quickly. "Table. Table. Wine. Railing. Ocean. Another table. What am I looking for?"

"The man sitting at the table behind them."

I zeroed in. "It's pretty grainy, but he's holding up a wine glass, almost as if..." I enlarged the photo. "As if he's making a toast. And he's..." I enlarged it again. "He's looking straight at the camera. That's odd. He's photo-bombing them." I checked Emy's notes beneath the photo. "She doesn't mention his name. Why would a total stranger want to be in their picture?"

"His face, Verity," my aunt said impatiently. "Look at his face."

I enlarged it one more time, squinted, then sat back, dumbfounded. "It can't be," I whispered.

"It can, and it is. Wait there—I'm coming over."

I was still scrutinizing the photo when we heard the thump-thump-thump of Adeline's crutch on the porch. Jeff got up to let her in. Her arm was tucked into a silk sling etched with roses. She and Gideon must have been planning a night on the town. Or karaoke at The Tipsy Jay, at least.

We made room for her on the sofa, and I placed the computer on her lap.

Jeff had downloaded a photo of Martin Griffiths from the police site, and we lined it up with the mysterious stranger in Emy's photo.

"It's him," Adeline said. "It's definitely him."

Jeff was more circumspect. "It could be, but a lot of people look the same. You can't tell from one blurry picture. Besides, why would he be following Emy and Lorne? And why would he go out of his way to be included in their photo? He'd have to know that you would..." His voice trailed off.

Adeline finished the sentence. "See it?" She turned to me. "Tell me again how Emy and Lorne won this vacation."

"I don't really know. It was a contest, apparently, but... Emy doesn't remember entering it."

We exchanged stricken glances. The vein in my throat started to throb, and I pushed the laptop away. A memory of Griffiths taking aim at Tyson Farrell came to mind. Followed by the image of Tyson crumpling to the ground.

"Emy and Lorne are in danger," I said.

Jeff's voice was calm, as always. "You don't know that."

"We have to go down there."

"No," he blurted. "It could be a trap. We can ask the local force to check up on them. That's the best idea."

Adeline nodded glumly. "Jeff has a point. It probably *is* a trap."

"I don't care," I said. "We can't let him get away with it. Are you suggesting we do nothing?" Rising to my feet, I paced the room.

"I didn't say that."

"Verity," Jeff said. "Let me check with the local force and see what they come up with. If the man in this photo is Martin Griffiths, they can arrest him."

"He won't be using his real name. The Syndicate will have set him up with a new identity. Jeff, we have to do something. Obviously, my aunt's in no condition to get on a plane and go anywhere, but I can—"

That's when I noticed her tapping away on the laptop. "What are you doing?"

She gave me a shifty look. "Shopping for bathrobes."

"You are not." Leaning over, I spun the computer around to check the screen. "You're buying an airline ticket."

"Two, actually." She swung the screen back. "Do you want an aisle seat or a window?"

"Ahh..." I cast a wary glance at Jeff.

He flicked his gaze from Adeline to me, and back to Adeline.

I waited, holding my breath.

"Make it three," Jeff said. "I'm coming with you."

My jaw dropped. "You can't. What about work?"

"I have vacation time coming."

"You're saving that for our honeymoon."

"If you get yourself killed, there won't be a honeymoon." He gave me one of those *don't-mess-with-me* looks. "When do we leave?"

THE END

To receive advance notice of upcoming books and special offers, please join my mailing list at www.rickieblair.com.

Reviews are very important for the success of a book. If you enjoyed *Doubt on a Limb*, please consider leaving an online review.

ALSO BY RICKIE BLAIR

The Leafy Hollow Mysteries

From Garden To Grave

Digging Up Trouble

A Branch Too Far

Muddy Waters

Snowed Under

The Grave Truth

Picture Imperfect

Doubt on a Limb

The Ruby Danger series

Dangerous Allies

Dangerous Benefits

Dangerous Comforts

ABOUT THE AUTHOR

When not hunched over her computer talking to people who exist only in her head, Rickie spends her time taming an unruly half-acre garden and an irrepressible Jack Chi. She also shares her southern Ontario home with two rescue cats and an overactive Netflix account.

Contact Rickie at rickieblair.com or on Facebook at facebook.com/AuthorRickieBlair/